"WHAT EVAN AND I HAD IS GONE FOREVER."

Amanda turned to her father, her gray eyes full of tears. "Now it's too late for us."

"Don't deceive yourself," Peter said almost gruffly. "You two shared something very rare, and you still do. Good marriages are hard work. There are days, even weeks, when things go so badly you wonder if you were ever in love."

"But what's the difference between those times and the end of loving someone?"

"The bad times pass and you see that person differently. It's like falling in love again. Because you say you love someone it doesn't give you the excuse not to learn what's in his heart, not to support him, stand by him, accept his weaknesses as well as his strengths."

"But—"

"No buts, Amanda. For your sake and for his, take the time to learn what's in Evan's heart."

ABOUT THE AUTHOR

Marisa Carroll is the pseudonym for the writing
team of two sisters from Deshler, Ohio. Having
been avid romance fans for years, the women
decided to try writing together in 1983. Since
then, they have sold five books. When they are
not plotting their novels, each author keeps busy:
one works as a bookkeeper for the family's oil
jobbing business and the other utilizes her
professional skills as a Red Cross volunteer.
Remembered Magic is Marisa Carroll's first
Superromance.

Books by Marisa Carroll

Marisa Carroll

REMEMBERED MAGIC

Harlequin Books

TORONTO • NEW YORK • LONDON
AMSTERDAM • PARIS • SYDNEY • HAMBURG
STOCKHOLM • ATHENS • TOKYO • MILAN

Published July 1987

First printing May 1987

ISBN 0-373-70268-X

CHAPTER ONE

"ALMOST GOT YOU that time, boss lady," the slim, elderly black man called down from his seat on the electric forklift.

Amanda Winston sidestepped the machine and laughed up at its grizzled operator. Eddie Nightengale had been at the *Sarasota Examiner* for as long as Amanda could remember. "If I didn't know you could stop that contraption on a dime, I'd have to find a new way to get in to work in the morning. And don't call me 'boss lady,'"she added in a friendly tone. "It makes me feel like I should be wearing chaps and a ten-gallon hat."

"You've got a point there." Eddie rested his arms on the forklift's steering wheel as he watched Amanda with bright, dark eyes nearly hidden in the folds of his laugh lines. "That's not your style at all." He eyed the tall, elegant outline of his employer's figure appreciatively for a moment. "Maybe I should take to callin' you Madam Executive. Especially now that you're gonna be marryin' Mr. Robert Tacett and movin' on uptown."

Amanda opened her mouth to retort in kind, but no words emerged. She stood quietly, letting her gray eyes adjust to the dim light in the lower level of the cement block building that housed the newspaper, while her body and mind absorbed the very faint jolt of unease Eddie's comments had provoked within her.

"You all right, Ms Winston?" Eddie inquired, all signs of drollery wiped from his voice. "I didn't scare you, drivin' up behind you like that, did I?"

"Of course you didn't, Eddie." Amanda shook her head to clear it of the unwelcome, fleeting memory of a pair of tawny-gold eyes. "I must have pre-wedding jitters, that's all. I've used this door every morning for the past three years, and every morning you've come sneaking up behind me on that thing."

"And will for a good many more, I predict. The Almighty willin', that is." Eddie grinned, his good humor restored once more. Amanda watched as he deftly maneuvered the prongs of the forklift under one of the huge rolls of newsprint and lifted it away from its rack. Deceptively static now, the giant rolls of new paper would soon begin their whirlwind journey through the maze of rollers that fed the greedy, noisy presses.

"Penny for your thoughts." Eddie was back, catching Amanda's eye with an expressive wave of his hand. "You must have the weddin' pretty heavy on your mind after all," he drawled in the casual soft-voweled tones of a native Floridian. Amanda tipped her head and made a quick negative gesture of dismissal.

"I was just going over a possible list of employees who could be retired early and save me a lot of headaches," she responded with a grin and a finger pointed right at the middle of Eddie's chest. Her threat didn't faze the driver a whit.

"Yes sir, that Mr. Robert Tacett, he sure is one lucky gent. Me and my wife would like to wish you all the best."

"Thanks, Eddie." Amanda smiled again, genuinely touched. "I appreciate your thoughtfulness. And I do believe you could charm the spots off a leopard without even bothering to get down off that machine."

"That's what my wife has been sayin' for near forty years." With a final wave in her direction, Eddie rolled off down the corridor toward the feeder doors and loading docks at the rear of the building. The smell of exhaust from the off-loading delivery trucks followed Amanda as she moved down the hall in the opposite direction.

She took a deep breath and shook off the faint, lingering tinge of sadness that had dogged her since Eddie's chance remarks about her upcoming marriage. Everything was on track in her life for the first time in years. In less than two weeks she'd be married to a wonderful man who'd give her the affection, companionship and stability that she'd always longed for. The paper was doing well, unlike many other smaller dailies across the nation, which were sinking into bankruptcy or being absorbed by huge, impersonal media chains; its circulation was up, and its revenues were at least keeping the cash flow moving in a positive direction. When the renovations and format update she and her father had been working on for over a year were completed, the *Sarasota Examiner* would be able to hold its own against the larger Tampa and Miami dailies that comprised their chief competition.

Amanda allowed another smile to play over her lips, relaxing her expression and softening the generous lines of her mouth as she returned the friendly greetings of her employees along the route to her office. In the three years since she'd returned to Florida from New York, these people had become something of an extended family to her. Working together, they'd turned the paper around, refocusing its objectives and tailoring its content to appeal to Sarasota's growing population, especially its new residents, as well as the multitude of winter visitors who descended on the area each autumn. She felt good, as if she truly belonged here, as if her contributions to her father's paper and to the community where she'd grown up truly counted for something. Such secure feelings proved to Amanda that her struggle to pick up the pieces of her personal life in order to start building a solid future was succeeding.

Amanda paused outside the double doors of the cavernous basement room that housed the presses. The latest issue of the paper had been on the streets only a few hours, but already the presses were being reloaded, inked and tested for the next run. The smells of ink and new paper were strong in the air. There was noise and movement all around her. The sights and scents of the big bustling room gave Amanda a quick, heady rush of exhilaration, banishing the last of her irrational sense of unease she had felt moments before.

Hers was a perfectly normal reaction, Amanda would recite mentally time and again, just as she did now climbing the short flight of steps leading to the main level of the building. A stray spark of multifaceted sunlight arced from the diamond solitaire on her left hand, tugging her thoughts once more toward the future. In less than two weeks, she would be married.

She'd made a mess of her first marriage; she could admit that now. She'd watched her fierce and all-encompassing love for Evan Cameron wither and die. She'd lost the baby she'd been nurturing within her, along with her self-esteem and her belief in happily-ever-after endings, all within a few short weeks. Any combination of those circumstances would affect a sane person's outlook on a second marriage. Add those losses together, and the anxiety could very well become paralyzing.

Perhaps saying she was happier than she'd ever been was an exaggeration of her present feelings, but Amanda was at least content with her life. Happiness would come with further healing, with being able to forget everything that had gone before. And after happiness—perhaps—love. Amanda was eager to prove she could be a loving wife to Robert. He was witty, intelligent, handsome and wise; he possessed all the qualities any woman could hope to find in a husband. And someday she would come to love him as he deserved to be loved. Someday...

"ROBERT, I'M TELLING YOU, I'm on to something." Peter Winston swiveled the big oak chair behind Amanda's desk and dropped both feet flat on the floor with a decided thump. He stared across the small room at his future son-in-law, who was standing by a bank of metal filing cabinets. It was almost ten o'clock on an unusually hot March morning, and the air conditioning was on the fritz, but Robert Tacett looked as if he'd just stepped out of the pages of *Gentleman's Quarterly*. Peter, on the other hand, looked as if he'd slept in his floral-print shirt and baggy linen pants, and didn't care. "Carmella is telling the truth. I'd stake my boat on it." He ran his hand through his thick, iron-gray hair in a gesture long familiar to his old cronies at the *Washington Post*.

"The woman is frightened, Peter. She's alone and friendless in a foreign country. When people get scared, they imagine all sorts of things." Robert moved to stand in front of the desk, picking up and then discarding a millefiori paperweight that Amanda's mother had given her daughter the Christmas before her death. Peter let a brief, smiling image of his wife float before his eyes, then tucked the precious spark of memory back into the private corners of his heart. "After all," Robert went on, "Carmella's only been in this country a couple of months. How long did you say she's been working for you?"

"A little over three weeks." Peter picked up the glass paperweight, cupping it in his hand for a moment before resuming the conversation. "I hired her directly from the refugee-placement center. My Spanish isn't much better than her English, but she got her point across loud and clear, if that's what you're getting at." He set the paperweight down very carefully, and ran his hand through his hair again, making it stand on end.

"It's not unlikely she believes that she sees danger behind every bush. She'll get over it when she settles in and realizes she's safe in this country," Robert predicted, running his hand over his own neatly cut dark hair in a reflexive action. He smiled in response to the older man's obvious excitement.

"You're damn right she's scared. Half her family's dead, the other half is in prison in Costa Verde for opposing President Alexandro's regime. She walked over a goddamned mountain and through fifty miles of rain forest carrying two little kids to get to the agency's mission after her husband was killed by an army raid on their village. If she says she recognized those two men at the shelter as being members of one of Alexandro's death squads, I damn well believe her.'' Peter's tone was pugnacious. Unconsciously, he balled his hand into a fist.

"The shelter's administrators, or the immigration authorities, should..." Robert began to argue, then stopped, his jaw tightening as Peter snorted loudly and derisively.

"They aren't going to take me any more seriously than you do at the moment. We're talking about a lay agency of the church here, with a worldwide reputation for humanitarian acts."

"That's my point," Robert said quietly, but with a hint of steel in his voice. Peter glanced sharply at his companion, then nodded in reluctant agreement. Robert Tacett was a shrewd and canny individual. His reservations, such as they were, could all be termed valid.

"If I go to the police or nosed this around to the immigration-and-naturalization people, those crooks would disappear into the mangroves so fast it would make your head spin. No way." Peter's voice was tense. His big, stubby hands cut through the air with slashing gestures that emphasized every word.

"Will Carmella be able to prove the men she saw being processed through as legitimate political refugees were terrorists or assassins?" In many ways, his daughter's fiancé reminded Peter of his ex-son-in-law, Evan Cameron. Both men were intelligent and quick to grasp the feel of a situation. However Robert was very different in all the ways that counted—in Peter's not-unbiased opinion. Not that he wasn't damn quick on the uptake. A man in his position had to be. The Tacett family holdings were spread all along the west Florida coast. Robert ran everything, had since his father's death seven or eight years ago. And he still managed to keep his eye on his own business concerns, which included some of the area's prime real estate, several beachfront condominiums and one of the best and most successful restaurants in the city.

Robert was thorough, solid and dependable, and he wanted to know the facts, all of them, before he committed himself one way or the other. Peter couldn't fault him for that, but he didn't admire Robert's characteristic caution much, either. The older man sighed; Evan Cameron would have jumped in with both feet, just like Peter himself wanted to do. Peter took a deep breath, readying his arguments, preparing to defend his reporter's instincts.

"By the time I get done tracking this story down, Carmella will not only be able to prove her claims, we'll have those guys put away for the rest of their lives."

Robert moved behind Amanda's desk to stare out the window at gently swaying palm trees and a bright blue Florida sky. "I believe you, Peter. If you're convinced the woman knows what she's talking about..."

"Her grandfather was beaten half to death by one of the men just two weeks before she escaped from Costa Verde." Peter's tone was cold with deadly certainty. "You don't forget a horror like that. She's sure, all right."

"Then I imagine the best way to proceed would be to go get some more concrete evidence."

"Right on the money," Peter said, nodding his agreement. He couldn't remember the last time he'd been so excited about the possibility of tracking down a story. It took twenty years off a man's age to have something with this much potential to work on.

"You need hard facts to lay in front of the refugee committee, Immigration, the police, or whoever it is you go to in a situation like this." Robert's voice hardened a fraction. "I'm not even going to suggest you follow the sane and reasonable course and hire a private detective, but for Amanda's sake, promise me you won't do anything rash. Go to the authorities as soon as you know anything for certain." Robert spread his arms, palms resting flat on the wood surface as he faced the older man across the width of the scarred oak desk.

Peter's dark, heavy brows pulled together in a frown, then he gestured abruptly, conceding the younger man's point. "I can't promise what I'll be doing until I figure out what I'm up against. Carmella trusts me, but only so far."

Robert had made some good points. But *damn*, this was a hell of a story brewing. He wasn't about to let it drop because Robert Tacett thought it was too dangerous, or because his daughter believed he was too old.

Peter Winston had been on the staff of the *Washington Post* for fifteen years before moving to Florida to take over the ownership of the *Examiner*. Amanda had been a small child at the time. He hadn't regretted his decision to leave the fast-paced world of investigative reporting behind, but like an old war-horse, when the battle trumpets sounded he was ready to go.

"Have you spoken to Amanda about this situation?" Robert turned to face Peter, his deep blue eyes searching the older man's face. "It could be dangerous."

"Don't worry about me." Peter spoke with feigned assurance to hide his own wariness at calling back into use old skills and reactivating professional contacts that were twenty years out of date. "I didn't get to be pushing mandatory retirement by being a fool. And Robert, I'd appreciate it if you don't speak to Amanda about this situation. I'll deal with her when I'm ready for her to know—"

"Ready for Amanda to know what? Dad, have you decided to give up the house and buy that condo out at the marina?" Amanda walked into the office, looking so much like her mother for a moment that Peter caught his breath. She had Moira Winston's fine bone structure, tall, slim build and porcelain-clear skin. Her hair was the same color, too, a rich deep shade of auburn, more brown than red. Coupled with the high-necked blouse and dark skirt she was wearing, it gave her the innocent, untouched look of a bygone day. But the illusion of cool, disinterested beauty was broken when she smiled.

Amanda's abundant, silky hair and cloud-gray eyes were a gift of her mother's Irish heritage, and her strong chin and straight nose had been bequeathed through his genes, but her smile was her own. It softened and lightened her features, bringing her face to glorious life.

"No, I am not selling your mother's house." Peter spoke roughly to hide the extent of his emotion. "We've been over that and over that, Mandy."

"I know, Dad, but a house is so much work..."

"For a man my age." Peter finished her sentence with a disgusted twist of his lips. "Mandy, when are you going to get off this retirement kick of yours?" He softened the sharpness of his tone, grinning abashedly as he caught the sparkle of mischief in Amanda's eye. She'd known he'd rise to that particular bait, and he had.

"When you pack up that disreputable old Royal portable and your golf clubs and learn to take it easy. Dad, we've discussed this so often." Amanda laid her hand on his arm to emphasize her point. "You've worked hard all your life. You've taken care of me and everybody else who came along needing a handout or a place to stay the night. Now I want to take care of you. I want you to enjoy yourself, that's all. You've earned the rest."

"Do you know what comes after 'rest' in the dictionary?" There was a wicked glint in Peter's deep-set brown eyes.

"No, what?" Amanda glanced quickly over at Robert, silently entreating his assistance. She sensed she was being set up for something, but she wasn't sure what.

"'Rest home,'" Peter answered succinctly if inaccurately. "Don't you two think you'd better be leaving for the courthouse? You'll be late for your appointment with the records clerk."

"He got you that time, Amanda." Robert chuckled, moving out from behind her desk to take his fiancée in his arms and give her a quick light kiss on the cheek. "I think the word that actually follows 'rest' in the dictionary is 'restaurant.' And if we don't get over to the license bureau and back before the lunch crowd starts coming into mine, it will be a zoo."

"I'm ready whenever you are," Amanda replied, and returned his kiss.

"Want to join me for lunch later on, Dad? Shall I make reservations for us at the Main Bar?"

"Can't make it, sweetheart. There's been a problem with the typesetter already this morning." Peter watched the exchange of embraces between Robert and his daughter appraisingly. Peter Winston, Pulitzer Prize–nominated investigative reporter, hard-boiled editor-in-chief of the *Examiner* was a romantic at heart. But he'd go to the rack before he let anyone know what was at the root of his disquiet over the prospect of Amanda's second marriage. Peter believed in love—everlasting, undying commitment to another human being—like the love he'd shared too briefly with Amanda's mother, like the love he'd thought Amanda had found with Evan Cameron once upon a time. He was worried that despite their good intentions, Robert and Amanda were both, in their own ways, going into this marriage for the wrong reasons. Amanda couldn't afford another heartbreak like the one she'd suffered over the breakup of her marriage to Evan. Robert didn't deserve that kind of bad luck, either. Peter would have traded his soul to save his child from any more emotional anguish in her life, but he just didn't know where to start.

"What's wrong with the typesetter, Dad?" Amanda asked, lifting a hand to rest on the gentle swell of her hip. "Why didn't you call me? I didn't have to meet with the florist this morning. I could have been here an hour and a half ago." She pursed her lips and eyed her parent severely.

"It's nothing serious. I've already been down to take a look. I called the repair people in Tampa. They'll be here in twenty minutes or so." He glanced at his wristwatch to confirm the time. "I'm not senile yet. I can still get this paper to press without missing a deadline."

"All right, all right." Amanda threw up her hands, admitting defeat. She laughed, seeing her own stubborn determination reflected in her father's eyes. "You don't have to belabor the point, does he, Robert?"

"We can both take a hint." Robert held up his hands like a referee in a prizefight as he entered into the spirit of the spiked repartee. "Come on, Amanda, let's get going before your dad changes his mind. Filling out forms at the county courthouse beats having you two stand here and take potshots at each other all day."

"I FAIL TO SEE the reason you need to know my mother's middle name in order to get a marriage license in this county." Amanda drew herself to her full height—all five feet, eight inches of it. Her low throaty contralto took on the quality of hauteur she usually reserved for recalcitrant display-advertising salesmen. The subtle intonation wasn't lost on the civil servant behind the Formica counter. Or on the tall, distinguished man at her side.

"Robert, tell me, what has my mother's middle name go to do with our getting married?" Long sooty lashes swept down to rest for a moment on Amanda's cheekbones as she struggled to bring her feelings under control. Her hands were sweating, and she wiped them surreptitiously on the folds of her skirt. "It's such a useless bit of knowledge, and we're in a hurry. What possible value can it be to anybody? It's no wonder this state is in such a mess."

"I don't think this is the best time or place to begin unraveling the bureaucratic tangles of Sarasota County," Robert said reasonably. "Are you okay? You look awfully pale all of a sudden."

"I'm fine." Amanda tried to meet his blue eyes, and her line of vision came to rest squarely on his chin. She gave a little start of guilty surprise, the explanation she'd been formulating dying before it reached her lips. Quickly, she raised her eyes to his before either man could notice her hesitation. *Damn!* She'd done it again. Robert was six-four, not five-ten. What was the matter with her this morning? Was she losing her mind? Or was she possessed?

The shadowy, mocking male figure superimposed between them was gone in less than the blink of an eye, had in reality never been there, of course. It was an aberration, a figment of her overactive imagination. It seemed that since she'd accepted Robert's proposal of marriage Evan Cameron's ghost had intruded on them at the most inconvenient times.

Like now, her ex-husband was at least six inches shorter than Robert. As a couple, Evan and Amanda had been nearly equal in height, in the length of their legs, in the way their bodies had perfectly complemented each other. . . .

She had only to turn her head, as she'd just done, to meet Evan's golden-brown gaze. He was all earth, wind and fire, his body toned with shades of teak and bronze, totally opposite to Robert's dark, sophisticated good looks.

"It's all right, Miss Winston," the clerk said patiently, "I'm used to nervous brides. No matter how trivial you feel the question is, I need to know your mother's middle name."

Robert watched Amanda closely, ignoring the other man. She reached for her fiancée's hand, her heart skipping a beat when he squeezed hers reassuringly, but the surge of affection she felt for him was bittersweet. He was so good for her. He'd never evoke the violent, all-consuming passion in her that Evan had been able to bring to the surface with his merest touch, but neither would Robert ever hurt her as badly as her ex-husband had done. "Her middle name was Catherine," Amanda answered quietly, apologizing for her bad temper with her eyes and a quirky smile meant for Robert alone. He smiled back, and some of her tension melted away.

The clerk's next question caught Amanda unaware. "Have either of you been married before?"

Robert answered firmly with a single word, still looking at Amanda's now-averted profile. "No." The little man behind the Plexiglas partition turned slightly, pencil poised above the form, myopic brown eyes peering directly into Amanda's white face.

"Miss Winston?"

"I've been married before." She swallowed, hoping her voice would come out stronger, more assured, when she spoke again. "I'm divorced."

"Your husband is not deceased?"

"He's very much alive." Amanda stared as he made a little check beside the appropriate box. Evan was more than alive; he was growing more famous with each book he published. His fourth and latest effort had been at the top of the *New York Times* bestseller list for fifteen weeks. His fifth book was due out in time for the Christmas rush. He was being hailed as the new Stephen King, a master of tales of terror and the occult.

"All we need now is a copy of your divorce decree, and we'll have this license issued in no time at all." The man looked up from his form expectantly. "You did bring a copy with you, didn't you, Miss Winston?"

"I..." Amanda stumbled over her words and came to a halt. The man looked bored. He must face situations like this every day. He couldn't begin to know what an earth-shaking experience this was for Amanda. She'd walked into this building on the arm of the man she cared for more than any other; the man with whom she expected to share her future. Now she was reliving memories of long ago and far away. "Robert." She looked at him helplessly. "I don't have a copy..."

"Where is the decree, Amanda? It won't take that long to run out to the key and get it." Robert was still watching her closely. His arm shot out and gripped her elbow as she swayed suddenly. Her eyes searched his as she struggled to find the best words to answer with.

"I don't have it at home. It isn't anywhere, Robert. I...I burned it before I ever left New York to come home to Sarasota. I thought I'd never need it again." Amanda finished the confession in seconds. She hated having to admit what she'd done three years ago in a fit of pain and anger. "I never thought..." She'd never thought she'd find another man to love and cherish; she'd never thought she'd marry again, but how did she tell Robert that in front of the awful little man behind the counter? Amanda shut her eyes and willed away the stinging tears of embarrassment and confusion that welled behind her eyelids.

"You can get a copy from your lawyer, I expect." The clerk blinked, looking mildly interested at the unexpected revelation, but remained silent. "We'll call your lawyer, right away." Robert's tone was quiet, carefully neutral, as if he feared any display of emotion on his part might push Amanda over the edge. He thanked the clerk, but his tone brooked no more interference from the bespectacled civil servant. He guided Amanda out of the office and through the glass doors of the building before she really knew what was happening.

Outside, the late-winter sunshine was bright and hot. Women with blue-white hair and sensible shoes strolled along the sidewalks. Old men in colorful tropical shirts and straw hats sat on benches near the Spanish-style building. Amanda and Robert got into his car without speaking. The traffic on Ringling Boulevard was light, and in only a few minutes they were alongside Island Park. A cabin cruiser, sleek and well cared for, much like her father's boat, glided by heading for its berth, paralleling their course for a short while.

"Robert, will we have to postpone the ceremony?" The thought suddenly came to mind.

"Do you want to?" He turned his head to watch the play of emotion across her expressive features. His own expression was guarded.

"I . . . no, of course not. It's just . . . the minister, the flowers. I'm confused Robert, and so damned sorry for the inconvenience. I feel like a fool." She tugged distractedly at the pearl stud in her left earlobe. "It's all my fault. I should have looked into the legalities weeks ago." They'd turned away from the water, heading back downtown in the general direction of the newspaper building.

"It's nobody's fault." Robert took his hand off the wheel, and Amanda placed hers within the warm confines of his grasp. He traced the rise of her knuckles under the skin, running his fingers over the bright gold band of her engagement ring. "Am I rushing you, Amanda? Is that why this little snafu is upsetting you so deeply?" He kept his eyes on his driving, giving Amanda a few seconds to gather her composure and answer convincingly.

"You're not rushing me. I want to marry you, Robert. I want to make you happy, to be a family." *Family.* The word caused another ripple of pain, sharp, and close around her heart. Robert didn't want children. He was past the age of wanting to be tied down with a family. She understood and respected his decision, but as hard as she tried to hide the truth from herself, the knowledge left an empty spot somewhere deep inside her. Had she agreed to marriage too quickly? Was this what she really wanted? "I want us to be together," she answered with all the sincerity she could inject into her voice.

"That's what I want, too, Amanda." There was a faint shadow of remembered pain darkening his chiseled features. Even watching him in profile, Amanda could sense the change in his expression. She wanted suddenly to be able to banish his sorrow. "I've been alone a long time. I don't want to be alone anymore. We're good together, Amanda. We enjoy the same things, we have other interests, also, outside our relationship, and we both have our careers. I want to make everything as easy as possible for both of us."

Amanda couldn't help smiling at the image of the debonair Robert Tacett being nervous about anything. "Robert, you've been so good to me..." Her voice trailed off, and she colored slightly. She was twenty-nine years old, for heaven's sake. Why should it be so hard for her to say what was on her mind? Robert had been patient, so loving, accepting her reticence about a physical relationship without a word of complaint, never rushing her. Even if sex so far hadn't entered into the scheme of things, she intuitively knew he would be a kind and gentle lover. She didn't love him in the same way she'd loved Evan. Perhaps,

Amanda reasoned, you only loved that strongly and that hopelessly once in your life, but she cared for him deeply and wanted to make him happy.

"I think it might be easiest if you contact Cameron and get his copy of the divorce decree." Robert returned to the subject at hand with his usual practical approach to difficulties of any kind.

Amanda couldn't be so detached. "No! I don't want to talk to Evan." She found she was suddenly close to tears, and that made her angry. "He's out of my life. I don't want to have *anything* to do with him."

"I know your divorce was difficult." Robert maneuvered around a double-parked car and pulled into the driveway of the *Examiner* building.

"It was a nightmare. I ended my marriage to Evan for two very good reasons." Amanda laughed and the sound sent a shiver of superstitious warning down Robert's spine. "We fell out of love along the way. And he couldn't seem to find time for me in his life." She shrugged and bit her lip. "He was unfaithful."

"You told me there was never another woman."

Amanda opened the car door, and the heat from the concrete parking lot rose around her in shimmering sultry waves. A fitful breeze off the Gulf tugged at stray curls of auburn hair and rustled the fronds of the royal palms lining the drive.

"It wasn't another flesh-and-blood woman. You're right, as always, and I'm being melodramatic. I never had a living, breathing rival for Evan's love. It was his writing that came between us. He needed his work, loved his work, more than he ever loved me. Only I didn't understand that until it was too late." Amanda lifted her shoulders in an expressive shrug that conveyed some of her bewilderment at how quickly her marriage had fallen apart around her. "It wasn't all Evan's fault, either. Losing the baby...well, it was so hard." She took a deep breath. "It's over and done with. I don't want ghosts of my past failures as a wife to intrude on our life together. I want to do it through the lawyers in New York. Can't you see? I don't want to have anything to do with Evan Cameron again as long as I live."

CHAPTER TWO

THE DISTORTION OF the wall-mounted security camera did nothing to improve Murry Nessman's squat, unattractive figure or to erase the scowl from his puffy face. "Mr. Nessman to see you, Mr. Cameron," the uniformed guard spoke into the monitor.

"Send him right up, Burl." Evan smiled at the belligerent expression he could detect on his business agent's face as the other man regarded the array of electronic devices in the lobby entrance.

"Right away, Mr. Cameron." The screen went dead. Less than a minute later the elevator deposited his friend outside the door of his apartment.

"Come on in, Murry, you look frozen. What in hell are you doing out on a night like this, anyway?" It was a rhetorical question. They both knew very well why his beefy agent was braving the sleet and cold of a bitter March night.

"This building gives me the willies," Murry muttered. "I don't know how you can live here. Four years that same guy has sat behind his desk. And for four years he's asked me the same damned questions every time I set foot in this place."

"It's his job, Murry." The older man stepped with ponderous dignity onto the black-and-white marble floor of the foyer. Amanda had hated the security in the cooperative apartment as much as Murry. Funny how such inconsequential things often conjured an image of her that lingered before his mind's eye, bringing with it the spectral scents of wildflowers and lemon-verbena soap. Amanda, as she'd been when they met: young and hungry for life, lovely in an angular, coltish way, her body willing and eager to learn love's delights with him. . . .

"I'm out running around in a damned blizzard because I want to know what the hell you think you're doing walking out in the middle of negotiations with those Hollywood types?" Murry's voice was rough and breathless. He smoked too much, drank too much, and was fifty pounds overweight. He was also one of the canniest agents in the city, and Evan trusted him implicitly.

Murry, however, didn't share his trust, at least as far as the "Hollywood types" were concerned. He never completely trusted anyone who didn't live and do business within one of the five boroughs of New York City. He struggled out of his overcoat, and Evan shut the door, trying to block the memory of Amanda's soft golden body held close in his arms. The effort was only partially successful.

Still muttering imprecations at the weather and at writers who were obviously out of their minds, and bemoaning the state of the world in general, Murry unwound the plaid wool muffler encircling his neck. Tossing the scarf on a spindly legged reproduction nearby and muttering about "a Louis something-or-other antique chair," he marched with heavy measured tread into the living room of the luxurious apartment.

"I can't understand it. Where did I go wrong?" He addressed the ceiling. "Six months I've been brow-beating those...those..."

"Gentlemen?" Evan suggested diplomatically, hiding a smile by the simple expedient of turning it into a cough and clearing his throat.

Murry snorted and went on talking as if he hadn't heard. "Into giving you damn near total artistic control over this screenplay, and you blow it all by refusing to go out to the Coast and show them who's boss," he ended dramatically while Evan motioned him to a chair. "I'm out all day trying to keep ingrates like you out of the poorhouse, and what do I find? A message from my service: Mr Cameron's canceling his trip to California. He's going to Florida. What the hell's in Florida, for God's sake?" Murry rolled his eyes heavenward and patted his pocket, searching for one of his ever-present cigars. "There's nothing but old people and crocodiles down there."

"Alligators." Evan stood before his friend and mentor and looked down at the portly figure slumped in the big chair. Trust Murry to find the most comfortable piece of furniture in the room and stake it out as his own.

"Alligators, crocodiles, what's the difference?" Evan held his peace, deciding it was no time to explain the biological differences between the two species of reptile.

"They all eat writers," Murry warned portentously, fixing his client with a gimlet-eyed stare as he puffed his stogie to life. "And fifteen percent of a dead writer isn't worth much." He finished with the air of a man who has had the last unassailable word.

"Settle down, Murry." Evan chuckled, holding up his hands in mock surrender. "Put your feet up, relax, and I'll get you a beer." Long association with his cantankerous business agent had conditioned Evan to his bouts of petulance. "I'm tired, Murry. I've done five books in seven years, one movie, and now there's another one in the works. I need some time off, that's all." He headed for the kitchen.

"You're a hell of a writer, Cameron, but a lousy actor. That little speech isn't good enough by a long shot."

"Maybe I want to see some palm trees and pretty girls in bikinis," Evan called out through the shuttered service opening in the wall that separated the kitchen and dining areas of the apartment.

"They've got pretty girls and palm trees in California. Where you're headed they've got orthopedic shoe stores and urologists. They call it 'God's Waiting Room,' for the love of Mike." Murry made a rude noise and took an agitated puff on his cigar. He knew there was only one person in Florida as far as Evan was concerned; he didn't even bother to ask the younger man's destination, taking it for granted that his client was going to Sarasota to see Amanda. "What possible reason can you have for getting mixed up with all those geriatric types? Most of them should be rocking on the rest-home porch, not out driving big gas-guzzling cars up and down the public streets." He paused for breath, wheezing a little at the exertion of so long a speech. "This is the best movie deal we're ever likely to make."

Since Murry was long past his sixtieth year himself, Evan wondered irreverently just what his friend considered geriatric types but decided not to ask. "I know you got me everything I wanted from the studio but the deal will keep for a week or two. I won't be gone longer than that."

"Why go at all?" Murry could be as tenacious as a pit bull when he put his mind to it.

"I'm going to see Amanda." Evan stood in the archway separating the dining alcove from the living area with two bottles of beer in one hand and two pilsner glasses in the other.

Silence greeted his disclosure. Only the hiss of flames from the fireplace and the wheeze of Murry's labored breathing could be heard in the apartment. Murry sat with his eyes closed, looking pained. Far below them on the street, the sounds of traffic underscored the sleet being flung against the windows.

A night like this, stormy and bitterly cold, always made Evan remember the last evening he and Amanda had spent under this roof as man and wife. They had barely been speaking to each other by then, each walled off in a cocoon of pride and misery. In his anger and pain he'd lashed out at Amanda, hurting them both, insisting she take the money he'd planned to use as down payment on a house in the country.

In his fantasies, Evan had dreamed that they could pick up the pieces of their relationship, away from the pretentious New York life-style they'd drifted into during the last year of their marriage. He'd hoped that they could find the magic again. He would have a garden, go fishing on long summer evenings, make babies with Amanda... Only their baby had died before it had been more than a promise of the future, and somehow their love had withered and died also.

He didn't love Amanda anymore. He was certain of that fact. But some nights, like tonight, he couldn't get her out of his thoughts. Maybe seeing her again, seeing her in love with, and happy with, another man, would cure him of the last of his feelings for her. He started toward Murry, the rugged lines of his face set with grim determination as he prepared to do battle with the ghost of a dead love.

Murry opened his eyes when Evan handed him the glass and the bottle of beer. "Why go now? Why, after all this time?" The staccato questions, voiced in a nasal Brooklyn accent, ricocheted around the quiet, warmly-lighted room like tracer bullets.

"She's going to be married again," Evan explained in a flat voice. "She hasn't got a certified copy of our divorce decree for some reason, and she needs one." He shook his head, looking perplexed. He wished he could get the echo of her distinctive, husky voice out of his mind before he tried to go to sleep tonight. "She left a message on my answering machine. She didn't give me a reason, and her message was disjointed. You remember how she jumbles her sentences together when she's excited or upset."

"Let those high-priced Wall Street lawyers of yours take care of it. I saw how much you paid them to handle the divorce. They owe you one."

"I don't want them involved. Lawyers make Amanda nervous." He dropped down onto the overstuffed sofa sitting at right angles to the bright burning fire in the grate. He faced Murry head-on.

"Then why don't her own lawyers get a copy of the papers for her?" Murry asked. "She surely can't be afraid to talk to them?"

"I'm not sure. She mumbled something about a computer error . . . some clerk somewhere pushed the wrong button . . . she said it *ate* a whole letter of the alphabet. Whatever the hell that means.'' Evan shook his dark-blond head and took a long swallow of his beer.

''Stay out of it.'' Murry struggled upright in the big, low chair. ''You'll only hurt yourself, and Mandy. Why stir it up again, now, after all this time?''

''For old times' sake, maybe?'' Evan shrugged expressively, his broad shoulders straining the bulky material of his rust-colored turtleneck sweater. ''I can't explain it rationally.'' He wasn't going to tell Murry his suspicion that Amanda might be pregnant by this nameless, faceless man she wanted to marry. He didn't have any evidence to support his fear, only a sharp, empty feeling in his gut whenever he thought of the possibility. Amanda married to someone else was hard enough for him to accept. Amanda carrying another man's child hurt too much to contemplate.

''What makes you think she wants to see you again?'' Once more, Murry's blunt questions summoned Evan back to reality.

''Because if she's…if she lost her divorce papers and the lawyers can't seem to come up with them, then I have the only other legal copy.'' Evan heard the sharp edge in his own voice and shut his mouth with a snap. He didn't want to have to justify his actions any further. His decision to go to Florida and confront his ex-wife had been a gut reaction to the sound of her voice and the news she'd dropped on him like a bolt from the blue. ''I'll deliver the papers personally.''

''Send them down Federal Express,'' Murry advised. ''Save yourself a lot of grief. Don't get involved again.'' He threw the statements at Evan with his usual rapidity, giving the younger man little time to formulate an answer. ''You don't have any say in her life anymore.''

"I have to be sure she's not making a mistake." Evan remained silent a moment, studying the bubbles rushing to meet the foamy head of the beer in his glass before he spoke again. "I feel responsible for her. Call it a guilty conscience if you want, but I put her through hell when I couldn't work my way out of that damned writing block. I knew she wasn't happy here. Then we lost the baby...and each other. I want to make sure she's not rushing into something now." He broke off, scowling, realizing that his argument didn't hold water. Amanda had been a free woman for three years.

"I still say you're only asking for more heartbreak. If you want to torture yourself, that's your business. And fifteen-percent mine. But you don't have any right to make Amanda miserable too. Let what's over and done with be over and done with." Murry's grating voice was unusually low pitched and almost gentle. "And for my fifteen percent, I think you're still in love with her."

Tawny eyes narrowed abruptly as Evan stiffened. He swung his legs down from the glass-topped coffee table where he'd stretched them out. He wouldn't admit, even to himself, that there was the slightest possibility that he could still be in love with Amanda. Sometimes he wondered if he didn't hate her just a little. She'd left him. She'd withdrawn into a shell of grief and silent misery after their baby had died. She wouldn't let him mourn with her, so he'd suffered alone.

What a mess his life had been in that winter! He couldn't write, and he couldn't understand why. He couldn't comfort Amanda or come to grips with his own grief. Then she'd walked out on him when he was as far down as he thought he could go.

No! He didn't love her. The idea was ridiculous.

"Keep your opinions to yourself," he said to no one in particular.

"Far be it from me to stand in the way of true love," Murry replied into thin air, following his own line of thought. He threw up his hands in a gesture of resignation. "I've never been able to talk your stubborn Scots head out of anything you were set to do, anyway. Go ahead, make a fool of yourself in Sun City or wherever it is you're headed."

I'm headed for trouble, Evan decided glumly, but he didn't admit the premonition aloud.

"You should never have let her go so easily in the first place." Murry sighed expansively as if accepting a heavy burden. He looked concerned. "I'll take care of those movie moguls. I could do with a little sun and sand myself. I'll probably get pneumonia in a taxi with no heater on the way to the airport, but who cares?" He waggled a fat finger in warning. "My medical expenses are coming out of your pocket, Cameron."

"It's a deal." Evan smiled, but the sunniness never reached his unusual topaz eyes. Had he been a fool to let Amanda go? Perhaps seeing her again would answer that question. He watched as his agent struggled to rise from the chair. "You always did drive a better bargain than I could."

"It comes with age. And greed," Murry said frankly. "Besides, who'd have thought three years ago that that baby would have been optioned by a major movie studio for a cool quarter of a million bucks?" Murry's voice lowered to the tender growl he always reserved for discussions that involved money. His computerlike mind swiftly calculated his own percentage of the deal as he worked at the buttons of his overcoat. "That's what a Book-of-the-Month-Club pick will do for you. Sorry that one didn't click sooner. It might have made all the difference to you and Mandy if it hadn't come so hard.''

"*Demon's Spawn?* I hated that book,'' Evan admitted. "It's ironic, or poetic, or maybe it's just a dirty trick it was the sequel to *Demon Seed*.'' He shook his head wearily. "But you're wrong about one thing. It wouldn't have made any difference in what happened between Amanda and me.'' His first book, *Demon Seed*, had hit the bestseller lists only two weeks before Amanda miscarried. The tabloids couldn't pick up fast enough on the coincidence in the real-life loss of the child and the plot twist in his book that gave bereaved human parents a preternatural child to raise and love and eventually set loose on a terrified world. Amanda had hated the publicity, and so had he, but he'd never told her so.

Murry watched Evan's face as his client relived the past, and he changed the subject back to business matters again. "I'll get started on the movie deal first thing in the morning. The more I think about it, the better it sounds. You always were too soft on those Hollywood guys.'' He wound the red-and-black muffler tightly around his ears. "Good luck, my boy. You deserve it.''

"I'll be in touch.'' Evan grasped the hand protruding from the sleeve of Murry's coat. "Thanks again, old friend.''

"Don't mention it. Like I said, you'll get my bill.'' He opened the door and turned to leave the apartment. His hand on the knob, Murry paused but didn't turn around. "And Evan,'' he added as he exited, "say hello to Mandy for me.''

PURPLE EVENING SHADOWS filled the carport, and crouched along the crushed-shell walkway leading to the house. Amanda closed her eyes, resting a moment before summoning the energy to open the car door and carry her heavy bag of groceries the last few feet to the front door. Her head ached. It had been a long, exasperating day, and she was tired.

A thud on the hood of the small car brought Amanda upright. A large white tomcat was regarding her with mellow green eyes. One paw was stretched out, tapping the windshield as if to attract her attention. "Max." Amanda addressed the cat sternly. "Where have you been? Not out romancing Mrs. Ellery's Siamese again, I hope? I'm afraid the next time Ming Le produces a litter of surprisingly long-haired kittens you won't be able to avoid your responsibility so easily." Max didn't bother to answer her accusations, stretching with lazy grace and hopping down from the car with a satisfied look on his face. Amanda shook her head, anticipating a visit from her elderly neighbor with another tale of forced seduction.

"You'd better start behaving, old boy, or I'll have you neutered." She slid out of the car but Max was already halfway up the path to the house and he paid the comment no more attention than it deserved.

He waited patiently by the door while Amanda fumbled with her keys, and then the animal ran past her into the dark room. The air was scented with jasmine, and Amanda lingered a moment in the cool twilight. Shadows were darkening the pines and oleanders that screened her home from the view of passing motorists on the road beyond. Not that there was much traffic this far out on the key to intrude on her solitude. Although Midnight Pass Road served all the residents of Siesta Key, hers was one of the few houses beyond the public beach, and the tourists seldom ventured that far.

Turning away from the growing shadows outside her front door, Amanda stepped into a world of glowing, jewel-tinted hues. Terrazzo floors stretched ahead of her, defining the living area with its rough-textured, off-white seating arrangement and angular chrome-and-glass accessories. The stark effect was softened by coral rugs and the green of living plants. The jalousie windows were screened by hanging ferns, and large pots of various exotic species were scattered around the room. Amanda loved growing things, and the miniature jungle outside her door was carried over into the room itself.

The sun was hovering above the horizon, a blazing orange ball sinking toward the line separating sea and sky. Max was seated in his accustomed chair in the breakfast nook, staring intently out to sea. Amanda watched also, seeing the setting sun transposed onto a cold metallic-gray sky. The skyline of a huge city rose around her, and she seemed to be viewing the murky sunset through another's eyes. A handsome man with a rangy, athletic figure was standing . . . alone . . . in the window of a large silent room.

Evan again! Thoughts of him had been popping in and out of her mind all day. She had gone against her better judgment and called Evan to ask for his help in obtaining a copy of the divorce decree. The sound of his voice on the answering machine had been enough to start this haunting of her thoughts for the rest of the day. She couldn't begin to imagine what actually speaking to him would have done to her.

Amanda fixed a salad and ate it standing up at the kitchen sink. She needed a walk on the beach, she decided as she rinsed the dishes. Although one of the older homes on Siesta Key, her twenties-era bungalow was in excellent condition. Amanda could never have afforded its prestigious location on her own salary. It was Evan's money that had paid for her present happiness.

Evan's money. Her hands tightened around the edge of the sun-warmed, yellow Formica countertop, but her thoughts took her back. A montage of their last days together flitted past the filtering censor of her memory, sifting out the worst of the pain, letting her see the past in distorted, out-of-sequence bits and pieces that made an incomplete whole.

Evan had promised that the advance check for *Demon's Spawn* would go toward a house in the country, but instead he stood by the institutional-sized, stark white refrigerator in the New York apartment looking down at the paper in his hand. "I want you to take this, Amanda. We both know everything's going sour between us. I want you to have something of your own— for all you gave up those first five years."

"Don't say that," she'd protested. Was that what they'd come to? Amanda had wondered. Believing they *owed* each other compensation for their love? She'd given up her own dreams of a career in newspaper publishing gladly enough. She'd settled for a dull copy-editing job on the small biweekly newspaper in the conservative Maine college town where Evan earned starvation wages trying to teach English Lit to a batch of upper-middle-class discipline problems and under-achievers. She enjoyed the dual roles of wife and homemaker more than she'd ever believed possible.

And Evan worked even harder; teaching, tutoring on weekends, writing every hour he could manage to steal or borrow. "Give the money back. Don't try to finish this book; it isn't worth the heartache."

"Not finish it." It wasn't a question. He simply repeated the words in a dazed voice.

"Yes, let it go. We'll go away for a while. You can rest, start on a new project. Please, Evan." It took all the strength she had to say those words. The shuttered, unreadable look on his face told Amanda before she finished speaking that she had failed to reach him again.

"I can't leave here until I finish *this* book, Amanda." His voice was filled with a desperate, quiet intensity that was even more frightening for its lack of passion. "I can't give up now, or it will finish me. I can't leave it alone. It's there inside me, fighting to get out, and I can't put it out of my mind, waking or sleeping."

Amanda almost wished her rival was a woman; she'd be able to fight for him then. Because from that moment on she knew with certainty that what she had always feared was true. The dark world Evan had created and peopled with demons and strange, disquieting entities was real. And it was capable of reaching out to cause his destruction and possibly her own.

She was frightened and confused, mourning the loss of her baby and what seemed to be the death of her love for Evan. She struck back in blind fury and outrage.

"Then you'll have to do it without me. There isn't enough money in the world to make me stay here and watch you destroy yourself over this book." Amanda held her breath. She was playing her last card, taking away all their other options.

Evan answered with bitter finality. "If I have to do this alone, I will." He didn't even allow her the dubious satisfaction of arguing with her. She was committed, condemned by her own hand and her own ultimatum.

"I want a divorce, Evan. I'm going back home. Soon. Back to Florida where people are sane and happy, not shut up in concrete boxes fighting terrors they create for themselves as well as the bleak reality of life out there." She gestured beyond the darkly reflecting windows where sleet chattered against the glass with nerve-wracking regularity.

He looked so tired, standing there in the harsh overhead light. He was drawn to a fine edge, working too hard, she tried to tell herself for the thousandth time, pushing too hard to finish this book and prove his talent was real and lasting. There was no question of his ability in her mind. Yet they had come too far down different paths to easily bridge the distance between them.

"You're leaving me just like that?" he asked, as if he couldn't believe what he was hearing.

"I want to go home," she repeated stubbornly, masking the total humiliation, the utter defeat of her femininity that she was experiencing.

"Then take the goddamned check at least."

She shook her head, squeezing back the tears that seemed to come so easily since she'd lost the baby.

"Take it and leave me a little pride." Evan's voice was as sharp as a blade, but Amanda scarcely felt the new pain. She hurt so badly already that one more wound went almost unnoticed. He ran a hand through his rough-cut mane. He needed a haircut. Who'd tell him that when she was gone?

"I don't want it."

"Mandy, for God's sake, take it, don't make me have to worry about how you're getting along on top of all the rest." He'd slammed the check down on the counter.

Perhaps if she could tell him that she wanted their parting to be as civilized as possible, that she was trying to make the break neat and clean so the edges of her broken heart would have a chance to heal... someday...he might listen. But the closed look on Evan's face froze the words in her throat, catapulting Amanda into confusion whenever she tried to speak.

In the end, she took the money he'd offered and watched in a daze as he walked out the door and out of her life. Like a zombie, she moved through the cold, legal formalities that dissolved their union and sealed the end of her girlish dreams of eternal love.

A few days later she left New York, returning to Florida and throwing herself into partnership with her father and the *Examiner*. And that was more or less how their life together ended, Amanda concluded sadly. Not with arguments and bitter recriminations, but with debilitating silence and the slamming of a door.

A FEW MINUTES LATER, Amanda wandered barefoot from her house down to the beach and onto the sand, brushing back a stray lock of sun-gilded hair, and smoothing her hand down the front of the denim wraparound skirt she'd changed into. The tide was on the turn, and a strong odor of marine life was borne across the sand by an otherwise freshening breeze. A brown pelican flew by with slow beats of its wings, heading for a piling where it perched, outlined sharply against the setting sun. Amanda watched the clumsy flight with troubled eyes as she walked aimlessly along the deserted beach. Max trailed along at her side. He was plainly bored with her meandering pace but seemed prepared to do his duty as an unofficial body-guard—at least, Amanda mused, as long as no more interesting occupation caught his fancy.

Digging her toes into the warm white sand, Amanda let the sharp edge of her thoughts remain. She was lonely. It was one of the reasons she had agreed to marry Robert. She wanted a home and someone to love and cherish. Robert wanted the same things. She knew she'd come to love Robert even more deeply when the twining of their lives had forged bonds with the passage of time.

Never again would she experience the joy that came with caring so strongly and so deeply you couldn't contain the wonder of it. But neither would she suffer the pain of loss if such a relationship went wrong. She'd learned some kind of a lesson from her divorce, even though she had trouble putting it into words. From now on Amanda intended to stand back a little from her life and evaluate relationships and feelings in an orderly, objective way. It would be better for every-body involved.

Amanda dropped down onto the sand, settling her-self comfortably against the trunk of a fallen palm. Max leaped onto her lap, purring with a strong steady beat. As the light faded, Amanda's musing enfolded her in a state of dreamy contentment far removed from her agitated, waking thoughts. She stroked the cat's soft, luxuriant fur and drifted closer to the release of sleep.

Silently, without warning, a form materialized beside her, and she smiled up at the male figure silhouetted against the rising moon. Shadows hid his features, but she wasn't afraid, and she held out her hands. It was probably only a distortion of the moonlight that shortened Robert's figure and broadened the sharp lines of his form.

It was quiet on the beach and only the call of late-flying birds disturbed the serenity of her hidden refuge. Robert didn't speak, further dispelling the last stirrings of reality. He gathered her into his arms as the large cat was swallowed up by the darkness. She was so tired. It felt good just to be held this way. She nestled closer to the hard curve of his shoulder. They would come to truly love each other if they could share such moments as this. She relaxed further into his arms and her thoughts of a happy future.

"I've missed you, Amanda." His voice was low and deep.

What a strange thing for Robert to say, Amanda thought with a flicker of sleepy amusement. They'd only said goodbye to each other three hours ago. His words were confusing, but she was too bemused by starlight and moonshine to seek an explanation. The unreality of the situation was clouding her senses. She was conscious only of a great desire to be held and caressed by the man beside her. As if reading her mind, he cupped her chin in his hand, turning her face up to his. She tried to open her eyes, but a dazzle of moonbeams made her shut them again, and a warm mouth covered her lips.

His tongue explored the supple curves with deliberate slowness, entreating their parting with deceptive gentleness before invading the moistness of her mouth. Amanda stiffened in surprise, her hands still curled in her lap. Robert had never kissed her like this before. He had never demanded a response so enticingly. Her lips parted willingly under his, inviting him with a mingling of tongues to explore further. It wasn't like Robert to be this aggressive, but she liked it. His kisses had never caused this singing of her blood, yet the sensations seemed like familiar memories.

It was exhilarating. She was once again a woman, whole and complete, desired by a loving, caring man. Her arms stole around his waist, lean and hard, and her thigh pressed against his. Strong hands spread across her back and reached up to tangle in the russet curls held back by tortoiseshell combs. They feathered along her throat, resting on the pulse beating wildly at the base, stifling the questions she longed to ask. His hands lingered a moment, as though testing the depth of her response, before they were replaced by a series of nibbling, arousing kisses on the soft white skin of her throat.

Boldly her hands closed over his, where they rested on the sensitized curves of her breasts, before moving up the hair-roughened skin of his arms to pull his head back to her lips. She needed to draw him closer, to extend and return his lovemaking. Her eyes remained closed as she drifted in limbo, anticipating the feel of his weight pressing her into the soft sand beneath them.

She didn't have to urge Robert to kiss her again, to move his body to match the pattern of hers, arousing her, turning her bones to liquid fire, shutting off her

breath until she was dizzy and light-headed and floating. He did all those things and more.

"Robert," she murmured against the searching lips.
"It's never been like this between us. I never knew you
could make me feel like this. I never..."

Her lover raised his head with slow deliberation,
breaking their embrace. He lifted her chin with strong
fingers. She knew he was looking at her, compelling her
to meet his gaze, but she resisted, aware the spell would
be broken when she opened her eyes.

"It's always been like this for us, Amanda. It always will be." The low, vibrant words rippled over her,
raising gooseflesh on her skin. Slowly, unbelievingly,
Amanda opened her eyes to meet and lock with glittering amber spheres.

"Evan!" She gasped, already starting to pull away
from her dreamworld. And her dream lover. "It can't
be you." Amanda's voice caught on a sob, the ecstasy
of the past minutes imploding into a hard ball of misery and shame somewhere in her middle. "I don't want
you here!" The last cry was wrenched from her.
Struggling back to reality, she fought against the
strength of his arms.

"You'll never be happy with him, Mandy." Evan's
voice was willing her to stay in this fantasy with him.
She fought to tear away the remaining film of dreams.
She could feel hot stinging tears on her cheeks, tears of
sadness and remorse.

"Go away! I can be happy with Robert. I will be
happy. It was you I couldn't make happy. It was you
who shut me out of your life—left me alone—you who
didn't love me anymore."

Amanda lunged away from his grasp but met no resistance. The dream was fading, loosening its hold on

her. She was alone. She always had been. The solid commanding figure was gone, dissolved into darkness by the salty wet tears rushing down her cheeks. Her hands tightened convulsively on the sleeping cat in her lap, further proof of the unreality of the last few minutes. Max had been with her all along, sleeping on her lap. She dashed tears from her eyes, as a gull called far out on the water and the muted echo repeated itself along the beach.

"Amanda! Amanda, are you out here?" Slowly she turned to face the sound of her name being called as the big cat stretched, kneading her with sheathed claws before leaping away.

The man coming toward her now was no figment of her imagination. He didn't move across the whispering water or travel along a path of silvery moonlight. His polished oxfords were kicking up sand with every step he took. He was blessed reality, strong and solid and very much a part of this world. "Amanda?" He was concerned by her silence and his voice showed it.

Amanda blinked and brushed a hand across her cheeks, removing the last traces of her silent tears. "Over here, Robert. I must have drifted off to sleep," she explained, trying out her shaky voice.

"You do sound as if you've been a thousand miles away. Look at you. You're all covered with sand." He dropped to his knees and eyed her indulgently. "It's getting chilly, and you don't even have a sweater with you." Another time Amanda might have resented Robert's efforts to mother her, but not tonight. Tonight she was just grateful to have him beside her. He bent forward to drop a light kiss on her cheek. Amanda turned her head to seek his lips, not certain why she needed to experience the contrast between the reality of

Robert's kisses and those of the phantom lover who'd visited her such a short time before. His kiss was light and quick, pleasant and arousing, but also very, very different from the kiss of the man in her dream. Amanda sighed, and tucked her bare feet up under her skirt.

"Don't tell me you aren't wearing shoes?" he asked with a smile, holding out a hand to help her rise from the sand. "I got your message. Did your lawyers really lose the only other copy of the divorce decree?" He folded her arm through his and held her hand as they walked slowly toward the house.

"It's ridiculous but true," Amanda explained with a weary sigh. "Somehow the computer swallowed up everything having to do with clients whose names start with *W*. I guess it only takes pushing one wrong button for something like that to happen. It's a fluke, but a damned awkward one for me. I had to call Evan," she finished, her voice sharp.

"What did he have to say?"

"I don't know. He wasn't in. He might be out of the country for all I know." Amanda fought to drive back the sensations her dream had revived, forcing the renewed doubts about herself and Robert that were surfacing as far back into her consciousness as she could manage. Taking a deep breath, she smiled up at him. "I don't think my message made a lot of sense. He'll probably call me back tomorrow."

"How do you feel about that?"

"I don't really know. Nervous and edgy, but that's to be expected. I'm not particularly proud of what I did. I'd like to get it over with. I canceled the flowers and called Reverend Markham. He was very nice about it."

"I had my secretary type up some notes for our friends. Just saying there had been a problem in the paperwork, and we'd let them know when we reschedule. Thank heaven we'd only planned a small wedding." He gave her hand a squeeze, then released her as they walked in thoughtful silence back to her house. They entered through the sliding glass doors that opened onto the wooden deck. Once back inside her cheery yellow-and-turquoise kitchen, Amanda felt better.

"At least the caterer won't insist on keeping the deposit." Robert's fine staff at his restaurant, the Sand Dollar, was in charge of the reception. She smiled, hoping no traces of her dream encounter still showed on her face. It was foolish to feel as if she'd betrayed Robert by dreaming of another love, but she did. "Oh Robert, you don't know how foolish I feel about this whole fiasco," she said.

Robert stepped forward and took her in his arms. "Don't waste any more time berating yourself. I'd much rather you directed all of that nervous energy toward becoming Mrs. Robert Tacett as quickly as possible." He leaned down to kiss her, and she waited expectantly. The contact was pleasant; she opened her mouth to welcome the tip of his tongue, but there was no sunburst of desire blossoming within her. She let her arms steal around his waist, drawing him close, but that didn't help.

"I said it this morning, and I think now, more than ever, that I may have been right. Have I been pushing too hard for this wedding?" Robert surveyed her face, studying the dark hollows beneath her eyes. Amanda watched him closely, too, seeing the flash of uncertainty in his blue eyes that she knew he didn't want her to detect. "It's a hell of a thing when you can't marry the girl of your dreams. I'll be in touch tomorrow so you can let me know if Cameron returns your call." With a last quick kiss, he stepped into the darkened living room and out the front door.

Amanda stayed where she was, her arms wrapped around her body, trying to hug away the chill that had suddenly invaded her bones. *The girl of your dreams.* But Robert, dear sweet Robert, wasn't the man in *her* dreams.

CHAPTER THREE

AMANDA GLANCED AT the calendar on the wall of her office. It was topped by a New England snow scene depicting what looked to be a sugaring-off party from a long-ago day. She'd been to a sugaring-off party when she and Evan had lived in Maine, and had enjoyed it enormously. But it wasn't the nostalgic winter scene that had initially caught her eye, or the fact that she was more than a little thankful to have come to the end of what was turning out to be the longest week of her life. It was the date.

The second Friday in March.

The day that would have been her wedding day if matters hadn't been so thoroughly fouled up. She hadn't heard anything further from her lawyers. Or from Evan. He hadn't bothered to return her call, and she hadn't been able to get up the nerve to dial him again. Robert, for his part, hadn't pressured her to do so, and she was grateful. Everything pertaining to her future was on hold.

"Amanda." Her father spoke from his seat in one of the hard wooden chairs that faced her desk. He was slumped down onto the base of his spine and looked very uncomfortable. For almost a quarter of a century it had been his desk, but three years ago, when she'd returned to Sarasota, he'd packed up his typewriter and his golf clubs and moved to an office three doors down, away from the busy city newsroom across the hall. "Are you listening to me at all? What do you want to bet she hasn't heard a word I've said?" Peter shifted in his chair to address his assistant, Teresa Harrington.

"I'm paying attention." Amanda leaned forward to emphasize her point. "I'm not that upset about postponing the wedding." Her lips settled into a rueful little smile as she regarded the two concerned faces before her.

"It's a shame that you have to be so inconvenienced." Teresa was a small, dainty creature in her late thirties. A Colombian by birth, with fine bone structure and huge black eyes, she looked fragile and sheltered. In reality, she was as strong and resilient as tempered steel. She had to be to have taken Peter's whirlwind approach to life and newspaper publishing in her stride all these years.

She'd come to work for the *Examiner* fifteen years before, shortly after the death of her husband in a car accident. She'd chosen to live in America and raise her young son. The boy was nearly seventeen now, spending the year in Colombia with his grandparents, learning to know and understand his mother's heritage.

"Robert and I have agreed to a three-week delay. I'm sure everything will have worked itself out by that time."

"That sounds like a sensible solution. I'm still going to be your witness, I hope?" Teresa tilted her head a little to one side and smiled.

"No one else."

"Good. You are two of my favorite people, you know." Teresa knew Robert well from having served with him on various fund-raising committees in the past. In fact, she'd introduced Amanda and Robert at the unveiling of a new baroque masterpiece at the Ringling Museum a little over a year ago.

Amanda waved her hand, a signal to change the subject, and Peter decided to honor his daughter's desire to move away from discussing her sidetracked wedding plans. "All the timetables for switching over to the new format are right on line." He watched Amanda closely as he spoke. "The new guidelines for Story and Art have been sent to the department heads for their suggestions and comments. We're starting to roll on this reorganization. Have I forgotten anything?" He finished his recitation with a theatrical flourish of his clipboard. It elicited an appreciative giggle from Amanda and a quick, bright smile from Teresa.

"Not that I can see," his assistant answered first. She had been checking off points against the master list she held. "Amanda?"

"A-okay." It hadn't taken Peter long to make up his mind about the future of the *Examiner* after Amanda had come back to Florida following her divorce. He'd taken one look at her thin, drawn face and sorrowful eyes and plunged them both into a reordering and revamping of the paper that was only now culminating in a total format change, bringing them in line with the big dailies in Tampa and Miami, while still retaining the character and friendly charm of a small-town newspaper.

Now Amanda was trying to talk him into retiring. He wasn't ready to be put out to pasture, not by a long shot. Especially not with what he knew now about Alexandro's corrupt regime, and Carmella's recognition of terrorists at the shelter.

"I've notified Accounting to be ready for the switch-over." Teresa's softly accented voice interrupted his thoughts. She was sitting beside him in another of the damned uncomfortable wooden chairs. Her soft dark hair was drawn back into a heavy roll at the base of her neck. Her skin glowed with a creamy luster that no cosmetic could duplicate. No matter how warm the day, how hectic the schedule, she always looked every inch the lady. "The necessary adjustments to the computer billing setup will be finished in the next few days."

"Good."

"Excellent." Amanda spoke exactly when he did. They both laughed at the coincidence.

"That's about it." He consulted his clipboard once more. He could feel Amanda looking at the hole in the sole of the disreputable old deck shoes he was wearing; he knew she was probably wondering from the back of what closet he'd unearthed them. His shirt and pants had come from the same closet. If he didn't get this meeting over with pretty soon, she'd be asking him point-blank why he was dressed like a bum. "The main press will be down about six weeks while we make the column-width adjustments. We'll use the small press for backup. I've made arrangements with the *St. Petersburg Times* in case we run into a snag. They'll print us in an emergency."

"I've got a new media campaign ready to run at the end of next month. There are some great radio spots I'd like you to hear, Peter." Teresa crossed her slender legs at the knee and leaned back in her chair for a moment before straightening up once again. "We're all ready to show this town a brand new paper."

"I can't wait," Amanda said with more enthusiasm than she'd shown all day.

"There's not going to be much more for me to do during the changeover, Mandy." Peter pushed the uncomfortable old pair of horn-rimmed reading glasses he'd found at the bottom of his desk drawer higher on the bridge of his nose. "I think I'd like to take a few days off."

Her father's request took Amanda by surprise. "Are you feeling ill? I can't remember the last time you took any time off."

"I'm fine. I just want to take the boat out for a few days." He grinned, but the smile failed to reach his eyes. "What the deuce is going on down in the lobby?" He swiveled in his seat, but couldn't see over the railing from where he was sitting. "Sounds like Bruce Springsteen just walked in the door."

Teresa lifted her shoulders in an elegant little shrug. Amanda didn't say anything, but walked around her desk and out the door before either of her companions rose from their seats. In the lobby at the foot of the wide spiral staircase leading to the executive offices, a bevy of secretaries was grouped around a ruggedly built man in a tweed sports coat and brown flannel slacks.

Amanda shrugged off a familiar, unsettling tremor of recognition. The man below her shifted position to answer a comment from one of his admirers. Amanda's heart skipped a crazy, painful beat. It was Evan.

Had he materialized out of the hot, stormy Florida day because she'd summoned him so wantonly that evening on the beach? Her hand tightened on the wrought-iron railing. She blinked hard to dispel the vision of her ex-husband. The figure didn't vanish.

When she opened her eyes he was still there, solid and very, very real, surrounded by chattering women. *A rooster in the henhouse,* Amanda thought waspishly, but her gaze wandered over him as avidly as the rest.

He still bought his clothes off the rack, she noted. And he still wore them as if they came from the most exclusive tailor. He'd gained back some of the weight he'd lost when they divorced, but his waist was still as narrow as she remembered. He had a runner's body: fluid, compact and tightly muscled. How well she recalled each and every line of its contours, the angles and hollows, the slopes and ridges of muscles...

"Well, I'll be damned. It's Evan." Her father's voice was a rough, pleased chuckle in her ear. "Go say hello to him, Mandy." Peter gave her arm a nudge with his elbow.

"I don't...come with me, Dad," Amanda said, giving in to a childish impulse for reassurance.

"Nope." Peter's tone was firm, but there was gruff kindness in the refusal. "It's up to you, Mandy. I'll be by later to say hello." He disappeared, with a curious Teresa in tow.

"Dad. Come back here." Amanda hadn't taken her eyes off the spectacle in the lobby as she spoke. Evan was handling his fans with ease and aplomb, something he'd never been able to do in the past. He had changed, obviously, but then so had she. Three years was a long time.

"Evan." Her voice was tight but steady enough. Amanda congratulated herself on that small victory and started down the stairs. The assembled women below turned to stare up at her as though choreographed by an expert hand. Evan didn't follow their lead, and that rankled. He unhurriedly concluded autographing the paperback copy of his book that Lilly, the receptionist, was holding. She grabbed it with a hasty garbled "thanks" and fled back behind her glass partition after one look at Amanda's set face.

"Amanda." Tawny gold eyes stared up at her as she halted on the steps. "Aren't you even going to say hello?" His voice was a low dark caress; the voice of her dream lover. Only a few casual words had been spoken, but already she could feel the pull of his attraction for her.

"I assumed you must be in California, since you didn't bother to return my call." Amanda resisted the urge to touch her hair as his amber eyes roved over her. Instead she tugged irritably at the cuff of her ivory silk blouse, controlling her apprehension, as well as her temper, with difficulty.

His hair was still as thick and sun-streaked as ever but it was shorter than he'd worn it when they were married. He'd evidently learned to make appointments with his barber all by himself. For some reason the thought made Amanda a little melancholy.

"I talked to your lawyers."

Amanda descended the last of the steps that separated them. She didn't like giving up the small psychological advantage the difference in height produced, but neither did she want their conversation broadcast all over the building. "How dare you." She meant the words to be haughty and arrogant, but her throat closed in the middle of the sentence, and she had to swallow hard to keep from choking on them.

"You have to admit your message didn't make a lot of sense." Evan made a quick, almost involuntary decision. Murry had been correct that day in his apartment. He'd been a fool to let Amanda go without at least trying to sort through their problems first. Maybe there was still a chance for them, a chance so small it was almost nonexistent, but a chance nonetheless. He frowned, moving closer to better judge Amanda's reaction to his next pronouncement. "I'm here to help bail you out of this mess."

His words were spoken in a lazy dangerous drawl that only added to Amanda's confusion and succeeded in sparking her anger. "How can you straighten this mess out?"

Evan didn't answer at once. He let his eyes move over her in silent intimacy, resting on her hair where it curled around her ears, lingering on the rounded curve of her breasts, the delicate rise of her belly. The need to know if she might be carrying another man's child assailed him again, as it had that first night in his apartment. Had she been living with a man, become pregnant by him and decided to marry? A lot of people he knew in New York never bothered to formalize their relationships until a child was conceived. It would explain the seeming urgency of her getting in touch with him after three years. It also hurt like hell to even contemplate the idea. Their baby had died. Was she going to carry another man's child and give it life?

"Florida agrees with you." He returned his scrutiny to her face, hiding his thoughts effectively behind an impassive expression. "Amanda..." His need to know was so great he almost asked her if she was pregnant, but he stopped himself at the last moment.

"Florida has always agreed with me." Was that a brief flicker of insecurity she saw cross his face? If it was, it was gone in the blink of an eye, and she couldn't be sure. "I'm not interested in your help, only in your copy of the divorce paper." That cut hit home; she could see it by the way his mouth tightened. She felt a momentary rush of satisfaction that quickly died under the weight of Evan's next words.

"That's just the point, my dear wife."

"Wife?" Amanda's voice rose an octave. She swallowed and cleared her throat. "We've been divorced for three years." Her words were more forlorn than angry, she suspected, and she glared at him to add emphasis to the sentence.

"Prove it," he replied in an obvious challenge.

Amanda felt her breath escape in a rush. He was right, damn it. She couldn't prove it. "We'd better discuss this matter in the privacy of my office." She capitulated with all the grace she could muster, gesturing for him to follow her up the spiral staircase. Her hands were shaking, and her knees knocked together so loudly she thought he might be able to hear. "I'll have your luggage taken out of the lobby. This is a newspaper, not a hotel for transients," she added with an edge to her voice. It seemed for the time being that the only part of her mind still functioning was a purely self-preserving sense of angry bravado.

Evan followed her up the stairs. Silently they moved along the carpeted hall, his shadow leading her like a dark nemesis, an agent of retribution for her foolish, destructive behavior. Amanda's heart banged so painfully against her ribs it hurt to breathe.

"Why did you come, Evan?" The door closed behind him, sealing her into the room with him. True to his word, her father and Teresa were nowhere to be seen. She was alone and on her own with a man who'd played havoc with her emotions and her intellect from the very first moment she'd laid eyes on him. "I didn't want you to come."

Her words were soft and tinged with deep sadness. Her voice had lost all its sting. She looked confused and defensive. Evan felt like a louse, but he'd started this scene and he'd have to finish it, whether or not he liked the way it was unfolding. "It seems my being here *is* necessary at this point. You see, Murry has my copy of the decree, and he's in Europe for six weeks."

"Murry Nessman? In Europe?" Amanda looked dazed. Her hands were clenched so tightly on the back of her chair that he could see her knuckles, now white, under the skin. "I never thought I'd hear you say that Murry had gone to Europe."

Hell, I've nearly blown it already. Murry is right, I'm no actor. "There's a first time for everything, Amanda," he told her in the hard tone he'd adopted downstairs when he took the first step along this trail of deception.

"And people change." She shook her head a little, wonderingly. Evan felt another twinge of conscience assail him. "You sounded as if it was urgent—your message, I mean." He stopped speaking for a moment, then went back on the attack, changing the subject before she could formulate an answer. "What happened to your copy of the decree, Mandy? The lawyers told me, reluctantly, about their computer glitch, but you never explained..."

"I...I must have lost it when I moved back from New York," she finished lamely. "It doesn't matter, anyway. It's gone." Amanda tried to smile, and almost succeeded. He looked so serious, the corners of his mouth drawn down, his brows knitted in a frown. It was almost the way he always used to look when he was creating a new scenario for a book. Amanda rejected the whimsical notion. "There's no other way to get a copy of the papers any time soon?"

She'd known instinctively from the moment she saw him in the lobby that another hitch had developed. Amanda looked down at her hand, where Robert's diamond sparked with a cold, clear light. She wished Robert was here now, to insulate her from Evan's pull on her senses. For a split second, back there on the stairs, she'd almost allowed herself to believe that Evan had come to take her away; that he would sweep her up into his arms and make all the world their oyster as he had in the beginning. But the momentary rush of pleasure was an illusion...no, a delusion—a flaw in the fabric of logic and sanity—as he'd described it in one of his books.

"The only way to clear this up any sooner is to fly off to Mexico or Haiti or wherever it is that they do these quickie divorces these days." *This is where my vaunted storytelling ability had better start to pay off.* He had to keep her off balance, keep her from asking logical questions and coming up with valid conclusions. Thank God it was Friday afternoon. His cockamamie story about the lawyers would hold up until Monday, and maybe by then he could come up with a better one.

"That's insane." Amanda clutched the back of the big oak chair so hard that it rocked. *Alone with Evan on some deserted tropical beach? Never...never again.*

"It wouldn't write. My publishers would laugh me out of the office, but nevertheless, it's true." Evan shrugged his shoulders, barely controlling an urge to cross his fingers behind his back, like an eight-year-old Tom Sawyer telling whoppers to his aunt. The gesture strained the fabric of his jacket. The wool tweed was too hot for Florida, but he ignored the discomfort, watching Amanda—his Amanda—closely. This was where his crazy spur-of-the-moment gamble worked, or where he fell flat on his face. Sweat broke out in a direct line down his spine. A muscle twitched along his jaw but thankfully Amanda was too preoccupied with her own thoughts to notice. He had to keep her off balance. He'd nearly blown it the first time he'd opened his mouth. He shouldn't have mentioned Murry's name. She liked Murry, always had. Of course she'd inquire about such an out-of-character act as a trip to Europe. He'd have to be more careful in the future.

Evan had known the moment he'd seen her that he couldn't just produce the decree and walk back out of her life. And still the question nagged at him. Was she pregnant? Had another man overcome her reluctance to conceive another child when he could not? The thought tore through him like a fiery sword. He wasn't going anywhere or giving her anything, until he knew the truth. Amanda wasn't vindictive. If he asked her, would she tell him? In the end, he lacked the guts to ask. He didn't want to know.

"Those are my choices? Wait on a certified copy from New York or fly off to God knows where with you?"

"Would that be so bad?" Evan swallowed a grin. She wasn't going to ask him any more sticky questions. For the time being she believed him. The fragrance of her perfume, cool and lemony and fresh as a summer day, was going straight to his head, making it difficult to think straight. He had to keep his wits about him, or he'd make a jackass of himself yet.

"It's not like you to play the knight in shining armor this way." Amanda inclined her head and regarded him suspiciously.

"I thought you might need help." He was on the defensive again. He didn't want to have to admit it was his own violent reaction to her garbled message that had brought him racing down here. The torturing thought that she might be carrying another man's child had already driven him to outright lies. And he still couldn't be sure. Not from the looks of her. Amanda had always been slim, but with a round woman's belly and softly flaring hips. Her hair was longer; that was all the change he could detect. She was wearing it up in some kind of soft intricate swirl on the top of her head. He liked that. In Maine, he remembered, she had occasionally worn it in pigtails or a ponytail. In New York she'd adopted a tightly pulled-back French braid. He liked this new sophisticated style. Had she changed her hair for her husband-to-be? "I've missed you, Mandy, so damn much..."

The soft utterance shocked Amanda out of her thoughts. *I've missed you too.* The words were poised on her tongue, where they had no right to be, when Peter burst unceremoniously into the room.

"Evan boy, they told me you were here. It's good to see you. How long can you stay?"

Evan returned the older man's handclasp with genuine fondness. He was surprised at the way Peter looked, almost as if he were spending the day working on his boat or cleaning out the eaves spouts, but he pretended not to notice. In all truth, he was too glad to see Amanda's father again to give much thought to the older man's wardrobe. He had never known his own father. His mother, a successful Boston attorney, had chosen not to marry her lover, and he'd always keenly felt the lack of a male parent in his life. He'd missed Peter almost as much as he'd missed Amanda. "It's good to see you again, sir."

"None of that 'sir' stuff. It was Peter before…" The older man hesitated a moment, staring hard at him before continuing. "It was Peter when you were married to my daughter. My name hasn't changed."

"It's good to see you again…Peter." He laughed, and Amanda felt a smile tug at the corner of her own mouth. Evan had the most infectious laugh she'd ever heard. That welcome fact hadn't changed, either. The two men before her would appear very dissimilar to the chance observer, yet were in fact so alike beneath the surface. They shared a quality of male arrogance, élan and self-confidence that was the natural asset of a successful man.

"He's not going to be staying, Dad," Amanda said, interrupting Peter's demand to hear about Evan's trip. She had to take a firm stand now, before he melted all her defenses.

"Mandy, girl." Peter spun around to face her. "The man has come over a thousand miles. He just told me that he had to lay over for eleven hours at Atlanta. You can't just hustle him off like a piece of junk mail. Anyway, you know as well as I do how hard it is to get a seat on a plane in or out of this town at this time of year. He can stay with me."

"Dad!" Amanda's tone was tight with anxiety. She opened her mouth to keep her garrulous father from officially tendering the invitation, when Teresa's entrance onto the scene halted her.

"You're not going to like this," she disclosed in a quiet but unusually tense tone. "The headliner is acting up again."

Amanda moaned her frustration. "What now, for heaven's sake?"

"It's mixing twenty-four-point type with sixty-point and garbaging the sports page."

"My Lord, what else can go wrong today?" Amanda shot a quelling look in Evan's direction. "Dad, will you give me a hand?" She could easily imagine their readers' reaction to a paper composed of gibberish manufactured by a temperamental, photosensitive typesetting machine. And she wanted her father where she could keep her eye on him. As for Evan Cameron, at the moment she didn't care where he went, as long as it was far, far away.

"I don't think so, Mandy," Peter said. "You can handle it. I'm going to take Evan down to the Main Bar for lunch." He smiled tightly and gave her a long, obstinate look. "I think it's time an old man like me gets out of the day-to-day, nuts-and-bolts hassle of running a newspaper."

"But, Dad." Amanda almost let the words come out as a wail, but she restrained herself just in time.

"Nope. You're right, Mandy. I need a rest. Come on, Evan, let's get some lunch, and you can fill me in on what exactly it is you're doing down here." Her father gave Amanda one more crafty look and started for the door.

Teresa stepped out of her boss's way and smiled, politely but noncommittally, at Evan as he moved through the doorway. She looked as flabbergasted by Peter's actions as Amanda felt.

"He's losing his mind," Amanda stated with conviction. "I don't know what to do with him." She moved toward the closet to take out a pair of white duck coveralls she kept for press emergencies such as this one. She'd found a long time ago that conferring with the composition crew of a daily newspaper was usually a dirty job. "I have the feeling that this is just the beginning of a very bad day."

"I don't want to be the one to add to your problems, but you have a call," Teresa said, nodding toward the blinking white light on the phone. Amanda had been so preoccupied with her thoughts and her ambivalent reactions to Evan's unexpected arrival that she hadn't even noticed the waiting call.

"Who is it?" she asked, looking resigned as she reached for the receiver.

"It's Robert..." Teresa colored slightly and went on. "It's Mr. Tacett on line two."

CHAPTER FOUR

EXITING THE DOUBLE METAL doors of the *Examiner*'s lower level late that afternoon, Amanda found herself smack in the middle of a violent storm careening in off the Gulf. She was tired, dispirited, strangely jittery and ill at ease. She felt like a child's toy that had been wound too tight. Evan Cameron was back in her life, and for the moment she didn't know how to cope with that reality.

Climbing into her car for the drive home, Amanda wished she could spend the evening with Robert. He would put things into perspective, make sensible, helpful suggestions on how to handle Evan's reappearance in her life. But his manager had called in sick, and even such a highly efficient and well-staffed operation as the Sand Dollar couldn't be left to run itself on a Friday night in the middle of the tourist season.

So they'd settled for a hurried and very public late lunch. Robert had been sympathetic to her state of mind, but somewhat distracted by his own concerns. Amanda had realized suddenly that she was on her own. She'd returned to the paper in a subdued mood, only to find that Evan had never returned.

Now, as she negotiated the road, she was beginning to wonder if the whole episode hadn't been a figment of her imagination. Or was it possible he'd taken her at her word and returned to New York immediately? The possibility that he had come and gone in her life so quickly that he'd barely stirred a ripple with his passing seemed hard to believe.

Yet why should he stay? He'd come to offer his help and she'd refused, adamantly, and with little grace. He was probably happy to be shed of his latent guilt over the breakup of their marriage. Amanda crossed the drawbridge connecting Siesta Key to the mainland as her little car bucked and swayed in gusts of sudden wind. That was the answer. Evan had already headed back to New York.

She almost regretted sending him away, if the truth be told. Robert had been right this afternoon. He had told her she should try to make peace with the past—and her past was Evan Cameron. She needed to come to terms with her first marriage so that she could let it go. Still, in retrospect, that seemed too dangerous a temptation. The attraction between them remained strong; that was what frightened her so. That was what she hadn't been able to tell Robert when she'd refused to consider his suggestion. She could feel the pull of Evan's spell, still, after all this time.

Pulling into her driveway, Amanda told herself for the hundredth time that she'd done what was best for both of them, no matter how callous or cruel her actions had seemed. She swung open the car door and raced for the house. Falling torrents of rain hit her with the stinging force of ball-bearing shot. As she struggled with the lock, a chilly wind swirled around her with a fury all its own. Wet and disheveled, Amanda stood panting inside the door, concerned for Max's well-being, as she let her eyes accustom themselves to the storm-darkened room.

The house was silent. Expectant. The roar of the wind was magnified by the unnatural quiet. No comforting, familiar rumble of the refrigerator motor or whir of the electric clock greeted her. Only the howling of the wind and the maniacal drumming of rain on the roof. The lights were dead. Apparently one of the downed palms along the road had taken some power lines with it.

A rustling among the branches of a six-foot Norfolk pine in the jungle-shadowed corner of the room raised gooseflesh on Amanda's skin. She wasn't alone. The building seemed to hold its breath, waiting for the next blinding flash of lightning to set it free. The atmosphere around her was ominous, pervasive, pushing down on her awareness with increasing pressure.

"Here Max, here kitty." Amanda was positive she'd allowed Max out to prowl that morning. Someone had to have let him back into the house.

No. The door had been locked. It had taken her two attempts to get her key inserted in the lock. Only her father knew where she kept the spare key. If he'd been here and let Max inside, that meant Evan had been here, also. She didn't want to think about Evan being in her home.

"Come here, Max." Amanda let her nerves get the better of her for a moment and was immediately angry with herself for the lapse. That's what seeing Evan again today had done for her; somehow the experience made even her own home assume the character of an entity from one of his books. Her imagination had made it a living, waiting being, filled with menace and unseen danger. "Max!"

Nothing. She felt a chill, and hugged her arms around herself. Her scoop-necked blouse was plastered to her, outlining the curve of her breasts beneath the lace of her bra. Her skirt was soaked, clinging to her hips and thighs like a second skin with every step she took. Amanda kicked off her wet sandals and moved toward the windows.

The storm outside was a sight to bring her fanciful musings about the supernatural back to the forefront of her thoughts. Boiling white-flecked breakers reached toward the clouds before their towering weight pulled them down onto themselves and sent each one roaring onto the streaming sand. No living creature moved on the face of the water. It was a world without color, existing in a limbo of gray and white save for the fire in the heavens.

Amanda couldn't help but be reminded yet again of one of Evan's stories. He always led his readers, and his characters, deceptively toward the terror that awaited them, giving them addictive glimpses of excitement and beauty before ensnaring them in a web of danger and evil.

She was still standing with her hand on the drapes when an especially brilliant flash of lightning raked across the sky. A roar of thunder split the silence. An unearthly keening howl erupted all around her, sending Amanda's heart leaping in startled response to unseen horror.

A white projectile hurtled toward her and fastened onto the hanging cloth of the breakfast-nook table. Amanda bit down hard on her lower lip to conquer a growing scream until she recognized the howling tomcat suspended in the folds of her favorite Irish lace tablecloth. Max dropped unceremoniously to the floor in a welter of linen, paper napkins and a crystal bowl of strawberry preserves.

"Max." Amanda's voice was still a little thin and reedy as she stooped to untangle the snarling cat. "Hold still, pest," she scolded. "You'll tear the cloth." Her words brought a new series of plaintive howls from the cat. Max hated storms.

Amanda began to laugh. She couldn't help herself. It was a scene straight out of Alfred Hitchcock. Or Evan Cameron. Just as she'd been imagining it—the storm, the shadows, the woman alone in a house, isolated from the outside world...all the classic trappings of terror and suspense.

Instead, this scene threatened to disintegrate into classic slapstick. Max didn't look like a herald of ancient evil, as cats were so often portrayed. He looked plain silly covered with sticky jam and shreds of clinging paper napkins.

"You ninny, Max. Look at you," Amanda lectured, as her own pulse and respiration returned to normal. "Let's find a candle and get you cleaned up. I suppose I must have left a window open somewhere. Is that how you got inside?" The storm was moving away, and the room was growing brighter with every passing second. The more Amanda could see of Max, the more her amusement grew. "It serves you right for scaring me half to death," she told him. Max stared at her with slitted green eyes, unamused. "Your little performance back there fit right into the plot line. All sound and fury." Max laid back his ears and growled low in his throat, apparently in no mood for useless chatter.

"All right, all right." Amanda started down the hall, bypassing the linen closet where she kept her emergency candles because Max was struggling so hard to get away. Bathing him was a major undertaking at the best of times. Today it would surely be war. "Now if this were one of Evan's books," Amanda told her pet, "the reader would heave a sigh of relief because the heroine and her cat had made it through the scary part, and then poor old Amanda would open the bathroom door and fall down the rabbit's hole." Amanda shifted Max's not inconsiderable weight, scowled at the closed bathroom door and swung it open.

Reality warped out of sync as she stepped into a room of shifting, dancing candlelight and the overwhelming presence of a terrifying figure emerging from the darkness. Outlined against the blue tiled walls, his reflection distorted by a dozen lighted tapers and magnified by the bank of mirrors above the vanity, was a pagan god's naked form.

"Judas Priest, Amanda. You just scared me out of ten years' growth."

"Evan? What the hell are you doing in my bathroom?" Amanda's usually throaty contralto more closely resembled the sound of a rusty hinge. She was tired of being frightened by unexpected events occurring in the sanctuary of her home.

"Taking a shower," came the prompt reply. It was all too obvious he'd just stepped from the shower. It was just as obvious that the noise of Max's predicament and the pounding rain and wind had masked his being there.

He might have been a warlock gilded by the refracting fires of Hades, or an ancient spirit bent on the acquisition of her immortal soul. But he invoked no darker power, as a character from one of his books might have done. Evan only laughed at her awestruck expression and reached for a towel from the rack by the shower door. He knotted it tightly around his slim waist and said, "Close your mouth, Amanda."

She did as she was told, but only so that she could open it again to speak coherently. "You shouldn't be taking a shower in the middle of a thunderstorm. It's dangerous." She kept her eyes safely at the level of his collarbone. She was determined not to let him see how shaken she was. But how could she have forgotten, for even a moment, the masculine power and beauty of his body?

"I like living dangerously once in a while."

"My father brought you out here." It was a statement, not a question, and Evan responded to it that way.

"Yes. I couldn't get a flight out, and I needed a shower. I've spent the last twenty-four hours in airports and airplanes, remember?" Droplets of water sparkled on his bronzed skin and in his unruly dark-blond hair. He gave his head a shake, sending water flying around the room. Max growled a warning in her arms, and Amanda caught her breath at the unconscious grace and assurance of Evan's movements.

"That still doesn't explain what you're doing in my house." Candles flickered on the marble vanity, limning the chiseled curves and angles of his body in shifting patterns of light and shadow, bouncing off the ceiling, the mirrors and the ferns hanging in the corner by the shower alcove. Amanda swallowed against the heat of longing stirring in her veins.

"I haven't anywhere else to go, Amanda," he replied softly.

"Don't try playing on my sympathy, Evan Cameron. I heard my father offer you a place to stay. And Sarasota is full of motels." Amanda stuck to her resolve to keep him at a distance with all the will she possessed.

"Your father offered me a place to sleep, and I guess I'll have to take him up on it, because there isn't a motel room to be had in this town without a reservation." Which was true enough, Amanda supposed, if you neglected to mention that you were *the* Evan Cameron. "It's spring break, you know. And your dad wanted some time to explain me to his housekeeper." Evan took a second towel from the rack and began to dry his hair. "Peter said I'd make her nervous." Amanda looked a little dizzy. The candlelight bouncing around off the blue walls and all the mirrors tended to create that effect. She seemed rooted in the doorway.

"Carmella just arrived from one of those small Central American countries. Costa Verde, I think. She evidently had a pretty rough time of it there. Dad's awfully protective of her."

Evan let out a long, low whistle as he toweled his arms and chest. "Costa Verde? If she opposed old Alexandro's regime, then saying that she had a rough time of it is probably the understatement of the decade."

"I don't know all the details. She lost her husband . . ."

Amanda remembered just in time that she wasn't going to be drawn into any kind of protracted conversation with him. "That's all beside the point. Carmella will have gone back to the refugee center by now. You can leave anytime."

"Please, Mandy. Don't shove me back out into the rain. I doubt if I can even get a cab to come out here as long as it's storming." He moved a step closer to her. She smelled warm and wet and very feminine. The thin material of her blouse did little to hide the loveliness of her body from eyes once familiar with its mysteries. "I thought we might have dinner together."

"I . . . I don't think so." Was it there again, that hint of genuine pleading beneath the cajolery in his words? A day's growth of beard roughened his jawline, and there were brackets of fatigue alongside his mouth, reminding her how tired he must really be.

"Are you afraid to spend even that much time alone with me?" The statement came out sounding like a soft-voiced challenge, but Evan didn't care. It had been a long time since he'd allowed himself to picture her face or recall the physical love they'd once shared. The excitement was still there between them; he could feel it.

"No." Amanda couldn't listen to that kind of seductive talk any longer. "There's nothing of that magic left between us, Evan. The fire burned itself out a long time ago." She felt the silken strands of his seductive web tightening around her and struggled against it. "I'm not afraid to have you here, but it's awkward."

"I'll go whenever you ask me to leave."

"Good."

She obviously wasn't going to back off an inch, but neither had she told him to leave, Evan reasoned. He relaxed slightly. He'd have to go slowly, take it one step at a time. This wasn't the best beginning, her finding him naked like this in her shower, but he hadn't been able to resist the temptation to get rid of his travel dirt any more than he could resist Peter's offer to show him the house in the first place. It was a beautiful little place, just the kind they might have picked out together.

"Please get out of my way, Evan. Max needs a bath." He blinked and shook his head to banish the power of his thoughts.

"Give me the cat, Amanda," he said, reaching for the bedraggled feline.

"You let him in before the storm, didn't you?" Evan was taking control of the situation away from her. She wasn't sure when it had happened, but suddenly she felt helpless and alone. Nevertheless she obeyed his request. Evan dumped Max unceremoniously into the shower stall and slid the glass doors shut.

"I'll take care of him in a minute." Max growled in annoyance, but that was all. "Does he always give up without a fight?"

"He's the terror of Siesta Key, actually." She looked around her, bemused. "Where did you find my candles, Evan?"

"Right where you've always kept them, second shelf from the top in the linen closet. You haven't changed all that much, have you, Mandy?" He was pleased with the conclusion. When she'd first confronted him on the stairway at the *Examiner*, he hadn't been so sure.

"Yes, I have." His tone had obviously stung her pride. He made a mental note to stop provoking her, but Lord, it was fun to indulge in one of the verbal sparring matches he'd always enjoyed so much.

"Not where it counts, love." He stepped closer. Now there was only inches between them. Amanda was backed against the partially opened door. "Are you sure you won't join us in the shower? There's plenty of hot water left, and you look darn near as miserable as Max does."

"It's still storming."

"Take the chance with me, Mandy." How could he forget the pain and misery they'd caused each other so quickly? Was there some kind of magic in the air, or was she casting a witch's spell over him? The hurt was still there, for both of them. He could see it reflected in her smoky gray eyes. He could feel it in himself, a tight hard lump in the middle of his chest.

And hell, as much as he wanted to, he couldn't pretend she was his wife anymore. She'd given her heart to another man. The diamond ring on her finger was a constant reminder of that commitment. Evan's face darkened and his eyes narrowed to slits as the bald truth hit home. Amanda loved another man. And it was still possible that she carried his child.

Amanda saw the darkening of his expression, and turned to flee. Long arms reached out to stop her. "You're soaked to the skin. Get out of those wet things now." Privately, Evan reminded himself that you never got anywhere without taking risks. This was the biggest gamble of his life. If there was any chance Amanda could still be his, he had to try. He'd let her go once without a fight. He wasn't going to give up so easily again.

"Let go of me, Evan." He was holding her by the upper arms. Her flesh felt warm and smooth beneath the thin, almost transparent fabric of her wet blouse. He moved his hand to the back of her head, burying his fingers in the soft swirl of auburn hair to hold her still. His finger grazed the line of her jaw before dropping to tease the soft swell of her breast below the open neckline of her blouse. He lowered his head, his mouth hovering scant inches from hers.

She put her hands on his chest to hold him away, but the contact was unnerving. Crisp, dark-gold hair curled across the tautly stretched skin. Her fingers tingled from the unexpected contact. Her lips parted to deny him again, but his mouth stopped her with a quick fleeting kiss that was over almost before it had begun.

"As I recall," Evan said in a teasing voice that still held an exciting hint of some darker emotion, "candlelight showers can be very beneficial to one's well-being." His agile fingers freed a button from its fastenings. His words were a verbal caress, as stimulating as his touch. Amanda struggled within herself, her re-awakening body swaying closer to his, her sense of reason pulling scattered, defensive barricades into position around her heart.

"I agree..." she answered with deceptive, breathy docility. "A warm, soothing shower can be very beneficial to a woman's well-being...when she takes it with the right man."

He didn't flinch as her words goaded him, but the fingers buried in her hair tightened painfully for a moment. Fine tremors ran through her, and she knew he felt them through the contact of her hands on his chest. The third button of her blouse met the fate of the first two, but she didn't step away. "Everything is better with the right man, Amanda."

"It's too bad for both of us that you're no longer the right man." She tore her gaze from his smiling lips, but not before they'd hardened into a dangerous line of steel. His hands ceased the sensual attack on her blouse. He lifted her stubborn chin with one long finger, snagging her unwilling gaze.

"Are you sure of that, Mandy sweet? Or are you whistling in the dark? Are you making the best of a bad deal? Do you love Tacett as much as you loved me?"

Are you carrying his baby inside you? he wanted to ask, but didn't.

"Yes, I love him." For a fleeting crazy second, Amanda felt trapped, like a character in one of Evan's books. It was a nightmare; he was an evil spirit bent on destroying her. She was trapped by his nearness, his appeal, and she couldn't find her way out of the sensual nightmare he'd created.

"What happened to your divorce decree, Mandy?" His finger cupped her chin, gently but firmly, keeping her from turning away, from running away. He stared deep into her stormy gray eyes for a long moment.

"I lost it." Amanda had no intention, ever, of telling Evan that she'd burned the document because she couldn't bear to see their dead love spelled out in black and white.

"I see." She had the strange feeling that he actually did. His words held a tinge of sadness beneath the sensuality that was so much a part of him. "I don't know why I'm here for certain either, Amanda."

"I don't understand . . ." She faltered to a halt under the continuing scrutiny of his golden eyes.

"I only know it isn't finished between us." The conviction in his voice couldn't be mistaken. "When you left New York you took a part of me, Amanda. A part of me I've never been able to find again. I want it back."

"Evan, what's gone is something we both lost. I'm sorry, but I can't help you find it again. Please let me go." She refused to look at him again and risk losing her serenity forever. He still didn't love her, surely? He couldn't. And she didn't want to love him, not again.

It hurt too much. Evan lowered his hands. She backed away, then turned, running into her bedroom, closing the door behind her, locking herself inside. Alone.

CHAPTER FIVE

"WHERE DID YOU ever learn to make hollandaise?" Amanda asked with grudging admiration. One bare foot swung free below her flowered cotton skirt as she balanced on a wicker stool at the kitchen counter. The storm had blown inland, leaving the evening air fresh and clear. She'd been able to corral most of her irrational fears about Evan's sudden reappearance in her life, at least for the moment. How many women could take finding a naked man in their shower with aplomb? Especially a man whose rough-hewn angles, whose hard, masculine lines and curves she'd known too well, had explored so intimately, had brought to the heights of passion time and time again....

"Amanda."

"What?" She couldn't keep her eyes from fixing themselves on his square, competent hands as he whisked the rich sauce in the top of a ceramic double boiler. It had been a gift from Robert, a gentle reminder that she was an excellent, if sporadic, cook. The trouble was, she seldom found time to oblige her fiancé with a home-cooked meal.

"Set the table." He sounded exasperated, as if he'd repeated the request more than once.

"You didn't answer my question." Amanda ignored his directive yet again. He seemed completely at home in her kitchen. His shirt was wrinkled, and he needed a shave, but those details only managed to lend a rakish air to his rangy figure. Evan had always looked good in just about anything. Or nothing.

"I took a cooking course a couple of years ago." Evan's throat was tight as he watched her from the corner of his eye. Her elbows were propped on the counter, her chin resting on her folded hands. Behind her, through the sliding glass doors, the sun was sinking in a glory of blue and rose over the Gulf. The lambent gleam picked out answering fire in her tumbled hair. He cleared his throat to ease the constriction there. "I got tired of eating my own burnt offerings after you left."

"You couldn't even make instant coffee when we got married."

"That was a long time ago." There wasn't a hint of emotion in his words, but Amanda felt an uncomfortable, guilty twinge in the pit of her stomach.

"What surprises me," he went on without missing a beat, "is that you even have a double boiler on the premises."

"It was a gift."

"From Tacett?"

"His name is Robert," Amanda informed him sharply.

"I know. Your father told me. Looks like this thing's never been used," he added in a pointed aside.

What had Peter told him? Not that she'd burned her divorce decree, surely. She'd sworn him to secrecy on that detail. "I'm afraid with all that's going on at the paper I don't have much time to cook anymore," Amanda said. "And Robert owns the most marvelous seafood restaurant in the city. Maybe even in the entire state."

"That's quite a compliment."

"I'd eat every meal there if I had the chance."

"Why don't you?" He lifted one eyebrow in a quiz-zical look that Amanda remembered well.

"It's on St. Armand's Key and really isn't that con-venient to get to. Mostly I don't go there because I lack the time. I spend so many hours at the paper that I'm usually too tired to drive out."

"So you come back here and throw a frozen dinner in the microwave, right?"

"Right."

"Well, no frozen entrée tonight. If you'll condes-cend to set the table, we can eat. Now. Salad's in the fridge." Evan smiled his special, quirking smile. Un-erringly he reached into the cupboard above the sink and brought out two plates and saucers and coffee cups. Pivoting on the ball of his foot, he slid open the silver drawer with equal accuracy.

Amanda glanced at Evan's rugged profile as he spooned delicately poached eggs over the ham and English muffins. "Why did you take cooking lessons? Why didn't you just hire a cook? Heaven knows you could afford to."

"Too much time to kill," Evan replied without turning from the stove where he was replacing the hol-landaise over steaming water in the double boiler.

Amanda felt she understood. He had his writing, of course. She had her work at the *Examiner*, her home to serve as the focal point of her daylight hours. But what of his nights? Had he been as lonely and at loose ends as she had been after the divorce? Not according to the gossip tabloids. Amanda stabbed a fresh straw-berry in her fruit cup. But those stories were always sensationalized. She had only to remember the bally-hoo after her miscarriage.

Evan had never told her how he felt about that painful experience; he'd ignored the publicity at the time. If he grieved, he had done so alone. The silence had contributed to the distance growing between them. Had it also added to the stress of his writing block?

"Don't you like your eggs Benedict? They're my specialty, you know." Evan broke in on her sad reverie with a soft-voiced question.

"They're fine. Far better than I could manage."

"You're a meat-and-potatoes woman, I remember." His lopsided smile came and went in the space of a heartbeat.

"I'm not the same person I was when we were married. You've changed too."

"Have I?" Evan asked. She was telling him they could be pleasant dinner companions, polite and civilized, but nothing more. "I guess that comes from being in charge of my own life for a change."

"And you weren't before?" Amanda looked disbelieving as she toyed with the spinach salad he'd concocted while she'd been in her room.

"If I'd been in charge of where my life was headed three years ago, I'd never have let you get away from me so easily. My drive to be the best ruled me. I don't allow it to anymore."

I'd never have let you get away so easily. They were treading on very dangerous ground. "You don't let your creative drive dictate your life?"

"I've harnessed it." Evan had the grace to look sheepish. "Although it's hard to treat writing as a nine-to-five career."

"I know," Amanda whispered.

"But I've improved my work habits, if that's what you're getting at. I'm a damned good storyteller. And a craftsman. Craftsmen need discipline, and I've learned that."

Why was he telling her this, now that it was too late? He had changed, it seemed, but so had she. They were two different people with two different lives. She tried another topic. "Is it very cold in New York?"

"Cold and wet and miserable. It was snowing when I left." He stared out at the amethyst shadings of the western sky, shaking his head in wonder. "It's another world down here."

"All I can recall about New York is cold and misery." Amanda paused, heard what she'd said, and was ashamed. She came to a stuttering halt, the last bite of her fruit cup suspended on her fork. "I'm sorry, Evan, that was small and petty of me to say."

"Cities tend to affect some people like that. Especially when they're unhappy." He pushed back his chair, helping her to do the same. The mood was effectively broken. "Coffee in the living room?" His voice was hard, noncommittal.

"Yes, please." Evan didn't hold any power over her that she wasn't willing to concede to him. They needed to talk. She returned to the subject when they were seated on the rough-woven sofa. "I didn't mean to sound so piously small-town in attitude. I know how much you love New York. You always said you need the vitality, the force of a big city, to do your best work."

Evan snorted, drawing a long breath back into his lungs. "Damn, I was a conceited bastard in those days. Even when I was doing some good work up in Maine. I told you before, Mandy. It wasn't my writing that caused problems as much as it was a lack of discipline and direction.'' Max slipped into the room and jumped proprietarily into Amanda's lap. He eyed Evan warily.

''I do understand.'' But not completely. Amanda was so used to blaming his writing for everything that had gone wrong between them that she needed time to adjust her thinking. ''It never occurred to me that you were insecure about your writing.''

''I was scared to death it wouldn't last.'' He hadn't intended to encourage any more reminiscences.

''I never knew.''

Evan didn't answer. He stretched his long, flannel-covered legs out before him. Amanda was aware, as she'd always been, of the latent power beneath his calm exterior. His body possessed a coiled vibrancy and strength, yet it was always controlled, held on a tight rein. Part of it was physical, part of it was mental, that ability of the serious writer to shut out the distracting stimuli surrounding him, to turn inward to the center of his creativity and draw on its inspiration to sustain him. He was so quiet he might have been asleep. Was that all she represented to him at this moment, Amanda asked herself, a distracting stimulus he could shut out at will?

Amanda hadn't turned on the lights. The only illumination came from the lingering glow of sunset outside the windows. It softened the roughness of white stucco walls and tiled floors. The floor plan of the house was open and airy, allowing the last of the sunlight to spill across the room and rest at their feet. Max stood and stretched, padding lightly across the cushions to knead Evan's thigh with his front paws.

''Is Max the only thing I gave you that you've brought to your new life?'' Evan scratched the big tomcat behind his ears. Max began to purr, evidently ready to forgive and forget their humiliating encounter in the shower.

"Yes." The word was sharp. Almost against her will, Amanda could see the tiny mewing creature Evan had presented her with their last Christmas as man and wife—just days after she lost the baby. Amanda had hated the big, expensive apartment, but they'd been happy that Christmas Eve, watching Max's kittenish antics, touching each other and feeling content. She'd been happy to see Evan more himself, no longer ridden by the inner devils his prolonged writing block had set loose to torment him. But the closeness, the sharing, had been as fleeting as the season. Before she knew it, she was alone with her kitten and her regrets.

Evan continued to watch the woman who'd held his heart in thrall since the day they met. Sorceress or angel? Was she remembering his gift of the skinny, half-starved young Max? Was she reliving the pain of their baby's death? He hoped not. Grief ate at him, as fresh and aching as a new wound, but he still didn't know how to tell her, or how to comfort her.

What would Amanda do if he took her in his arms? He wanted to hold her close, still her objections with kisses until she melted against him and begged for more. But why? So that he could free himself from her spell? Or so that he could rekindle the fire they'd always shared? And why did he want to do that? The question puzzled him as much as it would have gnawed at Amanda because there was only a single logical explanation. And he was no more ready to accept that answer than she was.

He'd come to Florida with all sorts of fancies in his head, all bounding around in no discernible order, like the stirrings of a new book. Many of his thoughts had been harsh. Did he want Amanda back because she belonged to another man? Was it revenge for his own pain that was driving him? Or was it some compulsion deeper, darker, and by far more binding on heart and soul that had called him to her? He turned his head, watching as Amanda's eyes drifted shut and her head dropped down onto her bare arm where it lay along the back of the couch. She looked soft and vulnerable and very, very lovely in the dim light. Her body glowed a rich creamy color. No suntan coarsened the smoothness of her skin or smudged the graceful curves and pure, sweet lines of her face.

In turn, she watched him from under her lashes, seemingly mesmerized by the movements of his fingertips along the cat's fur. Max was almost asleep, too, his green eyes closing in slow stages of relaxation.

If he turned now, and drew Amanda close, how would she respond? Evan asked himself. It seemed as if she floated somewhere between reality and the pleasure of a private dreamworld where suddenly he longed to follow. She looked flushed and expectant, as though waiting for a lover: his touch, his kisses, the pressure of his hands on her breasts bringing them to exquisite sensitivity. Hell, in a way she was waiting. For Robert Tacett. Not for him.

"Why are you in such a hurry to marry Tacett, Amanda?" Evan's question was harsh, taking her by surprise. His voice catapulted her out of the euphoria of her fantasy and the memory of her phantom lover. But he was no longer a phantom. He was flesh and blood, and only inches away. Amanda stiffened, hating him for so easily disarming her defenses, only to mount an attack and catch her off guard.

"I love him, of course." She said the words too quickly and too vehemently to be convincing. The indecision she felt must be obvious. She sat up straighter, brushing her hair from her warm cheeks, ordering her scattered thoughts. "We have everything in common," she added, folding her hands in her lap to keep them from trembling. "We want the same things from the future." But did they? She hated herself for even letting the question arise in her mind. She hated Evan for planting the seeds of doubt—no, not planting the seeds, but calling attention to them.

"You love him." He might have read her misgivings in her eyes. She looked away, unable to verify the statement without an outright lie.

"We have so much in common, and he's a wonderful man." She sidestepped the question. "We're comfortable together and that means a lot to me."

"Your dad says he's forty-five. Isn't that a little old to be starting a family?"

"Evan!" White-hot agony streaked through her. "That's none of your business."

"You always told me you wanted lots of babies." He set his jaw in a stubborn line, determined this time to find out if she was carrying another man's child.

"That was before I lost the baby. Now I'm not so sure. Robert . . . Robert supports me on that point. I don't ever want to go through the pain of losing another baby." She could be as unfeelingly blunt as he was. "Never."

"Lots of women have miscarriages and go on to have houses full of happy, healthy babies." Evan's voice was tight, almost devoid of inflection. He stared past her at the darkening sky outside the window. His eyes were dimmed by sadness, but Amanda couldn't see his expression in the twilight.

"I don't want to talk about it." The words came out thin and sharp. She reached over to turn on the floor lamp by the arm of the couch. The shadows retreated to the corners of the room. "Robert and I will make all our decisions for the future together. This isn't a whirlwind romance..." Amanda nearly bit her tongue in her effort to break off the words she'd been about to say.

"Like ours." He didn't contradict her as she half hoped he might. His tone was whimsical; his expression was not. Like a bird entranced by a cobra's deadly, beautiful dance, Amanda watched as he reached out a smoothly muscled, teak-brown arm to catch a stray wisp of her hair between his fingers. "No, Mandy, no more whirlwind romances for the practical, grown-up Ms Winston. How long have you known him?"

"For more than a year."

"Meeting, falling in love and being married in the span of fourteen days *is* a whirlwind romance." Evan's voice was deep with sensual intent, but his eyes looked through her to a time and place beyond the present. "It's a miracle that happens only to a lucky few." He blinked, snagging her gaze as his tawny eyes focused on her confused face. For a second she was convinced he was becoming entangled in the same gossamer net of recollections that held her captive. "Do you remember that little motel where we spent our wedding night?" His strong fingers toyed with the silken curl.

Unbidden and unwanted came the memories of those passion-drugged days, flashing through her mind with the speed of light, as his words tripped erotic touch-points deep in her soul. Amanda shook her head in a futile, negative gesture. Her eyes were glazed, her mind shimmering with an echo of sun-filled days and love-rich nights. Shudders rippled over her skin as she experienced again the heat of his lips on hers . . . his body pressing her down into the yielding softness of their bed...his knee between her thighs, coaxing her to open to him. . . .

With a choke of fury that was more a sob, Amanda tried to shake off his clinging fingers. On the heels of past pleasure came the agony; days and nights of wanting and needing, aching and crying for what was lost. "Our marriage was a mistake," she answered flatly, unable to keep her body from reacting to the siren song of old love, but not her brain. "And the motel where we spent our honeymoon is as past retrieving as our relationship. It's been torn down and replaced by a fast-food restaurant."

"But not our memories of it. Not what we shared there. Some little part of us will always remain. We carry some part of it within ourselves."

"My God, Evan. You're beginning to sound like some turn-of-the-century Gothic novelist instead of 'a worthy successor to Stephen King,'" she said, quoting one of his reviewers scornfully. She didn't read his books anymore, but that didn't stop her from following his career. "Our wedding night was a circus," she reminded him, acid etching her words. "It rained four inches in an hour and flooded that damn motel. Not to mention the cockroaches in the bathroom." Amanda shuddered, reliving the episode. "I cried myself to sleep in the car, and you ended up with bronchitis." She deliberately emphasized the words with a scathing look at the aggravating, intriguing man beside her.

"I wasn't referring to that motel—or that wedding night, Amanda," Evan replied with unnerving equanimity. His encompassing golden gaze riveted her to the seat.

It seemed impossible to the cautious, prudent creature of habit she'd become that they'd known each other only three short days before he'd spirited her off the campus of the University of South Florida. He was in Sarasota doing research on his first book and teaching a course in English Lit. She had been an undergraduate in Publication Management. She'd never been interested in following in Peter's footsteps as an investigative journalist. Since high school she'd wanted to be an editor and publisher. But suddenly, in the space of three short days, none of her dreams were as important as the reality of being with Evan. She'd told her father she was spending the weekend with friends; instead they'd driven far down into the Keys.

"Those little pastel-colored cottages." He had picked up the thread of her thoughts precisely. "The Gulf just steps away."

"We never used the beach." Amanda made one more attempt to free herself from his growing power over her.

"Only because we were far too occupied in our room." In the bed where he'd taught her body and heart the exciting games lovers have played throughout the centuries. They'd been married ten days later by a notary public. But that younger Evan and Amanda were gone, destroyed by time and circumstance. This woman beside him was someone totally different.

"It's all long over and done with, Evan." She jerked her head back, pulling her hair from his fingers. It hurt and he could see the tears fill her eyes before she blinked them back. "My relationship with Robert is based on something more than sexual compatibility." Her voice was coldly logical. It made Evan's skin crawl. "Our marriage will survive because there is more to it than physical love."

He stood, pulling her up with him. She stared at him with eyes darkened by old pain. Her lips trembled with the intensity of her feelings. "Will it survive? Or will it merely fail to die, Amanda? There is a difference."

"Stop referring to my private relationships as if they were living things."

"Aren't they living things? A loving relationship should be viable."

"I won't listen to you malign what I have with Robert. He's the man I've chosen to spend the rest of my life with." She sounded as if she spoke to reassure herself as much as him. Evan took the gamble that he'd read her reaction correctly. He reached out, grabbing her shoulders, pulling her toward him.

"You aren't getting away this easily. You've been avoiding my questions. I want to know why you're in such a hurry to marry this Tacett. You either love him so much you can't bear to be apart, yet there isn't a sign of him in this house, not even a snapshot on your dressing table." He watched her closely, but her gray eyes told him nothing in return. "Or you lied to me earlier. Are you carrying his child?"

CHAPTER SIX

FURY AND PAIN collided in Amanda's brain. "How, dare you ask me such a question." Her hands curled, into feral claws. Evan watched her warily, but didn't release her or move away. She balled her hands into fists, trying to control the spurt of rage and agony that built in the wake of his continued probing. "You have no right to ask me that."

"Hold still," Evan said harshly as she stumbled backward against the coffee table. "Hold still or you'll hurt yourself."

"I told you, Robert and I haven't decided." Amanda nearly choked on the lie. "I don't know if I ever want to be pregnant again." She couldn't take much more talk of babies and true love and the past. It hurt too much. Their discussion had pointed out all she had lost. Was she making the right choice about a family? "It's none of your business," she said at last.

"That's true, Amanda." Evan spoke quietly, ashamed of his outburst. "I forfeited any claim to you when you left me. I'm out of line. I apologize." He loosened his grip on her arms. The standoff continued—neither party retreating, or acknowledging defeat to the other force.

"There's nothing left between us," Amanda said quietly, needing to convince herself as much as him. "I'll prove it." She wound her arms around the strong, tanned column of his neck, pulled his lips down to hers and lost control of her universe.

Max awakened with a snarl, jumping from the couch to slink into the gloomy corners of the room, leaving Amanda to her fate. The table pressed against the backs of her legs, blocking her escape. Her breasts brushed tantalizingly across the fabric of Evan's shirt. She could feel the tenseness in every line of his hard body as he fitted her to him. She complied instinctively, as if she were the missing half he needed to make him whole. Indeed at one time she believed she was.

His mouth moved over her lips, paring them with tender insistence. She didn't have the will to resist; she welcomed the probing, tasting caress as though starved for it. And she was, she thought fatalistically. She was starved for his scent and his touch and his passion. The kiss was endless, provocative, intriguing, and over much too fast.

"I'm not passing judgment on you, Mandy," Evan said at last, apropos of something in his own thoughts that she couldn't decipher. He sounded sad, but his lips quirked irrepressibly, and she braced herself for his next comment. "I can see now that you're not pregnant." He ran his hands boldly over the soft rise of her stomach. Amanda pulled away from the fleeting caress, ordering her scattered wits with an effort of will that was almost physical. "But I do understand why Robert is in love with you, why he's so anxious to marry you and get you into his bed. You remember—I know better than any man what joy he'll find with you."

Fury leaped into Amanda's face. She welcomed the sharp release it provided from his growing erotic spell. She had asked for it, kissing him like that. She'd thought to prove herself immune to him, and she'd failed miserably. She'd gotten exactly what she deserved for such a foolhardy action. Amanda pushed at his chest with her hands, but she only managed to become more firmly ensnared in his arms.

"Don't make snap judgments about my love life or lack of one, Evan Cameron. Robert is a good, decent human being. He's the most considerate man I know...." She was digging a deeper hole for herself with every word and doing Robert a disservice as well. She was making him sound pompous and stodgy. And to make matters worse, she was having trouble coordinating her mental processes while he held her so easily.

"He's a damn fool," Evan said with certainty. A twisted smile tugged at the corner of his mouth. "You aren't pregnant. You've never even been to bed with the very principled Mr. Tacett!"

"That's not true," Amanda lied, protecting herself on an instinctive level. She was in too great a jeopardy to give him that piece of information to use against her. He'd shut her out of his life three years ago; now he was back, with as little explanation. She was asking for a second broken heart if she remained in his arms. She opened her mouth and lied again. "Robert is a magnificent lover."

"Is he, Amanda?" Evan's tone was abrasive. She watched his face closely. His eyes hid his thoughts so damn effectively she might have been looking at her reflection in a polished brass shield. "Does he make you moan aloud in the darkness, Amanda? Call his name in the night as you reach for him?" He lowered his head as if to kiss her and prove his point.

Amanda stood her ground. There was nowhere for her to run. His lips touched the skin of her throat where a pulse beat in wild confusion. His arms brushed down the length of hers, enticing them to lift and wrap around his neck. They did so, as if they possessed a will of their own. Her fingers curved to the breadth of his shoulders, as though they were attached to another woman's body. She was suddenly no longer herself, but a wanton creature who wanted nothing more than to spend her life in his arms.

"Does Robert's touch send that pulse in the hollow of your throat leaping the way it is now?" Evan placed his hand flat against her slim neck. Amanda could feel the thudding of her heartbeat echoing along his warm palm as he tightened his fingers the slightest degree.

"All those things." She wanted to scream the words into his arrogant face, but they slipped past her lips in a breathless sigh. Evan's hands slid lower to tease the swell of her breast.

"Tell the truth, Mandy." Was there a hint of desperation in the command? He shifted his weight, taking most of hers against him. His fingers twisted in her hair. Her head arched back to meet his questing lips. "Does Robert make you forget the world exists around you?" His lips touched her mouth lightly, stealing her answer, making her greedy for more. He pushed her down into the rough-textured cushions of the couch.

Amanda's eyelids fluttered closed as his face blocked out the lamplight. How dare he use his knowledge of her body to seduce her! It wasn't fair. She didn't want him kissing her. She didn't want to remember every moment of loving him. Yet her trembling arms around his neck and the rapid rise and fall of her breasts conveyed a different message.

The pressure of his caress increased; his mouth played over the smoothness of her cheeks before moving to cover her lips with provocative restraint. Amanda clutched at his shirt, pulling him closer, relishing the heaviness of his torso along her aching softness. Her fragmenting objections to being held in his embrace were shoved to a dark, dusty corner of her mind.

She drew him into closer contact with her longing body as her tongue darted with hummingbird quickness into the dark moist cavern of his mouth. Reality ceased to exist, as he had said it would. Or perhaps it was only unwinding, spiraling her back to the time when it had seemed their love would outlast the pyramids, to a place where other promises and other men didn't exist. He lifted his weight from her, supporting himself on his elbows, but his lips lingered near hers.

"You were never a very good liar, Mandy." His breath fanned her cheek. "You haven't made love with Robert Tacett at all."

The words brought her rudely back to the fringes of reality. "Evan, don't." Crystal tears of weakness and shame stung her eyes, even as she pushed into the exciting pressure of his thumbs on her budding nipples. "I'm going to marry Robert and build a life with him." She tried to use the words as a talisman against his power but they were too weak. She was belittled and humiliated by her weakness. He aroused a measure of primitive sexuality she'd kept carefully subdued for so long. She hated him for the ease of his victory.

His eyes glittered with a subtle triumph. He failed to see the tears shining in her gray eyes. "I knew you couldn't want him like this," he growled. "Your body never begged any hands but mine this eloquently."

Evan was too caught up in his own passion, his own memories of the love they'd shared, to really hear what he said. "I'm going to prove it to you." His fingers were already at the fastenings of her blouse. He slid the silky turquoise fabric from her shoulders, feasting his tawny eyes on the beauty of her clear ivory skin.

"Evan, stop it," Amanda whispered, fighting to regain control of her body and her will. She pushed at his relentless, caressing hands. She gathered her failing convictions for one last denial of her need. "Stop it now. You're too much of a stranger to me now." She made her voice as sharp as her panting breath would allow. "We can't recapture what we had." The strained words hinted at her passion, belying her intent.

"You feel the magic too." Evan watched her pale face, his own desire sharpening, hardening. He suppressed a shout of triumph. It was true. He didn't really know her anymore, but he remembered her this way so vividly. She had the look on her face he had always believed that only he could arouse in her.

"The magic is gone. It died for us."

"I'm not so sure." He lowered his head to place a row of kisses in the scented valley between her breasts.

"I don't love you anymore." Her body wasn't responding to the command in her voice. She was soft and pliant in his arms. Her hands pulled at the stubborn buttons of his shirt, tugged the tail from the waistband of his slacks. He shifted away from her to facilitate her movements. She refused to meet his eyes.

Her hands flitted over the ridges of his back and waist with fervent quickness, arousing his flesh, then soothing it. Evan knew he should pull back but he could not. She was a kind of madness, a fever in his blood. A few more kisses, a few more caresses, and sanity would return. Her hands settled on his shoulders, guiding his lips to her breasts, and he gloried in her passion.

"You won't admit it, will you, my stubborn Mandy," he coaxed in a low seductive whisper. "You've never made love to Tacett like this. You're still all mine." He knew the elation in his voice was too strong to hide. He slid his arms around her, lifting her slightly to unclasp her bra. He removed the thin barrier it presented to his inquisitive lips. Her breasts thrust upward, released from restraint. His eyes narrowed with desire as he surveyed their beauty. "You're so lovely."

"Damn you, Evan, I don't want to love you." Amanda groaned under the sensuous assault of his hands and mouth. She stroked the tautness of his thigh. Her sense of touch recalled every inch, every line and angle of him. Her fingers trailed with inviting, tantalizing slowness upwards along the tight column of muscle and sinew to tug at the waistband of his slacks. "This is wrong." Her words ended in a sob.

"I know, Mandy, I know." His voice was raspy with strain. He rested his forehead against hers for a long moment and took several deep, unsteady breaths. Amanda moved her arms up to circle his neck once again. "I think I'm going crazy. I don't have control of my own mind or body. I've never made love to another man's fiancé. I've never really made *love* to any woman but you, Amanda."

"I went a little crazy too," Amanda whispered, as he laid his cheek against hers, his weight still pressing her down into the cushions. How good it felt, how familiar, and yet how excitingly new.

"You've bewitched me, Mandy." He sounded as if he truly believed what he was saying.

"We can't let it go any further. We'll both hate ourselves after if we do." She didn't care if her words sounded trite or hackneyed. She meant them with every fiber of her being. She was almost beyond caring about the heartache she was storing up for herself, but she couldn't betray Robert's faith in her.

"You're right." Evan moved with easy grace as he rose from the couch. He knelt beside her, pulling her to a sitting position to help her fasten her bra and secure her blouse when her fumbling fingers couldn't seem to manage the task. "We've got a lot more talking to do before anything like this happens again."

Amanda took his large, strong hands between her own, compelling him to meet her troubled gaze. "This...won't happen again. I'm going to marry Robert as soon as possible. I..."

The telephone on the kitchen divider shrilled loudly in the charged silence. Amanda's focus on the world jumped back into clarity with painful suddenness. "Oh, Lord, it's probably Robert. I really don't think I want to explain what you're doing here. It's getting late." Where had the evening gone? The last time she'd noticed it was barely dusk, now it was dark and the moon was peeking from behind tattered clouds.

"Don't tell him anything." Evan didn't bother with the buttons of his shirt, and Amanda felt a wash of color stain her cheeks. She wished he would tuck in his shirttail and help her erase from her thoughts the potent recollection of touching his lean, strong chest.

"I won't lie to him, Evan. I told you we have a very good relationship. We don't play games with each other."

"I'm sorry, I forgot." His jaw was tight. The next ring of the phone brought Amanda to the divider in a few quick steps.

"Hello? Dad...is something wrong? It's getting late for you to call." She listened in silence for a few moments. Evan found himself pacing the length of the room. He liked Amanda's house. He hadn't really paid that much attention to his surroundings this evening, but when he'd first seen these rooms he'd felt the warmth and attention to detail Amanda had put into furnishing her home. He could be very comfortable in a setting like this.

"Dad, I wish you'd tell me what's going on..." Amanda sighed, and rubbed her hand over her temple as if her head hurt. Her hair was tumbled around her shoulders. She was barefoot and still a little flushed from their encounter on the couch.

Evan continued to ache for her, but he was also ashamed of himself. What was he, some green kid who couldn't keep his fly zipped? God, she'd felt good in his arms, under him, wanting him as much as he wanted her. And she had wanted him; he wasn't feeding his ego a lot of lies. The physical magic was still there between them. But emotionally...he couldn't be sure.

"Evan." Amanda's voice cut through his preoccupation. He stopped pacing and turned to face her. "Dad wants to talk to you. He's leaving town for a few days." She frowned, and two curved lines appeared between her brows. He'd always loved to trace the delicate arch of her eyebrows with his lips when they made love. He wanted to do it now. Instead he took the phone when she handed it to him.

"Peter, this is Evan."

"Are you straightening things out with my daughter?" The older man asked bluntly, his voice coming through loud and clear with just a hint of static in the background.

"We've done a lot of talking this evening." Evan kept his voice carefully neutral.

Peter wasn't fooled. "You'd better not cause her any more misery. I'm not sure Robert Tacett is the man for my Mandy, so I've done what I can to give you a chance to make things right between you," Peter went on without a hint of softness in his raspy voice. "But if you do anything to hurt her like you did before... you'll answer to me. Understood?"

"Yes, sir." Evan turned his back on Amanda as she tried to knot the heavy auburn mass of hair on top of her head.

"I'm leaving town for a few days. Carmella, my housekeeper, is expecting you. Thanks for giving me a chance to tell her you'll be staying at the house. She's had a rough time of it."

"Amanda filled me in this afternoon."

"Good. I'll skip the details, then. You're welcome to stay as long as you like."

"Thanks. I can use the rest. I might stay a week or so if I won't be imposing." A strangled groan came from Amanda's lips, but Evan pretended not to hear.

"No." She made a grab for the receiver. "Let me talk to my father. He didn't give me a reasonable explanation for this spur-of-the-moment trip of his."

"What's that, Peter?" Evan fended off Amanda with his free hand. "Fine. And don't worry. I'll treat Carmella with kid gloves. Most of the time she won't even know I'm around. Safe trip!"

"Don't hang up!" Amanda watched with compressed lips as he replaced the phone on the hook. "Damn it, Evan, you let him get away. I want to know what he's up to. And I don't want you here."

"We've got a lot of talking to do, Mandy." There was a hard implacable set to his jaw. Amanda couldn't meet his eyes for a long moment.

"No more. There isn't anything to settle between us. It was all over and done with three years ago." Tears sprang into her eyes, and she blinked them back furiously. "Move out of the way, please. I have to call him back." The knot of auburn hair on top of her head slipped sideways. She pushed at it ineffectually.

"You can't, Mandy. He said he was on his way out the door. Do you have any idea what he's up to?"

"No." Amanda burst into overwrought tears. "This is all your fault."

"No it isn't, Mandy, but I'm sorry I showed up without warning and complicated all your plans. I only meant to help." He drew her into his arms, resisting her struggles to step away. To Amanda's whirling senses he seemed to once again assume the proportions of an evil genie.

"Let me go!" Strands of hair curled wildly about her face and shoulders. "I can't think straight when you're holding me like that. Why did you come back, Evan? To punish me, to ruin what happiness I might find with Robert? Why?" Her voice rose on the last words.

"I've told you the truth, Amanda. I'm as mixed up as you are. I don't know why." Evan's hands clenched into fists against her back. Did she expect him to break down and tell her he loved her so she could throw the words back in his face?

"Then go back to New York. Why do you insist on staying when I've asked you to leave? If you wanted to see me squirm, to make a fool of me, to see me cry over you, you've succeeded. Isn't that enough revenge for one short day?"

"Amanda, don't say anything else we'll both regret."

"I haven't even started, Evan Cameron." She looked as wild and beautiful as some untamed forest creature. Her hair had tumbled out of its haphazard knot, and her breasts rose with each breath. Evan loosened his hold, and she whirled away from him toward the glass doors that led to a cedar deck and the beach beyond. "Did you plan all along to seduce me and spoil my life with Robert? Do you hate me that much?" Her face was set, her features etched sharply with anxiety, her eyes pools of gray misery.

"That's not true, Mandy, none of it." But Evan wasn't sure exactly what he should say. The events of the past few minutes had shaken him as badly as they had her. He knew there was something still between them, but he was as unprepared for the intensity of that passion as she was. He didn't know what to think or what to say. He hesitated too long to put his confusion into words.

"Yes, it is true," she whispered brokenly. "Every word." She was out the door in a flash. He hated her; and she wanted to hate him but she couldn't. Amanda flew toward the ocean's throaty roar, hoping to let its never-ending motion drown out the remorse of almost having betrayed Robert's trust. And the far more dangerous lure of her desire for Evan.

The wind off the Gulf was cold. Her bare feet sank into the soft sand as she watched starlight dance on the restless water. Her headlong flight had propelled her along the beach in a path most familiar to her flying feet. A few yards away, the dark bulk of the fallen palm and the shielding palmetto bushes offered their sanctuary.

Amanda dropped down alongside the tree trunk and rested her chin on her knees. How had her carefully laid plans gone so disastrously awry? Only four days ago she'd been ready to marry Robert and begin a new life as his wife. She'd believed that it was going to be a good marriage, based on a foundation of affection and trust.

Yet, with all the apparent ease of a wizard conjuring a spell, Evan had returned and shattered her dreams. His caresses and kisses had renewed a need to be physically loved and desired that threatened to sweep all her promises to Robert aside. The emotional turmoil he'd created was like a rushing whirlwind. Right now, Amanda could only think of the physical joy and pleasure he gave her. She still wanted Evan. She wanted him to hold her, to love her, to need her. And she was afraid she always would.

Remember the bad times. If he'd really loved you, he would never have let you go.

"Amanda! Where are you? It's as dark as Hades out here." Evan's voice was rough with a mixture of emotions she couldn't decipher. "Amanda, are you all right?" She stood up. She couldn't face him again. She started to run in a long-legged sprint that took her several yards up the beach before Evan spotted her and started pursuit.

He could see her hair streaming out behind her, catching glints of pale moonlight in its depths. Her skirt billowed around her long white legs as she ran.

She turned her head to gauge the distance between them, and he saw her eyes, wide and bright with tears. Her hesitation allowed him to catch up with her.

Amanda saw him close behind and knew she couldn't let him catch her. She didn't see the washed-out crescent of sand in front of her until it was too late. She stumbled into deeper water and lost her footing, tumbling to her knees. The water was cold, and her fall knocked the wind out of her. She sat down hard and gasped as the icy water washed over her breasts. Evan tried to sidestep Amanda's crumpled form and sprawled face first in the surf. He broke water with a spluttering roar of surprise and discomfort. Amanda couldn't help herself. First she started to giggle, then to laugh, and couldn't seem to stop. They both looked ridiculous.

Evan rose to his knees, shaking his head like a big, shaggy dog. "You did that on purpose, woman," he accused, resting his hands on his thighs and dragging deep lungs full of air into his body.

"I did not." Amanda tried to look haughty and disdainful, but she couldn't pull it off. She started laughing again as she got to her knees and pushed wet strands of hair behind her ears.

"I can't see a thing," Evan complained. It wasn't quite the truth. He could see her skirt floating around her in a circle. Her blouse and bra were so wet they were almost transparent. Evan made no move to leave the water for a few more minutes. The cool salty rush of waves over his skin helped clear his brain, cool the heat of desire burning within him.

"You've just got city eyes. You'll get used to it."

He held out his hand to help Amanda rise. She hesitated a fraction of a second, then allowed him to enfold her hand in his.

"I'm sorry I made you cry, Mandy." Evan reached out to trace the curve of her cheek. "You do believe that."

"I believe you." She looked down at their joined hands and sighed. "But you also have to face the truth." Her fingers brushed over the hard line of his jaw as he released her from the gentle bondage of his touch. "Our love is over and done with. It wasn't strong enough to withstand the stresses in our lives."

"Are you sure, Amanda?" He was watching her closely. The moonlight sparked deep within his golden eyes, hiding his emotions as effectively as a mirror's surface.

"I'm sure." How could she explain these hazy, hurting conjectures to this stranger who knew her body so well but who knew nothing, it seemed, of the woman locked within?

"It doesn't have to be that way...."

"Yes it does." She began to walk back to the house, water streaming from her clothes, her hair a fiery halo around her shoulders.

"Why?" Evan stopped her with a hand on her arm.

"Today was supposed to have been my wedding day." She looked sad and humiliated and defiant all at once. It was a potent combination. Evan wanted to take her in his arms and comfort her, but he did not. "That's why I feel so guilty, so disgusted with myself and so angry with you. I don't like thinking of myself as a woman who lets her baser instincts rule her head and her body." She sniffed and rubbed her cheek with the back of her hand.

He pulled her close, ignoring her struggles, kissing her hair in a soothing gesture, combing the tangled curls with gentle fingers. He held her until she gave up struggling against him and relaxed in his arms. "It wasn't your fault, Mandy. And I'll never ask anything of you that you're not willing to give freely."

"But you left me alone, Evan. So very much alone."

"Shh, no more talking tonight." He pressed a sweet, quick kiss on her lips. He didn't understand her last words, but he sensed that she was in no condition for any more soul-searching. He'd almost pushed her too far tonight, and he was sorry. "I'm taking you to your door and seeing you safely inside, then I'm heading back into town."

"You'll have a terrible time getting a cab in that outfit." Amanda gave him a wavering smile. She didn't even protest when he swept her into his arms and began to carry her across the hard-packed sand. She nestled her head in the curve of his shoulder, and his arms tightened a little around her.

"I've been on my own in the big city for three long years. I'll manage."

He didn't put her down until they reached her bedroom. Max had been waiting for them on the deck, and streaked past them as they stepped inside. He took up his accustomed place at the foot of Amanda's bed.

"Does he always sleep there?" Evan asked as he let her legs slide down the length of his. He leaned against the doorjamb and cradled her against him. There were puddles of salt water on the carpet all around them, but Amanda didn't care.

"I'm afraid so," she admitted before she realized what interpretation he would put on the words. "I've been too busy to break him of the habit."

"My money's on the cat." Evan's tone was provocative. With a flick of his finger, he lifted her chin. He might as well have said aloud that he thought Robert would never find his way past Max and into her bed.

"No more fencing." She met his tawny gaze head-on, despite the flush of heat rising to her cheeks. "I've told you. Robert is a wonderful man. Max is quite satisfied to have him in my life."

"But not, I think, in your bed." Evan's voice was a deep, velvety rumble, caressing even as he teased. "All right, Mandy, I promise, no more inflammatory observations." He held up one hand in a conciliatory gesture. "Good night. I'll lock up on my way out. And Mandy."

"Yes?" She lifted her head regally, despite her barefoot, tear-stained appearance.

"Pleasant dreams . . . if you dare."

CHAPTER SEVEN

PETER WINSTON SHRUGGED deeper into the thread-bare cotton jacket, making himself smaller, shabbier and more pathetic appearing still. He was getting the hang of this. He almost felt like a homeless street person. If they weren't so fanatical about cleanliness here at the shelter, he'd probably smell like one as well. A smile tugged at the corner of his mouth, but he held it back and slouched a couple of inches lower on the bench, staring off into oblivion, seemingly lost in a world of his own making.

He was actually watching the young woman sitting on the hard wooden bench across the crushed-shell walkway. Carmella Molina was reading a book and seemed unaware of his presence. As far as the rest of the inhabitants of the shelter were concerned, they were both only waiting for the bus into Sarasota. Carmella had just said goodbye to her children. If he turned his head, Peter could see the two little girls being led away by one of the staff members. Every morning, he'd learned, they had English lessons, and in the afternoons they were catching up on their schoolwork in Spanish. Carmella had confided to him, that she hoped to have a home of her own by fall, and also hoped that her daughters would be ready for public school. Peter hoped so, too. He didn't intend for Carmella to have to live in the same kind of fear in America that had originally driven her from her home in Costa Verde. Not if he could help it.

From beneath the brim of an ancient Chicago White Sox baseball cap that shielded his eyes from the glare of the morning sun, Peter watched people come and go. He wondered how his disguise was working out. He also wondered what Amanda would say if she could see him now. Beside him on the bench were two large plastic shopping bags stuffed with odds and ends of clothing and personal effects. He carried them everywhere: into the cafeteria for meals, hooked over the edge of the wheeled garbage bin he pushed up and down the halls with a broom and dustpan each afternoon. He even slept with his arms wrapped around them at night. It was damned uncomfortable, but it conveyed exactly the sense of quiet hopelessness he needed to project.

The other residents of the center pretty much left him to himself. He'd taken great pains to establish his eccentricity and his total ignorance of the Spanish language, and it seemed to be paying off. Last evening Carmella had pointed out to him two men she believed to be members of one of General Alexandro's death squads. Calling on skills he'd almost forgotten he possessed, Peter had ambled close with the broom he'd been wielding with convincing apathy and feebleness since his arrival at the shelter. The men had paid him no heed and gone on with their talk. In reality, his Spanish was passable to fair despite what he'd told Robert. He'd been more than a little disappointed to find that the men's conversation was casual and completely ordinary. The only thing of value he could overhear before he had to move on past the two was that they planned to meet someone in town today.

For the first time he regretted coming into this investigation alone. Teresa and Robert knew what he was doing, but he had no backup to assist him. He'd have to take the next opportunity to uncover more information when it presented itself. But not this morning. He had to make an appearance at the *Examiner*, or Amanda would begin to get suspicious. He couldn't worry her by confiding in her, and he didn't want to hear any more of her lectures about how it was time for him to slow down, not now, when he needed all the confidence in his abilities that he could muster. Besides, Amanda had enough on her mind since Evan had come back into her life. No, he'd have to be patient and sit this one out. He couldn't afford to blow his cover, not when everything looked as if it might be starting to fall into place.

Peter felt Carmella's eyes on him and let his cover slip long enough to give her a cocky grin. She was a pretty little thing, with huge dark eyes that mirrored her every emotion. Peter felt a prickle of unease skate down his spine. He didn't really know how Carmella would react when the chips were down. If Alexandro's men caught on to them...but he couldn't worry about the possibility now. She'd do what she had to do to protect herself and her children; she'd already proven that. And so would he do what was necessary to give them all the best possible chance at rebuilding their lives in a country where freedom and opportunity were taken for granted.

Carmella returned his smile a little tentatively, then more fully as she bowed her head once again over the Spanish-English text she was studying. She'd do well in her new life, Peter decided, returning to his slouched position on the hard wooden bench. She had even more determination and courage than Teresa had possessed when she'd been left alone in a strange land fifteen years ago.

Peter's brown eyes clouded, suddenly losing their confident directness, as his hands tightened around the plastic shopping bag in his lap. Someone was coming along the path. He could see the movement out of the corner of his eye. He had to watch himself, or he'd blow this story for sure. *The eyes always gave you away in the end.*

From beneath the rough brown cowl of his robe, a lay brother, a Costa Verde refugee, like Carmella and most of the others at the shelter, watched the silent exchange between the old man and the pretty, dark-haired woman intently. For a moment he'd thought he'd seen something out of character in the old derelict's behavior, and it had made him stop and take another look. Yet when he'd gotten close enough to be sure, he couldn't see anything but an old rummy dozing in the sun, waiting for a bus into town so that he could, no doubt, spend the day prowling the streets before returning to the shelter to avoid the chill of the late-March night.

The cowled figure bowed slightly as he passed the young woman, his hands folded serenely within the rough robe. His body was tall and straight beneath the concealing garment. Carmella Molina bore watching. Her husband had given the regime a hard time before his providential death in a skirmish near a mountain village. The old man slumped on the bench gave a grunting snore and seemed to wake himself with a shake. He'd been mistaken about that one, obviously. He could be dismissed, but not the woman.

Carmella looked up and met his eyes, hidden deep in
the shadows of the hooded robe. Her expression was
tense and wary, but she showed no signs of recognition. Good. For the moment he was satisfied that his
anonymity was secure. She did not know him, of that
he was certain. He would have seen the fear in her eyes
immediately if she had. *The eyes always gave one away
in the end.*

EVAN RESTED THE HEELS of his hands on the rim of the
stainless-steel sink and watched the ashes swirl into the
garbage disposal. The acrid smell of burnt paper filled
the air. He flipped the switch on the exhaust fan above
the stove as he listened to the disposal grind away. He
didn't want Carmella wondering about his sanity any
more than she probably already did. He'd tried his best
to be pleasant, but it wasn't easy, considering the mood
he was in.

Saturday morning, when she'd arrived to water the
plants and straighten the kitchen, they'd exchanged a
few words in Carmella's broken English and his frac-
tured Spanish. She'd offered to fix him lunch and he'd
refused, politely but firmly. She shrugged and finished her chores, returning to the refugee center in the
late morning. Sunday she'd been off, and he'd spent
the day wrestling with his need to see Amanda and his
own unsettling reactions to his ex-wife. Yesterday the
rental agency had delivered a small compact sedan, and
he'd spent the day exploring Sarasota and its envi-
rons. Today he intended to do the same—except today
he would also see Amanda.

So he'd done it. He'd burned the damned divorce
papers. He couldn't face her again and lie, bold-faced
and unrepentant. At least not until he could sort

through his own feelings. Now, if he had to repeat his idiotic story about Murry and Europe and nonexistent safe-deposit boxes, he could at least be convincing when he got to the punch line.

Evan spoke the words aloud into the empty kitchen in a mocking voice, testing the sound of them on his tongue. "I don't have the papers, Mandy. They aren't in Murry's safe-deposit box. I burned them." Damn it! She'd think he'd lost his mind. He reached for a half-empty cup of coffee and grimaced at the lukewarm, too-strong taste of it. He poured it down the drain and shook his head in self-disgust as he turned off the disposal. He just couldn't think of any other way to keep Amanda free for at least a little while longer. A couple of weeks, she'd said; that's how long it would take to get an official copy from the New York courts. That was all the time he had to come to grips with his feelings for her. All the time he had to decide what to do about the future. Their future.

If they had one.

Burning the divorce decree was probably the stupidest, most childish stunt he'd pulled in a long time. But it was done. And all at once Evan felt as if a weight had lifted off his shoulders.

TUESDAY MORNING also found Amanda behind her desk, but business could not be said to be proceeding as usual. At least not to her way of thinking, which admittedly was none too clear these past few days. Outwardly, perhaps, she was functioning as her usual efficient, attentive self but inside things were changing. She was changing: reluctantly reevaluating her wishes for the future and her behavior in the past. She couldn't stop thinking about Evan.

Was it because he'd made himself so conspicuously absent over the weekend? She'd wanted to spend the time with Robert, but the only time they'd been together was for brunch at the Sand Dollar on Sunday. His manager's illness, at first only thought to be a case of the flu, had instead been diagnosed as appendicitis. He'd undergone emergency surgery early that morning, and wouldn't be able to work for at least two or three weeks. Both Amanda and Robert had pretended that their postponed wedding plans had been a blessing in disguise, but neither of them had laughed very long.

Amanda got up from her desk and began to pace the floor in front of the window. She missed Robert's sane and loving counsel. But she was also aware that she needed to work through this uncertainty about their marriage so that she could give herself, body and soul, to a caring, patient man who deserved no less than everything she had to offer. Evan's growing importance in her thoughts was both dangerous and exciting. It was as if a volcano were growing beneath the quiet surface of her life. It was surely only a matter of time until it erupted in a cataclysmic rain of destruction that would leave her safe and sheltered world in ruins.

Teresa cleared her throat with a soft cough. Amanda wasn't sure how long the other woman had been standing in the doorway watching her. She banished the frown that seemed to be settling permanently between her gray eyes and summoned a smile. "Good morning."

"Good morning, Amanda. Why so thoughtful?" Her friend looked cool and competent in a white linen suit and tailored jade-green blouse. Amanda had to glance down at her own pumpkin-colored skirt and cotton sweater to recall what she was wearing at all.

"I was wishing I could be with Robert, but he has a business meeting at lunchtime."

"I know." Teresa glanced down at her shoes. Her accent was slightly more noticeable than usual. "He's lunching with me. We're both on the promotional committee for the Medieval Fair. I called to ask him to reschedule for today because our regular meeting will fall on the week you're planning to be on your honeymoon."

"If things straighten themselves out."

"No word on the arrival of the divorce decree?"

"Nope." Amanda toyed with the phone cord, pulling and stretching the elastic spiral while she talked. "And since it's you Robert is lunching with, I suppose I'll have to stop hoping his appointment gets hit by a bus." Amanda laughed but was rewarded with only a slight smile from Teresa in return.

"Robert and I can reschedule if you want...."

"Of course not." Amanda held up her hand. "That was a bad joke. Just because our lives are so mixed up at present doesn't mean I want to see everyone else's disrupted, too. Just ask him to call me sometime this afternoon." Teresa still looked ill at ease, so Amanda turned the conversation to business matters. "Are the Wednesday flyers ready to go?"

"Yes." Teresa sounded relieved. "And your father's back. He wants a conference with Accounting and Advertising. He'll be up in a few minutes." She dropped gracefully into one of the wooden chairs in front of the desk. "Everything is going like clockwork for a change. Even the headliner is behaving itself."

"Teresa? Amanda? Where are you two?" Peter's gruff voice preceded him down the hall. He appeared in the doorway, dressed in a clean, neatly pressed shirt and white duck pants. The only thing about him out of keeping today was the three days' growth of stubble on his chin. But that was understandable, too, if he'd spent the weekend on the Gulf and only returned home to shower and pick up a change of clothes as he often did.

"Hi, Dad. How was the trip?"

"Uhhh, fine, honey. Weather was good all weekend." Peter exchanged a quick glance with his editorial assistant. "Where have you two hidden the advertising accounts? Nobody down there can find a thing."

"Right here." Amanda opened the second drawer of the desk as she vacated her seat.

"I knew I'd trained you two to be better organized than that batch of yuppies downstairs." He dropped into the heavy swivel chair, and Amanda leaned over the back and gave him a quick, hard hug.

"It's good to have you back, Dad."

"Then quit trying to put me out to pasture." He scowled down at the untidy pile of folders he was creating. "Ahh, here we go. Anticipated revenue. Classified run-throughs. It's all here. Thanks, ladies."

"You're welcome."

"How was your weekend?"

"Quiet," she responded warily, moving to his side to extract a folder from the pile, buying a few seconds to formulate an answer he would accept. "I walked on the beach, and I did a lot of thinking."

"Come to any conclusions?" Peter asked, picking out the folder he wanted and returning the rest to the drawer. He shut it with a bang.

"Just one." Peter lifted an inquisitive eyebrow as his eyes met hers. "Your only daughter is a very confused woman this morning." Amanda tried to sound flip, but her very real distress was apparent.

"I can't help you very much with this one, Mandy, but I'll always be there to listen," Peter said, putting his arm around her shoulders. It was the closest he ever came to hugging her in public, even when the only other person in the room was Teresa.

"Just being here to listen if I need you to is all the help I intend to ask." Amanda gave him a peck on the cheek, but her words were firm. "Evan is here in Sarasota whether I want him to be or not. He's my problem. I'll work out my own solutions, because somehow I don't think he's going to disappear back into the mist like a character out of one of his books."

"That's never been his style," Peter chuckled, amused by some private memories of his own. Amanda gave him a sharp look, but he returned her scrutiny blandly. "I know you can solve your own problems, but just remember one thing, Mandy. Don't let your head run roughshod over your heart."

Amanda didn't say anything. Her father was already on his way out the door, and she couldn't find a suitable way to answer his parting remark.

"THIS PLACE IS as fascinating as I remember." Evan seemed preoccupied. He stood with both arms resting on the wooden railing of the walkway jutting out into the shallow, weed-choked lake.

"It's been ages since I've been this far out in the country." Amanda laughed softly as she spoke. She looked around her. They were alone, as they had been since she'd ignored her common sense and accepted a ride with him when he pulled up outside the *Examiner* building as she was leaving for a belated lunch. "Come out to Myakka," he'd called, with his special quirking smile curling his lips and making him look as young and carefree as when they'd first met. "I want to see an alligator." She'd agreed, because his enthusiasm was infectious and it *had* been a long time since she'd been away from the noise and bustle of the city.

It had also been a mistake.

It seemed as if the entire world were deserted, enhancing the feeling of isolation that had dogged her since the moment Evan had walked back into her life and cut her off from the security of the calm, orderly routine she'd been following since she'd returned to Florida. Myakka River State Park was only a short drive east of the Sarasota city limits, it was true, but it was definitely the back of beyond in Amanda's opinion. "It seems like the end of the world," she confessed, running her palms over her forearms to rub away superstitious gooseflesh.

"Or the beginning of a brand-new one...."

"That too, I suppose." Amanda's response came out a little sharper than she'd intended. Warning signals were going off inside her brain, and a dull ache spread downward to her heart. *Don't talk about his writing,* she chided herself. He was losing himself in his imagination again. She could feel him pulling away, and it was almost as uncomfortable as it had been when they were in love with each other and his periods of intense creativity left her lonely and alone. She should never have come with him.

But why should today be any different? He'd always had this effect on her. She'd spent most of the last three days thinking about him, wondering what he was doing, who he was seeing, rehearsing speeches to make him see reason and return to New York. It was almost as if the discipline of three years of suppressing every conscious thought of the man had been wiped from her mind.

"The beginning of a new world." Evan repeated the words, unaware of Amanda's agitation.

"I'm only comfortable out here when there are a couple of dozen bird-watchers on this platform." Amanda laughed again to demonstrate how relaxed she was. The sound echoed shrilly off in the distance. On the far shore, startled water birds took flight from the cedar stumps jutting out of the shallow lake. A bull alligator roared his defiance. Somewhere behind her the nervous grunting and rooting of wild pigs answered the call. Amanda had noticed several of the animals on the winding road leading into the park. Black and wiry, with lean, square faces and tough-looking snouts, they bore little resemblance to the fat barnyard porkers she had seen. The palmetto swamp was full of them. Amanda shivered and rubbed her hands down her arms again.

Closer in, ducks and other migratory fowl swam among the reeds. Amanda was half-afraid to look down because she might see one of them disappear with a squawk and a flurry of feathers, as had happened once a long time ago when her father first brought her out to the park. Instead, she kept her gaze fixed on the water, where the arrowing wakes of the alligators were not so menacing as the one or two yellow-eyed reptiles she could spot almost under her feet.

"Look at them." Evan made a wide sweep with his left arm. "Don't you think this place feels like somewhere at the beginning of time?" He spoke softly, following his own train of thought. *Is he shutting me out? Or merely being caught up in the creative process?* Amanda wondered.

"Evan." He didn't answer and Amanda tensed, but somehow she didn't have the feeling he was withdrawing from her in the way she'd always used to hate. "Evan." She repeated his name more loudly.

"This is where they would have come seeking a new world to colonize." His voice, always compelling, took on a new quality. He looked at her and smiled, and Amanda realized he was inviting her to share his mood and his fantasy. "I've been mulling over a story that would explain how the ancestors of the demon child from *Demon Seed* and *Demon Spawn* came here from their own dying, watery world. How would those superior beings have influenced our evolution? Manipulated events…waited patiently through time…for just the right moment…just the right hosts…."

"Just the right woman to bear their messiah?" Amanda waited, fearing to see him withdraw into himself as he'd seemed to do so often toward the end of their marriage. She wished there were other tourists on the platform studying the huge glass-enclosed index of birds, arguing amiably over the identity of the ducks feeding in the rushes at the end of the raised walkway.

"Their messiah?" He blinked and the smile grew broader. "That's a good angle, Mandy." A lock of dark-blond hair fell forward onto his forehead, and he brushed it away absently, a frustrated grin lifting the corners of his mouth. "Damn, I wish I hadn't forgotten my tape recorder. I don't want to lose this mood."

"Tape recorder?" Amanda was interested in spite of herself. "You never used to resort to taking notes. At least, not more than a few scribbles on the back of an envelope or on some poor kid's midterm." She watched him closely, amazed to see a dark red flush stain his high cheekbones.

"Mandy, how many times do I have to tell you I've changed?" She looked flustered, almost frightened.

"Back then, all I thought I needed to create was my brain and my fingers. And time..." Evan shook his head and laughed ruefully. "I used to believe that if I didn't get it down on paper as soon as the inspiration came to me, I'd never capture it again."

"And now?" Amanda sounded matter-of-fact, but they both knew that they were exploring wounds that had only partially healed.

"I told you the other night," Evan responded wearily. "Now I know better. It won't disappear overnight, not my ideas or my talent. And I use all the mechanical help I can get. I even own a word processor, but to tell the truth, I still use that beat-up old portable as much as ever." He reached out and covered her hand with his where it rested on the splintery wood railing, as if to forestall her turning away from him. "Why can't you believe that I've made peace with myself and my writing, Mandy?"

"It isn't that." Amanda wasn't certain he had changed all that much, but for the moment she would give him the benefit of the doubt. And, in all honesty, it was the subject of the two books that had stirred the most hurting and painful memories to new life.

"Then what is bothering you, love?"

Amanda ignored the endearment. He only meant the word casually. In the New York circles he now moved in, "love" must be as common as "good morning." She decided to be truthful. "Memories. It seems that's all I have on my mind since you came down here. I don't like thinking about the past so much, Evan. I've tried so hard to forget it these last three years." She spoke bluntly to cover rising tension that threatened to clog her throat with tears she couldn't let fall. "Talking about those books brings back the bad old days." She gave him a wavering, apologetic smile, and turned to stare back toward the parking lot where his rental car was hidden by the trees. Her hands were buried deep in the pockets of her full cotton skirt. She balled them into fists.

"The bad old days." Evan shifted his weight to rest his hip against the railing. The movement pulled his khaki pants tight across his thighs. He brushed at a speck of lint with his hand. He wondered if Amanda could ever understand just how torn up he felt about those days? Would she ever let herself understand, now that time and distance made the gulf between them almost impossible to bridge? His eyes picked up the gold of the westering sun and reflected the light back, hiding his thoughts as he turned his head to face her again. "You're talking about losing the baby, aren't you, Mandy?" His words were as blunt as hers had been.

"No, of course not...." Amanda whirled away, the deep orange of her skirt making a bright splash of color against the somber greens and browns around her. Her hair brushed against her cheeks with the movement, and she wished again that she'd taken the time to pull it back off her face. "Why do you think that? I wasn't..." Her voice trailed off unconvincingly.

"Yes, you were. I know you were because so was I." Evan held up his hand to forestall her next remark. He knew as well as she did that it would be another denial. "Why are you shying away from the subject, Amanda? You told me you were over the trauma of the miscarriage. You said you don't want any more children. Surely then, it shouldn't be so hard to talk about it. You must have discussed the subject with Tacett numerous times. Not having children isn't a decision a couple makes on the spur of the moment, after all."

Amanda made a violent negative motion of her head when he lifted his hand to make the gesture with the fluid economy of motion that was so much a part of him. He was coming too close to the truth. Robert, of course, had made his decision logically and with a great deal of thought. But she hadn't. She'd pretended to listen to her fiancé; indeed, she suspected she'd jumped on the suggestion almost as quickly as he broached it. Her arguments in favor of not having children had been glib and obviously convincing. Robert was no fool, and he had seemed satisfied with her sincerity.

But was she sincere? Or was she deceiving herself? Could it be that as loving and caring a man as Robert was, she didn't want to have a baby...his baby... because it wasn't Evan's? No! That couldn't be the truth of the matter.

"I've already told you that Robert and I have come to the decision, together, not to have children." Amanda's voice was cold and stiff because he had made her doubts come rushing to the tip of her tongue once again. She had to make herself keep them from spilling out into words. "It isn't any of your concern,

Evan. Drop the subject. Please.'' The last word was softer, and her large gray eyes spoke even more eloquently of her distress. Since Evan had made his unexpected reappearance in her life, she'd been forced to look inward more deeply than she'd done in many months. She didn't like some of the things she was learning about herself. She resented him for being the cause of her distress.

"The subject isn't closed." He followed her along the walkway. They were still almost close enough to touch. Evan gritted his teeth in an effort to put his thoughts into words. "Why don't you want to have Tacett's baby, Amanda?''

"I..." Amanda put her hands over her ears in a vain and childish effort to shut out his probing. "You don't have to have babies to function as a fulfilled woman in this day and age. I'm only exercising my rights." She lowered her hands deliberately. Tears filled her eyes, making them sparkle like mica chips in the sunlight. Why did he have the power to see past her defenses so easily, to make her open up to him no matter how badly she wanted to keep her feelings secret? She took a deep breath and faced the familiar, perceptive stranger before her squarely. "I don't want to lose a baby ever again. Please, Evan. Don't let us discuss this anymore. I realize it's different for a man. Our child wasn't even a baby yet, not really." She let the bitterness she'd kept bottled up so long seep into her speech. "The doctors still referred to...it...as a fetus, remember? I can't expect you to understand...."

"Why not?" Evan found his hands on her shoulders. He was shaking her, his fingers biting into the soft skin of her upper arms. He knew he was causing her discomfort and tried to relax his grip. The effort required to do so was tremendous. His hands seemed molded to the shape of her with a will of their own. "Why do you think I don't understand your grief? That I don't share it? It was my baby, too. Our baby."

"You never said that," Amanda spoke furiously, letting go of some of the pent-up anger she'd held back for so long it had almost become a part of her. A small corner of her was surprised and appalled to find that the rage was still there, strong and insistent, now that it had a chance to break free of the restraints she'd imposed on it. "I can't believe you because you never even cried for our baby." She began striding swiftly back along the walkway, blinking tears from her eyes. Evan's next words were low and strained.

"How do you know I never cried, Amanda?" Did she actually believe he hadn't cared at all? "You wouldn't let me near you those last few weeks. You were locked up inside your own sorrow. How do you know how little or how much I grieved? Or how much I still grieve?" His voice was harsh, not with anger but with tears.

Her foot was on the step leading down to the parking lot when Amanda realized the depth of Evan's emotion. She stopped, stood still for a long few seconds, then looked back. Their eyes met, and their gazes locked and held for a moment of mutual anguish. "Did you cry for our baby, Evan?" she asked wonderingly.

"Yes." He broke the intimate contact of their eyes by looking out over the water once again.

"You never told me."

"You never asked." Evan's tone held bitterness as great as her own. What had they done to each other during those long silent months in New York?

"Did you resent those horrible stories in the damn checkout tabloids as much as I did?" Amanda couldn't stop herself from venting another of the old, aching hurts. "Did they tear you apart inside like they did me?" He'd never said anything about the sensational headlines, the leading stories, the ridiculous thinly veiled innuendo and outright lies that had torn at her fragile emotions and lacerated her shattered nerves.

Evan's hands clenched at his sides. The fabric of his shirt strained across his chest and shoulders. She was going to make him say it out loud, damn it. He'd needed her then as much as she'd needed him. They'd both failed. It wasn't anybody's fault anymore. Yet they had done a great deal of damage to themselves in their ignorance. Now one of them had to make the first move to heal old wounds, take the first step to start them back along the path of understanding... together.

"What could we have done, Amanda? Suing them would only have made it worse, kept the story in the public eye for months, never let us forget." He ran his hand through his hair, standing it on end with the violence of his movements. Amanda's fingers itched suddenly to smooth it back, to brush the stray waves of dull gold off his high forehead and erase the lines that had settled there. Yes, it would be very nice to let her fingers linger on his skin and smooth the frown from between his amber eyes.

"I've never stopped crying inside, Amanda. I've never stopped hoping that someday, somehow..." He broke off, aware he'd already revealed too much. Soon he'd be asking her to recall how they'd both wanted a big family because they'd been lonely as only children themselves. He was too close to saying all sorts of things that shouldn't be spoken aloud . . . yet. He swallowed and started again on a different note, his tone stronger, less vulnerable. "I still want to have children someday, Mandy. I want to watch them grow into healthy, loving adults with a woman I love. I haven't changed in that respect. I can't believe you've changed so much either."

He'd backed her up against the trunk of a huge cypress tree. His pursuit, like his questions, was relentless. She had nowhere to go. She couldn't escape him, and perhaps it was time she stopped running away. Evan didn't have to remind her of any of the promises they'd made each other so long ago. "I never meant to imply you wouldn't make a good father, Evan," she answered obliquely. "You love children, you'll be wonderful with them." Amanda reached up on tiptoe to kiss his cheek and take the sting from her words. She had meant to add the qualifying word *someday* to her sentence as Evan had done, but he turned his head and their lips met instead. Amanda held her breath, ready to resist. There was no need. Evan didn't deepen the kiss but savored the slight contact for long heart-stopping seconds.

"I always thought you would be the mother of my children," he said quietly. "I have trouble picturing another woman in the role." His voice was husky, and he did nothing to hide the emotion in his eyes or the arousal of his body boldly against her softness.

"Evan, you're going too fast again." Amanda pushed desperately at his chest with the palm of her hand, noting fleetingly the sparkle of gold and diamonds on the cream-colored cotton of his shirt. She was appalled at her own willingness to believe and rejoice in his admission that it wouldn't be easy for another woman to take her place in his life. Ruthlessly, she set the traitorous thought aside and hardened her heart, unable to trust the promptings of so unstable an organ. "Maybe I have been too hasty in deciding not to have a child with Robert. I honestly don't know," she said candidly. "I have to work it out in my head, along with everything else."

"You will think about it. Discuss it with Tacett before you decide." Evan's words were strained but steady. There was an almost imperceptible ring of triumph in his voice. He waited for Amanda's response, holding her lightly in his strong embrace.

"I'll think about...everything." Amanda gasped as Evan pulled her tighter in the circle of his arms, his hands riding low on her back, pressing her against him for a timeless moment. Oddly, he didn't try to kiss her again, merely held her close and searched her eyes for answers she wasn't ready or able to provide. Amanda closed her eyes so he couldn't see the confusion mirrored there.

"Consider long and hard, Mandy. For both our sakes." Evan lowered his head and touched his lips to her eyelids. His breath was warm and smelled slightly minty where it brushed her skin. "I can accept, if I have to, the fact that you don't want to have a child with me again." His arms tightened for a fraction of a second and Amanda gasped. "Maybe our magic really is dead and gone, as you said that night on the beach." He sounded sad and tired and defeated. Amanda's eyes flew open, but his face was composed and his unusual hazel-and-gold eyes told her nothing.

Evan released her but took her hands in his. Amanda looked down at her slim wrists, held so effortlessly in his grasp. He was already acquiring a tan. The golden hair on his forearms was bleached even lighter than usual below the rolled-up sleeves of his shirt. She brought her straying thoughts back to attention with a sharp mental reprimand. It wasn't right to let him hold her like this. It was even less right to enjoy it so, to wish for more. Amanda moved as far away from him as their joined hands would permit. Evan allowed the subtle withdrawal and smiled sadly. "Promise me this. Don't deny yourself the joy of raising a child because of what is long over and done. Promise me just that one thing, and I won't ask for anything more."

She couldn't look away from the passionate sincerity in his eyes or the warmth in their beckoning depths. "I promise, Evan."

He did kiss her then, long and lingeringly, with all the tenderness she'd craved so desperately when they were drifting apart. If only they could have talked like this during those bleak, cold winter days. Would it have made the difference? Would it have given her the strength to stay and help him work his way out of his writing block? Or would it only have made it harder to go? Amanda didn't let herself kiss him back. After a few seconds Evan drew back of his own accord.

"You're not going to let me change your mind about anything else today, are you?" he asked quizzically, but there was a ghost of his special smile lurking at the corners of his mouth and eyes.

"No, nothing more." It was too late for them. Didn't he understand that? It was all happening too late. She'd promised herself—her heart and her body—to another man. Some of her thoughts must have communicated themselves to Evan, because the smile died on his lips and in his eyes to be replaced by a studied blankness. He let her go so quickly she stumbled backward.

"I'll take you home. It is getting late." They walked hand in hand the short distance to his car. They rode back to Sarasota in silence, not touching again. Evan dropped her beside her car in the *Examiner* parking lot and drove away without looking back. Amanda found herself alone again, with even more disturbing questions to ponder, solutions to devise to problems she'd deliberately refused to even consider for almost three years.

She didn't know where to start.

CHAPTER EIGHT

"TELL HER PLAYING hooky from her desk for one day won't land this newspaper in bankruptcy court, Robert." Peter grinned mischievously as he spoke.

"I have work to do." It was Friday again. Evan had been in Sarasota for a week, and nothing had been resolved between them. Nothing had been resolved between herself and Robert, either. Amanda felt as if she was living on the edge of a cliff and her footing was crumbling away beneath her. She needed the security of her routine at the *Examiner*; she didn't want her schedule interrupted.

"It will do you good to get away for a few hours, Amanda." Robert spoke so kindly that Amanda didn't have the heart to contradict him, although her nerves were so tightly stretched she had to bite her lips to keep from doing so.

"Just how do you intend to spend this free time you're manufacturing for us?" she asked her father instead.

"I'm the boss. I don't have to have an explanation." Her expression was one of preoccupation, but when she looked at him, Peter caught a glint of teasing laughter in her eyes. He relaxed slightly as he leaned against the doorframe. "I'm practicing up to be semi-retired. Isn't that what you wanted?"

Amanda hesitated. A week ago she would have been overjoyed by her father's announcement. Now she wasn't so sure.

"You've been after your dad to slow down for months, Amanda," Robert said sensibly. "You'd better encourage him."

"He's right, Mandy. Indulge an old man's whim. I've got an idea for a new series of articles." Peter chose his words carefully. Amanda was no fool. He knew she'd been congratulating herself on getting him to slow down. For a while he'd paid lip service to that idea. But he couldn't do so anymore. He needed access to the *Examiner*'s data banks and communications equipment.

"A series of articles?" Amanda snorted inelegantly. "You mean a series of prizewinning editorials, don't you? I suspected all this talk of retirement was rolling too glibly off your tongue. What have you got in mind, Dad?"

Peter moved out of the doorway so that Teresa could enter the room. "What am I missing?" she asked, coming to an abrupt halt as she spied Robert's tall figure rising from the corner of Amanda's desk. "Hello, Robert. It's good to see you again," she said softly. A faint, pearly blush tinted her cheeks, then faded away. Amanda had been checking her desk calendar and didn't notice the reaction, but Peter did. He eyed his assistant shrewdly. Robert was watching her, also, and smiling as he did so.

"Dad's got an idea for a new series of editorials," Amanda informed her.

"Articles, Mandy. Feature stories, really."

"I see," Teresa said mildly. Her eyes never left Peter's face. They'd been taking turns to make sure one of them was always on call to intercept any messages coming through from Peter's contacts in Washington. So far, his old buddies at State and Defense had been maddeningly silent.

"What's your subject?"

"Foster grandparents." Peter saw the stricken look in his daughter's eyes, and stopped speaking. "Mandy, what's wrong?"

"Nothing, Dad." She waved aside his solicitude. "I just wasn't aware that you're interested in the foster-grandparent program, that's all."

"I wasn't, until Carmella started bringing the girls out to the house. I like having them around. They make me feel young."

"It's a wonderful idea, Peter." Teresa broke the uncomfortable, lengthening silence.

"Sure it is." Amanda looked down at her hands. She couldn't look at Robert or her father. Her hands were folded so tightly together that her fingers hurt. The pain was both physical and of the soul. Why was her father, one of the best investigative journalists of his generation, talking of doing a series of feature stories on foster grandparents? The excellence of the organization aside, it made her sad to think her insistence on his slowing down had resulted in such a great change in his attitude toward practicing his craft. She thought of what he would have done with a story of adversity and courage like that of Carmella and her daughters a few months ago, and she wanted to cry.

And grandchildren. He's never told me that he missed having grandchildren of his own to love and spoil. If I marry Robert, he'll never know that joy.

"I'm taking Carmella's daughters out to the Ringling Circus Museum, for a start. Want to tag along?"

Peter studied his daughter intently. There was sadness and confusion lurking in her big gray eyes. She might have fooled someone else, but not him. She didn't think much of his feature-story idea. Nonetheless, he wanted to keep Carmella and the girls close by, and away from the shelter as much as possible. It was only a matter of time until his friends in Washington came through with a name and an identity to put with the description he'd telexed last night. He was close. Very close.

"I think I'll pass on the sight-seeing tour," Amanda said, with a pretty shrug of apology. "Robert and I were going to try and get away together for an hour or so this afternoon." She swiveled the chair enough to smile up at Robert as he stood by the window.

"We're going to take the boat out later," Peter said in a coaxing tone. He'd write the editorials Mandy wanted. When this whole thing was over and done with, he'd have another Pulitzer nomination under his belt. Maybe he'd even win the damned prize this time.

"Go ahead, Mandy. All I can offer you is a cup of coffee in your own snack bar." Robert's tone was rueful, his smile apologetic. He put one hand on the high back of Amanda's chair and leaned forward. "I've got a lost load of stone crab legs somewhere between here and Tampa. If they don't show up by two, I'm going to have to do something about tonight's menu. Sorry."

"Don't be." Amanda tried not to let her disappointment show. They'd spent so little time together over the last week. And it seemed that the more they were apart, the easier it was for her thoughts to become obsessed with images of Evan Cameron.

"Since I'm already here, can I borrow Teresa?" Robert asked with an engaging grin. "We might as well finish up the business of the Medieval Fair so that will be out of the way. I'm not about to be dealing with madrigal singers and off-key troubadours on our honeymoon.''

Teresa was staring down at her shoes. Peter watched his daughter smile at Robert, a friendly smile without a hint of vexation and very little disappointment, either. "Of course, if she can spare the time. Teresa?''

"Yes, oh, certainly. Would it be convenient now, Robert? We can use my office.''

"See you later, honey.'' Amanda lifted her face for his kiss. It was quick and light, and over in the blink of an eye.

"Perhaps tomorrow?'' she asked hopefully.

"Tomorrow?'' He waited for Teresa to precede him out of the room. "I'll do my best.''

"We're leaving at two.'' Peter had returned to his lounging position in the doorway. "The boat's at the house dock. I moved her up the canal from the marina last night.''

"At the house?'' She looked up quickly. "What about Evan?'' She hadn't seen him since their last conversation.

"He's working on an idea for a new book. I haven't seen much of him the last two days, to tell the truth. He doesn't eat. Doesn't sleep much, either.'' He regarded Amanda shrewdly. "From that sour look on your face, I'd venture to guess you don't approve of the man's industry?''

"He's a writer,'' she shrugged as if the gesture explained everything. "That's how they are.'' So new ideas had come to him, found fertile soil and taken root. Had his love for his work taken him away from her yet again?

"I'll see you at two then? It's ten-thirty now, so that should give you plenty of time to finish up here."

She was going to prove to everyone, herself included, that she was over Evan Cameron. "I'll be there."

"DAD? CARMELLA?" Amanda didn't raise her voice as she stuck her head inside her father's front door and called. There wasn't anybody home. At least not anybody she wanted to see. There was only one car parked under the carport, and that was Evan's rental sedan. She glanced down at her wristwatch, half hoping she had read the time wrong and that she was early. No, it kept perfect time, and it said three minutes past two.

The house was quiet. The familiar blue-and-green wallpaper was dappled with afternoon sunshine from the bank of windows alongside the front door. The parquet floor of the foyer gleamed with a fresh coat of wax. The house smelled clean and well cared for. Carmella was responsible for upkeep, and Amanda was pleased that she cared enough for Peter to take the extra time for little finishing touches like the colorful, fragrant vase of fresh flowers on the gateleg table along the wall.

Amanda stepped inside and closed the door silently behind her. The girls had probably cajoled her father into stopping for ice cream or some other treat. They'd only be a minute or so, she guessed. She'd wait for them out on the patio, near the boat dock. With any luck, she could avoid Evan altogether. He was probably locked in her father's study scribbling furiously away, oblivious to everything else. That's how it had always been in the past.

In the past.

She ought to fine herself a quarter for every time she used that phrase. She'd soon have enough to make this month's car payment if she did.

The door to the study wasn't locked, she noticed out of the corner of her eye as she hurried past. In fact, it was standing halfway open. Despite her good intentions, her steps faltered and she stopped. The room was very quiet. She listened for a long time after her own heartbeat slowed and steadied. She could hear Evan's breathing; it was deep and regular. He was asleep. Horrified by her actions, Amanda watched her hand lift and push the door farther open as if it were controlled by a force not of her own making.

"Evan?" There was no answer. She hadn't really expected any; her voice was so low pitched she could barely hear her own words. She wasn't prepared for how poignant the sight of him asleep would be. So often she'd seen him like this, relaxed and vulnerable in a way he never allowed himself to be at any other time. He hadn't changed much at all, physically. There were a few more lines fanning out at the corners of his eyes. And the indentations from nose to mouth were slightly more pronounced than she remembered, but that was all.

He was sprawled on the couch, spiral notebooks and loose sheets of paper scattered all around him. His left arm lay across the back of the early-American sofa her father had never bothered to get rid of, even though its cover was so shabby it was nearly worn through in places. He still had several pieces of paper clutched in his hand.

Coffee cups and soda cans added to the static chaos of the scene. A sandwich, barely touched, was drawing flies on an end table beside the equally shabby wing chair set at an angle to the sofa. Amanda pursed her lips. It was a familiar, frustrating scene. What had her father said this morning? Evan hadn't been eating or sleeping for the last two days. She wondered how much longer he would try to keep up such a killing pace.

Amanda didn't turn and leave the room as she wished she could do. If she woke him, offered to make him another sandwich and a fresh cup of coffee, it would end the same as it always had. His intriguing, tawny-gold eyes would focus on her for a moment, then drift back to his work, shutting her out of his thoughts, and he'd be lost to the creations of his imagination yet again. What did she care how he abused his health anymore? It wasn't any of her concern, thank goodness.

She wasn't responsible for the man any longer. She didn't have to put herself through hell worrying about him. She could just walk away, out of this room and out of his life, and that was exactly what she intended to do.

Evan came awake abruptly, just as the mental command to leave the room was forming in Amanda's mind. He stared at her with perfect comprehension. This was something else about him that hadn't changed. He never came awake in bits and pieces as she did, befuddled and groggy and not quite ready to face the world. His eyes were always bright and clear, regarding her unblinkingly as Max so often did.

"How's it going?" she asked, finding her tongue at last. She nodded toward the notebooks and sheets of paper, her hands stuffed deep into the pockets of her lightweight lime-green jacket to hide the tremors running through them.

"Good." Evan swung both feet onto the floor and regarded the papers in his hand as if seeing them for the first time. "It's good." He laid the papers on the table. "What time is it? I must have dozed off."

"It's a little after two. And you were sound asleep," Amanda corrected, hiding a smile that insisted on peeking out of the corner of her mouth. Dozing, indeed. He'd been out like a light.

"You're right," Evan conceded with a huge yawn. "I must have been really gone to have developed such a crick in my neck." He lifted his hand to his shoulder and rotated his head wearily. It didn't take an expert masseuse to see how uncomfortable he was.

"Here, let me do that," Amanda offered before she could think better of it. "That's one thing I do remember how to do exactly the way you like." She slipped out of her jacket and walked around to perch gingerly on the arm of the couch. She hesitated only a fraction of a second before placing the palms of her hands on the spot between his shoulder blades that had always bothered him the most. Evan dropped his head forward onto his chest and sighed with pleasure and relief as she worked gently at the knotted muscles.

"Thanks, Mandy. That feels better already." He let his hands dangle between his knees and sighed again. "Murry may be the best business agent in New York, but he isn't worth a hoot when it comes to giving a massage."

"I've missed him. Is he well?" Amanda smiled at her own mental image of Evan's irascible agent trying his hand at being a masseur.

"He's fine." There was amusement in Evan's tone, as well, and Amanda realized with a start that their thoughts were following a similar path once more.

"This is how I remember you best," she said to shut off thoughts of their mutual telepathy. She kept her voice deliberately neutral, devoid of emotion. "Completely lost in your writing." She had to keep her mind on the present, on the issues that divided them, because she knew how easily just being with this man could make her forget.

"Not exactly lost, Amanda. I never used to fall asleep in the middle of a brainstorming session. Lord, some nights I would have given half of everything I owned just to be able to lie down beside you and sleep." His laugh was self-mocking. "In the end, I did lose half of myself." He spoke so softly Amanda wasn't sure what he'd said. His next words were perfectly audible, however, and once again, self-mocking. "Do you suppose this falling asleep in the middle of a work session is a sign of advancing age? After all, I'll be thirty-five on my next birthday."

"That's eight months away," Amanda said. He'd never been able to joke about his writing before. "I'm not sure what it means, Evan, except that you're overworking as usual," she answered seriously.

"Cut it out, Mandy." Evan jerked away from her ministrations and stood up, suddenly towering over her. Loose papers flew off the coffee table and floated to the floor unheeded. "This is my job. Can't you understand that anymore? It's how I earn my living. It's not some mental aberration or moral failing. Quit making such a big deal out of it." He stalked away from her, crossing the room to stare out the windows that faced the back of the house and the canal. His hand went back to soothing the tenseness in his neck.

Amanda looked down at her hands and folded them in her lap for want of something better to do with them. "It was a big deal to me," she whispered.

"Have you talked to Tacett about having a baby yet?" He asked the question suddenly, catching her off guard with his change of subject. He had to know if the other man had come to his senses and agreed to give Mandy the child he still believed she craved.

"Why, no... I've been so busy. Robert's been spending a lot of hours at the restaurant." Her words dwindled as she heard how feeble her excuses sounded. It seemed as if she were far too involved with her own concerns, and Robert, seemingly, in his work, for them to even spend a modicum of time together.

"I thought you might ... might have come to some understanding about what we discussed the other day." Evan was watching her closely, and she couldn't return the scrutiny. The light coming in the window at his back helped to hide his expression effectively.

"I haven't come to any conclusion about having children, Evan. Robert and I will discuss the matter when the time is convenient."

God, she looks lovely with her head held high, her eyes flashing silvery lightning. Evan knew that he'd made her angry again, deliberately so. It seemed the only emotion he could willingly draw from her. And in Amanda, anger had always been very closely aligned to passion. "You're begging the question, and I don't have time to..." Evan didn't finish the sentence, but inside he was suddenly buoyant and confident once again. *She hasn't spoken to Tacett.* That meant she was working through her own feelings. There was a chance. A chance for him, for them, and he was going to take it.

"Señor Cameron, are you here? We have been to the circus." Carmella's daughters erupted through the study doorway. Evan turned from the window. They'd been so involved in their latest altercation that he hadn't even heard the front door open. Neither had Amanda, judging from the stunned look on her face. She stood up and smoothed her hands nervously down the front of her ivory-colored terry running shorts.

The two little girls stopped abruptly at the sight of her. They must be around seven and nine, or so, Amanda guessed. They were dressed identically in pale pink shorts and pastel-striped T-shirts. They shared Carmella's dark, brilliant eyes and snub nose. And her good manners. They both bobbed curtsies to Amanda as Peter introduced her.

"We are pleased to meet you, *señorita*," said the youngest. Linda's English was less clear than her sister Juanita's, but they were both doing very well.

"How do you do," Amanda responded with a smile. Both girls returned the smile and went back to describing their day to Evan. He couldn't have met them more than once or twice, but they were treating him like an old friend.

"Ringling Brothers," Linda said, very pleased with herself. She glanced over her shoulder at her mother to check her pronunciation. Carmella nodded proudly.

"The Ringling Brothers and Barnum and Bailey Circus Museum," Juanita corrected her sibling with big-sister disdain.

"There were no animals," Linda said, disappointment evident in her tone.

"Because it was a museum. There were many other interesting things to see." Juanita spoke haltingly. "We will go to see the real circus when they come home from their tour of . . . *señor*?'' She looked to Peter for guidance.

''I believe the circus is in Europe right now, honey.''

''Ringling Brothers and Barnum and Bailey,'' Linda repeated stubbornly. Peter picked her up and swung her around in a circle. She squealed with excitement. She was still laughing when he set her down.

''You've got it this time, sweetheart.'' Peter laughed out loud, and even Amanda managed a smile. He would make a wonderful grandfather. ''The Greatest Show on Earth, old John Ringling saw to that. Now let's get started on that boat ride. Go change into your slacks, and don't forget a jacket. It will be cold out on the water.''

The little girls ran off, white-ribboned braids flying out behind them. Carmella called out in Spanish, and they halted their headlong pace for a more ladylike ascent of the stairs.

''Pardon,'' she said softly. Her English was heavily accented, but easy to understand. ''They are very excited about this special day. Señor Evan, would you like for me to make you something to eat?'' She glanced severely at the abandoned sandwich, then inquiringly toward Peter. ''I am sure that there is time to do so.''

''No, thanks, Carmella. I'm going out for a drive,'' Evan responded. ''I'll pick up something at the deli out on the Trail.'' He was already sounding like a native, Amanda noted with a flicker of amusement, referring to US 41, the Tamiami Trail, by its familiar nickname.

''If you wish.'' Carmella looked slightly offended and more than a little put out that he seemed to prefer deli food to her home cooking.

"Later, before you leave for the night, if it isn't too much trouble, you might leave me a sandwich in the fridge?" His special quirking smile worked every bit as well on Carmella as it did on every other woman he'd ever met.

"Of course, *señor*," she said with a radiant smile. "I will fix you a very special salad also, full of wonderful things. And Señor Evan. Thank you very much for the copy of your book. It was very... how do you say?" She turned to Peter and spoke a word so quickly in Spanish that Amanda missed it altogether.

"Spooky?" Peter nearly choked on his laughter as he repeated the colloquialism in English.

"Yes... spooky," Carmella replied, relishing the word. "I almost could not close my eyes to sleep for fear that those demon people would come out of the darkness and carry me away." She shivered from the aftereffects of a deliciously scary recollection. "I can not wait to read the..." She paused to search her vocabulary for the correct English word.

"Sequel," Evan supplied gently.

"Sequel," Carmella repeated smugly. "But alas, I do not believe it has been translated into Spanish as yet. And my English, while very much better, is not yet good enough." She looked downcast for a moment, then shrugged philosophically. "But I will be very much improved when this book is ready." She gestured to the papers strewn over the coffee table, "And I will read it in English."

"You'll have the first copy off the press, I promise you," Evan said with a gallant bow.

Carmella smiled again, and her eyes sparkled flirtatiously. Amanda felt herself stiffen as she saw how pretty the other woman was when she was happy and animated. She recognized the unusual emotion prompting her reaction: jealousy. *Impossible,* she thought.

"Come with us, Evan." Peter's gruff voice and invitation effectively ended her introspection. "You look as if you could use the fresh air. We're taking the boat out for a spin. I'm going to show Carmella and the girls what Sarasota looks like from the sea."

"I'd like to, but I can't." Amanda's spirits had soared unaccountably at her father's unexpected urging for Evan to join them. Now they plummeted just as quickly when he refused. "I'm waiting for a phone call from New York. And I've got to make some kind of order out of this mess before then." He shook his head as if he'd just seen the untidy sprawl of papers clearly for the first time. "It's going to take some doing. How about a rain check on that cruise?"

"Sure thing." Peter dismissed the idea. "Ready to go, Mandy? I hear the girls thundering back down the stairs. I think they actually make more noise than you did at that age."

"Well, that's saying something, Dad," Amanda quipped. "You used to tell Mom I made more noise than a jet plane taking off."

"I wasn't exaggerating, either." Peter grimaced at the clatter of small feet over the wood floor. He motioned for Carmella to precede him out of the room. "Let's go, Mandy." He directed the command back over his shoulder.

"Coming, Dad."

"If you haven't got other plans, I'd like to spend tomorrow with you, Amanda. I can't stay down here indefinitely. We have a lot more to settle between us."

Evan moved around the couch to cut off her path to the door as he spoke.

"As I told you earlier, I haven't seen much of my fiancé for several days." She stressed the words ever so slightly and was rewarded by the narrowing of Evan's golden eyes. "I'm hoping Robert can arrange to get some time off this weekend. His manager is out with a ruptured appendix."

"So you told me. I'd think Tacett wouldn't have a lot of free time, judging by the hordes of tourists I've seen waiting in line outside the Sand Dollar." She was so close he could smell her perfume, and it took most of his willpower not to reach out and take her into his arms.

"You've been there?" Amanda cocked her head and stared up at him. She only had to tip her head slightly to look him in the eye. He'd always liked the fact that their bodies so nearly matched.

"I've driven by. You're avoiding accepting my invitation because you're afraid to be alone with me." It wasn't a question; it was a statement. He put one hand on the doorframe, not quite blocking her exit, but making it hard for her to leave the room in a dignified manner. "Will you spend tomorrow with me?"

If you dare. The words hung unspoken in the air between them, but Amanda had no doubt whatsoever that he intended to add them to his sentence. Was he deliberately trying to remind her of his parting challenge the night he'd carried her to the doorway of her bedroom? *Pleasant dreams... if you dare.* Well, she hadn't had any pleasant dreams since that moment. But was that, too, because she didn't dare?

"Tomorrow is all yours, Evan." She put her hand boldly against the side of his face. Her nerves tingled from the scratch of his beard against her fingertips. She wanted to jerk her hand away from the warmth of his skin, but pride came to her rescue and she trailed her nails languidly down the hard curve of his jaw. "If you can tear yourself away from your writing, that is." She didn't say those three simple words aloud, either, but her intention was clear. She glanced meaningfully at the paper-cluttered table one last time, avoided meeting Evan's eyes as she ducked under his arm and sailed regally out of the room.

"CARMELLA AND THE GIRLS seem to be enjoying this day very much." Amanda looked down from her seat in the raised wheel deck of Peter's boat. Carmella was sitting with her feet propped up on a canvas-cushioned deck chair and matching stool. Her eyes were closed as she drank in the friendly warmth of the afternoon sun.

"They needed a break. The shelter is as good as those places come, but it's still a pretty grim spot to be raising two little kids." He set his jaw and abruptly changed the subject. "What were you and Evan talking about after we left the study?"

Amanda decided not to pretend she didn't understand. "I think I'm losing my mind letting Evan back into my life like this. The whole thing is just a mess. I never imagined his being here would complicate my relationship with Robert so."

"Then you've been kidding yourself, Mandy. Evan Cameron's had the power to unnerve you since the day you first met. You've told me so often enough yourself in the past." Peter never took his eyes off the water, but Amanda knew she had his full attention. They were moving slowly, paralleling the shoreline, to give Carmella and her daughters the best view of Sarasota and its adjacent keys. The strategy was only partially successful. Carmella was indeed enjoying the ride, but early on in the trip the girls had disappeared into the cabin, which was complete with its own miniature galley. They were having a delightful time playing make-believe in the dollhouselike interior.

"I can't make any sense out of the whole week. Do you really think Evan was staying away from me these last few days for my sake? For our sakes, Robert's and mine? He said it was so that we could come to some kind of decision." The steady purr of the powerful diesel engines gave Amanda an illusion of privacy while she was seated beside Peter, away from the other passengers.

"What decision?" Peter pounced on her words so quickly Amanda almost didn't have time to regret speaking them. "Are you considering canceling your engagement?" Her father was far too shrewd a judge of human character, hers in particular, for it to be safe to be caught thinking out loud in his presence.

"Of course not," she answered just a shade too quickly and too loudly to be convincing. Amanda winced at her inadvertent confession. Or had it been inadvertent? She needed her father's support, and his advice, whether she liked what he had to say or not.

"Then what are you talking about?" Peter sounded exasperated, and Amanda couldn't blame him. She wasn't even making sense to her own way of thinking.

"About our decision not to have a family. I told you at Christmastime, when I accepted his ring, that Robert and I had decided not to have children."

"And I told you what I thought of that lame-brained plan then and there." Peter set his jaw in an obstinate line. "Don't ask me to change my mind to help make your rationalizations easier. You always wanted to have kids of your own, ever since you were a little girl yourself and knew you couldn't have any brothers or sisters. Remember?''

"I remember,'' Amanda sighed. No one she knew seemed likely to allow her to forget that. "People change, Dad,'' she said far more sharply than she'd intended to. She was tired of having to defend her position. "I've changed,'' she added defiantly.

"Have you?'' Peter didn't sound convinced. "What does Robert say about all this sudden soul-searching you're doing?'' Her father was playing devil's advocate, she was certain, but his barbed questions caused her discomfort nonetheless.

"I haven't discussed the matter with him as yet.'' Amanda didn't know her puzzled expression and slight hesitation told her father more plainly than words that she did, in fact, regret her decision not to have children. At least she did in her heart, for the regret showed most plainly in the sadness mirrored in her cloud-gray eyes. "It's as though Robert were in on this conspiracy in some way.'' She laughed, a short harsh sound that was nothing like her usual chiming giggle. "I haven't had more than five minutes alone with him since Evan showed up here last week.''

"Perhaps there are stronger forces at work here.'' Peter's tone was teasing, but Amanda wasn't in the mood to be teased. She answered very seriously indeed.

"It is almost as though another of Evan's supernatural forces is manipulating my life.''

"Mandy!'' Peter snorted in derision of the fanciful musing. "Will you stop and listen to yourself for a minute?''

Amanda laughed, too, after a moment's thought, and the sound this time was much more natural and relaxed. "Good Lord, listen to me. I sound like I've gone straight off the deep end! Maybe I should have myself locked away for a couple of weeks till the whole thing blows over."

"Will it blow over, Mandy?" Peter was deadly serious all at once. For the last three years, since the day she'd shown up on his doorstep with two suitcases and Max in a straw basket on her arm, Peter had been staunchly on her side. He seldom mentioned Evan's name, but Amanda was aware that he followed his ex-son-in-law's career closely. How often did her father wonder what the younger man was doing, if he was happy in his success, if he was content with his life?

"Dad, please don't make this so difficult for me." She spoke quietly over the throb of the engines. Carmella had left her deck chair to check on the little girls whose giggles and quick, light voices drifted up to Peter and Amanda now and then.

Amanda wanted desperately to bridge the gap she felt growing between herself and her father. She couldn't stand being estranged from Peter at such an unsettled time in her life. His nature wasn't demonstrative, but she knew that he loved her very much and she didn't want anything to jeopardize that love.

"I couldn't stay with Evan," she explained. "He didn't need me anymore." Her voice cracked as she spoke, and she turned her head to stare blindly out at the passing scene. The downtown buildings glistened and wavered in heat waves coming off the pavement. "When I returned from the hospital after losing the baby, he shut me out. Completely. Can you understand how much that hurt?" She lifted her hands to make small, soothing motions over her temples, but the dull ache growing behind her eyes refused to lessen.

"No, Mandy, I can't understand that," Peter returned bluntly. "If you love someone, you stick together through bad times and good times. You kids managed the hard times. When you didn't have an extra dime to your names you never let anything come between you. But when Evan made a success of his writing you let your marriage fall apart. That's something I can't comprehend or accept. You two had something special and very rare."

"I can't explain it. Evan just . . . left me . . . left me alone inside where it hurts so badly you can't do anything to dull the pain except cut yourself off from the source of it. And for all this time, I haven't had anything to blame it on but bad memories. And Evan's writing." She still wanted to blame their estrangement entirely on the stress of his writing block, but now it was hard to, honestly.

Amanda tugged at a stray lock of hair that burned like a curl of living auburn flame in the sunlight dancing off the water. "I thought I knew him as well as I knew myself, but I was wrong. And I never realized that I didn't know him until he began to have so much difficulty writing. There are depths to the man that I never guessed at. There's a dark, brooding core that he kept completely hidden from me. And when things started to go wrong it became so strong the bleakness reached out and destroyed our marriage."

"Amanda." Peter's fist came down on the teak wheel of the boat, sending them into a slight swerve to the right. Amanda's line of vision focused on the imposing marble facade of the Ringling mansion, *Cap'D'Zan*. It glowed rosy in the sunlight and looked even more pretentious from the water than it did from land. "You're letting your imagination run away with you," Peter continued. "You knew Evan was a writer when you married him. You've been around enough creative people to know how driven they can become. But it doesn't affect the way they feel about the people they love."

"I can accept that... now," Amanda said softly. "I'm still making excuses for my own behavior and for the way I thought Evan's writing ruled our lives. We should have talked, not shut ourselves away in separate rooms of that big, cold apartment. But we didn't do any of those things, and now it's too late for us. I'm going to marry Robert. I gave him my promise." The words were a plea for understanding. Surely her pledge to Robert would mean something to an honorable man like her father. "Robert will give me what I want. A life here in Sarasota, the freedom to pursue my career, a home and..."

"Children." Peter finished for her. His words went straight to Amanda's heart and lodged there with a swift sharp pain.

"I don't know. But I do know all Evan will give me is heartache."

"Mandy." Peter took her arm and tucked it under his elbow, pulling her close. He didn't look at her; his eyes were still on the other boat traffic, both motor and sail, that shared the calm, sparkling bay. "Sometimes heartache with the right person is better than feeling nothing at all with the wrong person." Amanda knew he was thinking aloud about her mother's death and all that they had shared during her short lifetime. She slipped her arm down around his waist to give him a hug.

"I still miss Mom too, Dad. And I know what you two shared was very special. But it doesn't apply to my situation."

"Don't try and deceive yourself that you and Evan didn't share that same *something*. Even I could see it, and you know fathers are notoriously critical of the men who take their daughters away from them." He chuckled wryly. "Look into your heart, Mandy. Are you doing the right thing in marrying Robert? Was it truly Evan's writing you couldn't accept? Or was it something else? How much were you at fault? Perhaps you need to examine your own actions and motives. I'm not going to do it for you. Good marriages are hard work, especially the best of them. There are days, even weeks, when things go so badly you wonder if you were ever in love at all."

"And how do you tell the difference between those times and the end of loving someone?" Amanda asked honestly.

"The bad times pass, and you see that person in a different light, a different set of circumstances, and it's like falling in love all over again. Because you say you love someone it doesn't give you the excuse not to learn what's in their hearts, not to support them, stand by them, accept their weaknesses as well as their strengths." Peter took a deep breath and gave her shoulder a squeeze. "The gospel according to Winston." He almost uttered the last sentence without a break in his voice, but not quite. Peter cleared his throat and went on.

"You're making excuses now, Mandy, claiming not to know the man you loved. Or is it the man you still love?" he amended as she made an inarticulate little sound of protest. "I won't push you to tell me, but you should have had confidence enough to give Evan the freedom to make room for both you and his writing three years ago. Are you sure you did that?''

''I can't be sure of anything anymore, Dad. I don't love Evan. I can't. I promised Robert I'd marry him.'' She felt desperation circling like a harpy, just above her head. ''I can't deny that Evan has a part of me. He always will have. You can't live with someone for almost seven years without giving a part of yourself away. But he didn't want me to stay. I've learned my lesson the hard way. You can't go back and undo your mistakes, no matter how much you might want to try. You can't go home again.''

''Can't you, Mandy?'' Peter questioned, his tone rough with suppressed emotion. He shook his head. ''You were always the one to try and reason away rainbows. Miracles do happen, sweetheart. You can go home again. It only takes a lot of hard work. And a little bit of magic.''

CHAPTER NINE

THERE WAS MAGIC in the air.

Amanda leaned back in the festive green-and-yellow plaid lounge chair and stared out over the railing of the cedar deck. From behind the tinted lenses of her sunglasses, she watched the foam-capped waves rolling toward the shimmering crescent of white sand beach with unusual concentration. Was the sea the source of the subtle disturbance that had communicated itself to her when she entered the house a few minutes earlier?

Or was it coming from someplace beyond her range of vision? She kicked off her shoes and crossed her slim ankles, stretching her arms skyward to relieve the tension in her neck and shoulders. It was rather pleasant to be alone, or it would be, if it didn't give her thoughts another opportunity to start their endless circling back to the subject of the two men in her life.

She'd spent another restless night turning over in her mind all the things her father had had to say yesterday on his boat; remembering everything Evan had said to her each and every time they'd been together; rehearsing all the things she should say to Robert, discuss with Robert, if and when they were ever alone together again. The possibility of a frank conversation with her fiancé frightened her a little. She was having trouble even picturing his face, and it was unsettling, as though *something* was working to keep them apart.

But her father's words remained strongest in her thoughts and in her heart. Their conversation had done nothing to help her make her decision. Instead, his words had made it harder for her to keep to the path she'd already chosen. She couldn't—or wouldn't—deal with the questions Peter had raised. Not now, when the unwelcome pull of Evan's attraction was so strong, and the warring voice of her conscience kept reminding her of her promises to Robert. It was growing more difficult to hold on to her resolve with each hour that passed. Now, if she closed her eyes against the dazzle of sun and water, it would be the golden-eyed phantom of her ex-husband who answered her mental summons, not the kind, generous man whose ring she was wearing.

Amanda sat up, her eyes flying open, scanning the beach. The tension in the air was back, dancing along her skin like invisible sparkles of static electricity. The source of her discontent was out there somewhere, she was sure. The sun was bright on the water, and the stiff breeze from the west sent waves crashing onto the shore in long monotonous rows. The sea oats at the foot of the deck bobbed and nodded with a soothing rustle. Amanda settled back in her chair. The salty air brushed across her face with a warm caress, scattering her reflections, while the calling seabirds caught her attention, helping to distract her from the endless treadmill of her deliberations.

The strange force around her receded. She adjusted her sunglasses, and wrapped her arms around her knees with a little sigh of relief and chagrin. She was being incredibly silly about what was probably nothing more than a change in the barometer. Her turquoise-and-cream-striped skirt rode high on her thighs, baring a long curve of satiny skin. The combination of warm sun and cool sea breeze felt good. The strange feeling that kept coming over her was nothing more than her own unsettled state of mind. She'd made her conscious choice when she'd accepted Robert's ring. Neither Evan's persuasive kisses nor her father's arguments could undo that reality.

A figure materialized around the curve of the beach that cut her off from the neighboring houses and gave her the feeling of living at land's end. It was Evan. The fizzing, popping surge of electricity was back in the air, bouncing off her arms and legs, dazzling her eyes, shortening her breath.

His tall, rangy figure moved with sure, easy strides along the sand as Max appeared from beneath the shade of a nearby palm. Ming Le was with him. They touched noses briefly, and the other feline moved away, a sinuous brown against the brilliant white sand.

Evan's low laughter carried on the wind as he bent to scratch the cat's ears. Max regarded him intently and remained by his side as Evan straightened and looked around, as if he was sensing another's eyes on him. His feet were bare, his shoes tied together and slung over his shoulder. He was dressed very casually in gray sweatpants and a sleeveless black T-shirt. The wind tossed his dark-blond hair so that it looked like a boy's ruffled mop. Yet the traitorous coiling of longing deep within her wasn't for a small boy, but for the man he'd become.

Amanda stood up, allowing Evan to see her. He propped his sunglasses on top of his head and waved. She waved back, responding automatically to the lure of his summons. He would be gone soon enough. And so would her paralyzing indecisiveness. Soon Robert would be free of his extra duties at the Sand Dollar, and they could spend more time together, time they needed to get their relationship back on the right track.

But she had also promised Evan today, and she was a woman of her word. For the time being she would continue to flirt with disaster, to walk the thin line between pleasure and heartbreak and enjoy the heady intoxication of his company. She walked sedately down the steps to meet him, aware, as always, that her control over any situation involving Evan Cameron was tenuous at best.

"Where did you come from?" she asked airily. "I don't see your broomstick parked anywhere around." She made an exaggerated production of looking for his nonexistent mode of transportation to hide the sudden catch in her throat that had made her first words too breathy and low. Max regarded her unblinkingly from where he sat at Evan's feet. He, for one, wasn't fooled in the least by her attempted lightness.

"I hid it in the palmetto bushes back there." Evan motioned behind him with a jerk of his head. "Can't have any of the neighbors complaining about low-flying aircraft on the beach, can we? Especially Mrs. Ellery. Max is already in her black books." He included her in his conspiratorial grin.

"I always suspected you were a witch." Amanda laughed, but the sound was strained and not very strong. "Max. You promised to behave," Amanda scolded. "How on earth did you learn Mrs. Ellery's name? It isn't on her mailbox, and nowhere on the beach side of her house." A superstitious shiver ran down her spine.

"I talk to cats." Evan lifted his eyebrows and looked menacing.

"That settles it; you are a witch." Amanda pretended horror.

"Mandy, if you're going to be calling me names, at least quit confusing the genders. A male witch is a warlock. I know you don't particularly like my books, but I thought you knew that much about the occult."

"My mistake," Amanda apologized with mock seriousness. "Where's your car?"

"A good warlock would have cast a spell, made it invisible and parked it on your front lawn. I left it down at the public beach." Evan broke the whimsical mood with the prosaic statement, "I was a little early, so I decided to walk along the beach. We can go back together to pick it up later. I'm at your disposal this afternoon." His tawny-gold eyes challenged her to pick up on the leading statement.

"I truly wasn't certain that you could tear yourself away from your writing. I was wrong, I see. I apologize." The words came out stiff and hard.

"I always try to keep my word. And I've given enough of myself to that idea for a few days. It will be all the better for a short rest, and so will I." He held out a square brown hand, letting the touchy subject of his writing drop. "I could get addicted to this weather. It's probably snowing back in New York."

"I never thanked you for the money... to buy the house. I love living here." It was something she had to say.

Evan let his hand caress the length of her arm. Her skin was cool beneath the creamy, almost transparent fabric of her blouse. "You're always willing to give, Mandy." His fingers drifted upward to tangle in her hair where it rested in a riot of curling tendrils around her shoulders, while his thumbs subdued the auburn curls whipping about her flushed cheeks. "But some-where along the way, you didn't learn how to take in return." His lips brushed hers with such infinite tenderness that she closed her eyes to stop the tears. Was that what her father had been trying to tell her yesterday also?

Ignoring her small sigh of protest, Evan lifted the sunglasses away and drew her into his arms. His lips cajoled and caressed until hers parted in anticipation of his seeking entry, until Amanda no longer listened to the confusing clamor of her thoughts. She leaned into his embrace, twining her fingers into the taut fabric of his shirt as she returned the joy Evan gave her with her own searching tongue and, above them, the sun stood still in the blue, blue sky.

"I don't know what you're talking about," she said in genuine puzzlement as the kiss ended. Amanda took a deep breath, and the mist cleared from before her eyes. The earth moved again in its age-old path around the sun, and Evan held her away from his chest with a smile lighting his rugged features.

"That's the trouble, Mandy sweet. I truly believe you don't understand that loving is taking as well as giving. Allow me to show you how." Events were conspiring against him. He had deadlines to meet, obligations to Murry and his publishers as well as the motion picture deal to finalize back in New York. He couldn't afford to stay down here indefinitely. He was tired of waiting. He wanted Amanda back. She'd always been his. It was time she accepted that fact.

She was his because he'd never stopped loving her.

"I don't think that's wise." She searched Evan's features for some sign of what he was feeling, but the shuttered depths of his golden eyes were as unfathomable as ever. She couldn't admit her uncertainty about her future with Robert, her steadily growing longing to return with this man to a time and place that couldn't exist again, no matter how hard she wished that it might.

"Shhh, Mandy. Let go just for a little while. Feel, don't think." His hands moved from her shoulders to her back, drawing her closer. The thin cotton of his shirt was stretched tight across the hard wall of his chest. She put up her hand to hold him off and the low steady thrust of his heartbeat against her palm ignited a spark of liquid fire deep within her.

"We were going to go sight-seeing." She stammered a little on the last word in her haste to escape him. His eyes continued to hold her as firmly ensnared as his arms.

Evan shook his head in the negative. "No more sight-seeing."

Amanda felt a thrill of nervous excitement all the way to her sandy toes. She sensed new purpose in him, a new directness. He was tired of waiting.

She deliberately broke the contact of his golden eyes and focused her gaze on the sand at their feet. Evan's fingers began massaging the taut muscles behind her shoulders, just as she had done for him the day before. She didn't tell him to stop; instead she let a small sigh of relief sift through her lips as the nagging tension in her muscles faded away.

"Do you like that, Mandy?" Evan questioned softly, never ceasing the smoothing circles of his fingers. They were still standing face-to-face. His arms rested heavily on her shoulders, but it was a comfortable heaviness. His lips were scant inches from her hair. She could feel his warm breath stir the heavy autumn-tinted strands beside her ears.

"Yes," she replied after a short hesitation that spoke more eloquently of her surrender to his erotic spell than she realized. "I haven't had anyone to do that for me . . . for a long time."

"We were good together."

"Yes." She would do it all again, she knew in her heart, just to have him hold her like this. The touch of him brought her such joy and satisfaction. Knowing she was betraying her feelings for Robert, she still wanted Evan to hold her. She wanted to recapture the magic of their past, no matter how fleeting the rapture might be.

Evan cupped her chin in his hand and lifted her face to his. "We made so many mistakes, Mandy." His compelling gaze burned deeply into her soul. "We read each other wrong so often. We almost let the magic fade away."

Hearing the word she'd been using in her thoughts spoken aloud woke Amanda from her sensual musings. "Yes, it faded away, and it's sad." The sun was beating down on the top of her head, making her dizzy and light-headed. Or was it merely Evan's proximity that made her feel so off balance? She veiled her eyes with long, smoky lashes to hide her tears of regret. "We can't go back. There's no way to hold onto a rainbow," she whispered, and the words were full of longing and sorrow. "It's a lesson I learned three years ago, and the cost was very dear." She stepped away from him, turning back up the beach with tear-blinded eyes.

"We can try again," Evan went on quietly, ignoring her last words. "We can take time to know each other as we are now...."

"No. I've made a new life, with new commitments. You have a life in New York that doesn't include me. Do you want to give that up? Don't ask for the impossible, Evan. We can't go back." She strove to regain the clarity of purpose that had brought her this far. Why was it she could only bring Robert into the forefront of her thoughts to banish Evan's growing influence? By rights Robert should always be her first consideration.

"Yes, we can." Evan's voice held all the confidence in the world. He slid his hand behind her knees and lifted her into his arms. His face was so close that she had to close her eyes to keep his features from blurring. "We can go back. If you dare."

If you dare. The words shimmered with invisible power in the air around her head. She was certain he hadn't spoken the words aloud, yet she was equally certain she'd heard the soft-voiced challenge with her ears as well as her brain.

"No more." Her lips were suddenly so dry she had to moisten them with the tip of her tongue. She tried to free herself from the steel band of his embrace. The sensation of his nearness, the heat of their bodies, the strength of his arousal pressing into her hip were communicated through the thin fabric of their clothes, unsettling her even more because she knew he was aware of an answering need in her.

Amanda was unnerved by the extent of her longing for Evan. She could see desire in the deep gold of his eyes and gloried in her power; but at the same time she was frightened enough of those same feelings to wish she were someplace else entirely, someplace safe. Robert would probably never ask her to make love on a beach, as she and Evan had already done in the past; and she would never agree to the request, should he make it. But Evan could touch all the special, secret places of her body and anticipate each response. He would heighten her pleasure with every movement of his body, every caress of his hands, and she would be lost again to the passion and the joy.

The blinding glare of sunlight disappeared, to be replaced by the cooler shade of a strand of small pine and water oak that separated her property from her neighbor's. It was one of Max's favorite trysting places.

"Mandy, come back to me, sweet." Evan let her stand, then pulled her down beside him on the soft dry carpet of pine needles. "Your dreams must be very powerful." He moved his hands down over her waist to rest on the rounded fullness of her hips.

"I wasn't dreaming," she denied too quickly. "I was only thinking..." She was very close to forgetting herself. It would be so easy to give way to her increasing longing to remain in his arms. She was beginning to believe, at least with her heart, that he already understood her need to be an integral part of her man's life, his partner whole and strong. The Evan she was rediscovering so reluctantly and so inevitably would respect those needs. He would never cut her out, shut her off from his work and his feelings as he had done in the past. And for that new and more mature Evan, she could be all that she herself was capable of being.

"Your eyes are dreaming." He didn't move closer, but somehow Amanda found herself pressed more intimately against the burning hardness of his lower body.

"Have you always been able to read my thoughts?" she asked, a puzzled little frown etching twin lines across her brow. "I must be horribly transparent."

"I've never been able to read your thoughts," Evan replied seriously. "But I've always watched you. Your face is so very expressive." He touched his lips to her blue-shadowed eyelids in a caress light as butterfly wings. "I watched you as you slept, when you were dressing, or bathing, after making love to you...." He felt Amanda tense as if to flee, and his arms tightened around her. "Watching you has been one of the chief joys of my existence." He really wasn't sure how much longer he could play this waiting game, yet one false move on his part would scare Amanda away as quickly as a frightened woodland creature caught unawares.

"I've never been able to understand you," she replied softly, regretfully. "I thought I did in the beginning, but I was wrong." Evan reached out a large brown hand to brush a loose strand of auburn hair back from her face.

"I don't think I was able to let you understand me before. But it would be different now, Mandy."

"Would you let me into some of the secret places of your heart?" she asked in a voice so low he had to bend his head to catch the words.

"Yes. And will you do the same for me?" He leaned closer, brushing her cheek with his hand as he reached behind her to pick a creamy white orchid from the plant growing on the tree that shaded them. He offered her the bloom as a silent pledge.

"I . . ." Amanda didn't know how to finish the sentence. Was she complete enough within herself to offer him the freedom he needed to pursue his demanding craft? Was he secure enough in himself to give her the same freedom? She wasn't sure. And she needed to be sure before taking the risk of going back. Amanda took the flower silently, sadly, and held it in her trembling fingers while tears threatened to spill over her cheeks. Evan turned her face up to his with a gentle touch.

It wasn't difficult to read her thoughts. Her reservations were plain to see. "Shhh, Mandy. Don't try to answer all the tough questions in the space of a heartbeat. I don't expect you to. Do you know your hair is even redder than I remembered it?" His tone was thoughtful, full of wonder. "The sunlight makes it glow like fire."

Evan lowered his head to cover her parted lips with his own. Amanda didn't deny him, opening to his caress like the petals of a summer flower drinking in the warm, renewing rain. He felt her control, and its restraint on her actions, slipping away as the secluded arbor transformed itself into their Eden. The tip of his tongue followed the honeyed outline of her lips, lingering to taste the corners of her mouth with languid temptation.

Amanda's arms twined themselves around his neck. Her mouth met his, capturing the warm invading moistness of his tongue in her turn, drawing him deeper inside her, straining his control. He knew he should end the embrace, let her leave his arms and his life if that's what she wanted, but he could not. The quiet seclusion of their surroundings seemed to have worked a small miracle, lulling her defenses into submission. Everything that was happening seemed right, ordained. The rest of the world might not have existed beyond the boundaries of their embrace.

Evan's hands drifted over her glowing ivory skin, exploring and arousing her flesh as knowledgeably as

they had always done. Amanda pushed back the last
clamoring remnants of her conscience and followed his
lead. It was as if time had rolled away. She was his. He
was hers. She delighted in finding pleasure in the ridges
and furrows of his lightly-muscled body. Her hands
roamed at will over the broad line of his shoulders, the
tapering smoothness of his back beneath the sweat-
dampened cotton of his shirt. She let her hands slide
lower to press the taut curve of his buttocks more
tightly against the soft, desiring places of her body.

His kiss tapered off gradually, leaving her lips open
and willing, to trail across her cheek and down to the
hollow of her throat where the betraying pulse beat
wildly under his seeking lips. Her excitement told Evan
all too plainly that any resistance she might offer him
was purely reflexive. He inhaled the flowery scent of
her perfume and the spicy undertone of her passion as
he nuzzled the skin of her neck. The last of his own
reservations about asking her back into his life melted
in an inferno of renewing, awakening desire.

He'd been a fool to think he could stay away from
her any longer. They belonged to each other. She would
believe that as firmly and as unshakably as he did, if
only he could make her his once again. He kissed her,
stilling the protesting murmurs she was making deep in
her throat before they could leave her lips. Evan cradled her in his arms, protecting her from the sharpness of the dried pine needles, but she was beyond
noticing physical discomforts.

Evan lowered his weight onto his elbows and held her
tightly beneath him, their clothing a small barrier to
passion, their lower bodies pressed close. For long
seconds she returned his embrace, her eyes closed tight
against reality. He held her head, his fingers buried in

her hair so that he could taste her mouth, mingle tongues, exalt in the slight saltiness of her skin, respond to passion long suppressed and beautiful memories long denied.

"Stay with me, Mandy. Love me." His voice was low and raspy. It washed over her skin with almost tactile power. Her fingertips grazed the clear, smooth line of his lips as he spoke. He turned slightly as the pearly nail slipped over the even whiteness of his teeth. He caught and held her fingertip in a painless, sucking bite. Amanda groaned and caught her breath in response to the subtle, wordless invitation. She pulled back slowly, letting her finger glide over the inner softness of his bottom lip in lingering acquiescence, before lifting her hand to brush the stubborn, unruly wave of dull gold hair back from his forehead.

"I can't make love to you here, Evan." Her words were breathy and low. Her stomach contracted, and a slow, melting heat spread outward and downward as he bent his head to kiss the skin at the juncture of her neck and shoulders. The buttons of her blouse parted beneath his touch.

"Yes, you can. You are." He was adamant, no longer to be sidetracked by her qualms. His hands brushed aside her blouse and the fragile lace of her bra. Her nipple signaled her delight and passion more eloquently than any words. He pushed the narrow straps of her bra away, exposing a porcelain globe to his admiring eyes and hungry mouth. Amanda's eyelids fluttered down over bottomless, desiring, gray pools as Evan captured a rosy bud between his teeth. He tugged gently, sending a bolt of passion spreading like liquid fire through every inch of her being. She moaned lightly in answer to the pleasuring caress.

Evan growled deep in his throat. Something primitive stirred within him. She was his woman; no amount
of civilized posturing, no popular theories of equality
could override that elemental fact. He moved over her,
taking possession of her mouth yet again, reminding
them both that he knew her body better than she did
herself, that he could easily orchestrate its response,
urging her to accept the truth and let them both glory
in its strength.

Amanda surrendered, not wanting time to creep
forward unless it was to bring her craving body to full
satisfaction. Her hands roamed over the muscles of his
back and shoulders, moving upward to pull his head
back to her lips whenever his meandering caresses kept
them too long apart. His hand kneaded the fullness of
her breast; his touch was warmer than the sun. She
thrust her tongue deep inside his mouth, silently im-
ploring a contact more intimate and more fulfilling
than the tempting caresses they were exchanging.

"Your body knows we belong together, even if you
won't admit it with words, Amanda. Please spend the
rest of this weekend with me." Evan pleaded with her.
He was aware with the small portion of his intellect still
functioning that he was rushing her again. He looked
down to see his hand gently stroking the ripeness of her
breast, felt his demanding body pushing against the
softness of her hips, felt the beat of hot blood in his
veins and couldn't stop himself. She was his, damn it.
Amanda was quiet beneath him, her great cloud-gray
eyes regarding him with dreamy allure, yet he sensed
the war within her, the battle between inclination and
will.

She was a woman of honor, and he was asking her to
deliberately and with forethought break her promise to

another man, yet he couldn't halt the words. "Come with me, Mandy."

"It wouldn't be right." Amanda covered his hand with her own, beseeching him to pull her clothing back into place. She was trembling, and suddenly icy cold. "I've been so mixed up these last few days." She lifted her hand to touch his cheek. Evan turned his head to place a kiss on her palm.

"So am I, but don't you see that's why we need more time?" He had to convince her that he was speaking the truth. "We've come so far. Before this week we would have argued...maybe...or more likely just shut ourselves away in that damned big apartment. But we never, ever, would have talked as we have been doing since I've been down here. We owe it to ourselves..."

"I owe something to Robert, too." Amanda pushed at him to lift his weight from her lower body. The passion that had flared so abruptly between them dwindled and faded as reality came back in a great flooding rush. "Please, Evan, going away with you is out of the question," she insisted, her words sharp with pain and anxiety.

"It's only forty-eight hours out of the rest of our lives. Tacett doesn't need to know."

"What could we prove alone somewhere on a deserted beach but that we..." She heard what she'd said and set her lips in a tight, straight line, shaking her head. "No. It's impossible." She sat up, forcing Evan to do the same. She hugged her arms around her knees, rocking slightly. "I won't go."

"I wouldn't expect you to make love with me, Amanda." Evan raked his hand through his hair, his jaw set. "I've got a few scruples of my own, if that's what you're worried about."

"Yes, I am worried," she replied candidly. "That part of our magic is still very much alive. I don't know if either one of us is capable of controlling our desire for each other completely." She went on, sadness evident in her tone and in her posture. "But that isn't the point. How many times do I have to repeat it? You can't go back. *We* can't go back."

"Well, I sure as hell can," Evan said, anger tightening his voice. He stood, planting his feet, holding out a hand to help her rise. He was tired of playing the gentleman and so frustrated he could barely speak coherently. He turned on his heel and marched away.

Amanda watched him go in silence. White-hot reminders of their sunlit encounter remained like vestiges of some exotic opiate in her blood. She narrowed her eyes against the full glare of the afternoon sun. Her sunglasses were gone, nowhere to be seen. Her head ached. She needed to be able to sort out her conflicting emotions, to rub away the patina of desire Evan had cast over her and hold on to the hopes for the future she wanted for herself and Robert.

Yet, just as insistent in her thoughts were her father's words to her that day on his boat. He was right. She did try to reason away rainbows sometimes. Would she be hurting anyone but herself if she went away with Evan and worked him out of her system? Robert would never have to know. She would be able to come to him with a clear mind and an untroubled heart.

"Evan, wait!" He was standing on the beach, holding her sunglasses in his hand. Amanda walked toward him slowly, still a little uncertain.

"You've changed your mind," he stated simply as he handed her the glasses.

"I've changed my mind," she said with sudden conviction. "There are a lot of things we don't know about each other anymore. I'm discovering there are a lot more things I don't know about myself these days. Maybe it's time we did find some answers...together."

CHAPTER TEN

"DO YOU WANT TO try to call your father at the paper again?" Evan asked as he sat straddled across the chair to her dressing table, his crossed arms resting on its high spindly back. He was watching her in the mirror while Max regarded Evan's reflection benignly from his favored position at the foot of the bed.

"I'll leave a note at the house when we stop by to pick up your things." It would be easier that way. Her father would receive a short note saying only that she was going away with Evan to sort things out and not to worry. She would also have to explain everything to Robert when she returned, but she didn't want to think about that now. "But I have to be back by noon on Monday," she stated emphatically.

"I won't keep you from your work."

"It's just that Dad's been...well...preoccupied lately," she felt compelled to explain. "He comes and goes at odd hours...sometimes he just disappears altogether, like today. I'm worried about him."

"I'd say one of the perks of being semiretired is being able to come and go without checking in at regular intervals."

"You're probably right." Amanda sounded doubtful. He pushed away from the chair and stood up. She'd talk herself out of going away with him if they kept this up much longer.

"Is this ready to go?" He took the thin cotton nightgown she'd been holding in her hands and placed it on top of the clothes in her suitcase. She colored slightly at the sight of his strong tanned hands among the delicate wisps of her peach-and-ivory satin underthings.

"I'm ready. I just have to put Max in the utility room. Mr. Greer, next door, knows where the extra key is. He'll come and put Max out this evening and in the morning. They like each other." She bent down to pick up the big white cat. Evan snapped the locks on the suitcase.

"It's not that I don't want my father to live his own life," she said, returning to the subject they'd been discussing. "But I think he should slow down, and he's fighting me every inch of the way. Now, I'm not sure what he's up to, but there's something going on. I can feel it." She shrugged and gave a nervous, embarrassed giggle, brushing her cheek against Max's soft fur as he rested his paws on her shoulder and watched Evan following them down the hall. "We're going to have a long talk when . . . things get back to normal."

Max stuck out his tongue, and sharp white teeth appeared momentarily in an eerie feline grin. Evan scowled back at the cat. *So she isn't going to come easily into my arms now that the immediacy of passion has faded.*

He'd nearly forgotten how obstinate and strong-willed Amanda could be when she put her mind to it. More and more he could see how unlike herself she'd been those last months of their marriage, apathetic and withdrawn. The woman before him was much more like the girl he'd married than he'd thought just a few short days ago. She was solid and dependable, though paradoxically mercurial and delightfully impetuous when she allowed herself to be. She was, as the saying went, one in a million.

Yet, on this occasion at least, their shared past was working to his advantage. The last time he'd had her alone for forty-eight hours on a Florida beach, she'd agreed to be his wife. He'd make history repeat itself. "It'll work out right in the end," he said for his own benefit as much as a response to her last statement about her father's peculiar behavior.

Amanda didn't answer, bending to let Max out of her arms and then shutting him into the utility room off the kitchen. "Sorry, old friend. There's plenty of your favorite food and water, and I put fresh litter in your box. I won't be gone too long, I promise." Max howled miserably and gave Evan an inimical glare as the door shut in his face. He clawed frantically at the closed door. "He hates being penned up in there."

"The rest will do him good," Evan replied dryly. Amanda stared at him accusingly.

"I do believe you're jealous of Max's amorous exploits."

"No, only in awe of his prowess with the ladies. He's told me all about it." They both laughed, and the tension eased between them. "Where do you want to go, Mandy? Disney World? Sea World? Back down to the Keys?" He tried to keep things light, but his voice thickened on the last words. He dropped the suitcase he still carried in his hand and pulled her into the circle of his arms. "Tell me, please. I want you to be comfortable. I want this weekend to be perfect."

"It doesn't matter where we go. Just so long as it's private and we have . . ." The telephone's ring cut into her words.

Neural alarms went off inside Evan's skull. "Don't answer that," he commanded, not certain why he was obeying the mental warning, except his intuition was too strong to be ignored.

"Why ever not?" Amanda laughed. She had a hand on the receiver before Evan could make a move to stop her. He didn't even need to hear the booming voice on the other end of the line to know his uneasiness had been justified.

"Mandy girl! Is that really you?"

"Murry? Murry Nessman. It's good to hear your voice." Amanda laughed delightedly and smiled across at Evan. He couldn't smile back. His very fragile house of cards was threatening to tumble around him.

"I need to talk to Evan, and they gave me this number to try when I called the *Examiner*. That young fool took off in such a hurry that he didn't leave me a number where I could reach him. It's taken me half the day to track him down." Murry ended the sentence with a series of wheezing coughs. Amanda didn't even have to shut her eyes to see him in a baggy, ill-fitting suit with the ever-present cigar in his hand or clenched between his teeth. "Are you two patching things up down there?" he demanded with his customary lack of tact. For a moment Amanda regretted that he'd managed to catch his breath again so quickly.

"Evan's standing right here, Murry." She could almost smell the smoke from his cigar, so strong were her recollections of the man. "You're lucky to have caught him. And we are working some things through, but don't read extra meaning into his being with me, please." She turned her back to Evan and cupped both hands nervously around the receiver. If she had to consider going away with Evan much longer, she might have second thoughts and she didn't want that to happen.

"The connection is very good, isn't it?" Somehow she'd always thought overseas calls would be full of static and strange unidentifiable noises of one sort or another. "Are you doing a lot of sight-seeing on your trip?" Amanda pounced on the change of subject much like Max pounced on lizards on the beach. Behind her, Evan sprang into action, spinning her around to face him.

"Give me the phone." His voice was rough and strained. He ran his hand through his hair in agitation. Amanda stared at him in amazement. She put her hand over the mouthpiece and smiled. "Murry isn't going to chew your head off because you forgot to leave him a phone number where you could be reached. Relax."

"Give me the phone, damn it."

"All right." Amanda was too puzzled for the moment to be offended by his high-handed actions. "Murry, I'm going to turn you over to Evan. He's about to arm-wrestle me for the phone, so I assume it's because what you have to say to him must be very important."

"It sure is. These Tinsel Town yahoos are driving me to a coronary."

"Tinsel Town?" The words almost didn't make it past the constriction in her throat.

"Yeah. Glitterville. Tinsel Town. You know, Hollywood. Didn't Evan tell you I'm out here working my butt off for him while he's loafing around in the Sunshine State?"

Amanda fended off Evan's attempt to take the phone away, bewilderment and sudden mistrust darkening her gray eyes almost to charcoal. "Aren't you in Europe, Murry?"

"Europe? Whatever gave you that notion? I haven't set foot over there since V-E Day. Hell, no, I'm trapped in the land of schizos and megalomaniacs. Two of whom are the producer and director on this picture deal we're putting together. Evan's gonna have to come out here and put some pressure on these guys, or the only recognizable thing he'll get out of this script is his name on the credits. And I ain't guaranteeing they'll even spell that right."

"I see." But Amanda didn't see, not at all. "I'll put Evan on, then. These calls must be costing you a fortune." She was babbling, and she couldn't seem to help it. Evan had lied to her. He'd been lying from the very beginning. But why? She'd been ready to give up everything she'd worked for just to spend two days alone with him. Lord, what a fool she was. "Take it easy, Murry. It's been great talking to you. Here's Evan." She refused to look at him, thrusting the phone blindly in his direction. Even with the mouthpiece two feet away from her head, she had no trouble hearing Murry's last words to her.

"It's been good to hear your voice, Mandy. I'm glad you two are starting to work things out."

She walked blindly, stiffly, over to the utility room and let Max out of confinement. He rubbed against her ankles once in a perfunctory gesture as she knelt to scratch behind his ears in wordless apology for shutting him inside the small room. He shied away from the attempted caress and stalked into the living room, his dignity offended.

Amanda stood and veered off toward her bedroom, blocking out the sound of Evan's voice raised in a one-sided altercation with his manager. It didn't matter what he said to her anymore, what seemingly plausible explanation he came up with; her logic had been correct all along. Her heart, as usual, had been untrustworthy. She retrieved her suitcase and put it down on the exact center of her bed. Max ambled into the room and watched her closely as he washed his front paw and applied it methodically to his immaculate whiskers. Deciding something was wrong, he hopped up beside her when she sat down dejectedly on the old-fashioned, tufted-cotton spread. Next, he butted his head against her arm. Amanda reached out to stroke his long, white fur. Max purred loudly, all indignities forgiven.

"We've been made a fool of, cat."

"Mandy, that's not true. You have to let me explain." Evan was standing in the doorway, looking almost as miserable as she felt.

"I'll drive you to your car." Amanda was pleased with how level-sounding and unemotional her tone was.

"I'll only be gone a day or two at the most. I'm coming back, Amanda. I'd ask you to go with me now..."

"But I would interfere with your work," she said bitterly.

"No. Because I'm going to be tied up day and night. It isn't what I had in mind for us this weekend." He laughed, but it was a short, mirthless sound that caused her skin to crawl and Max to growl warningly low in his throat. "What is it they say about the best-laid plans? Murry says *Demon Spawn*'s going to end up as a Busby Berkeley musical if I don't get out there and exercise a little creative control. God knows, I made Murry work hard enough to get it for me. He says the producer and the director..." Evan stopped short and looked slightly sheepish. "Well, I'll spare you Murry's description of the pair. Let's just say he's accusing them of practicing a pretty bizarre kind of alternate life-style."

Amanda didn't even afford his small attempt at humor the ghost of a smile. "I'll get my car keys," she said dully, plucking at the material of her sunny yellow skirt. He hadn't tried very hard to talk her into going along with him. When it came down to his writing, she would always have to take a back seat.

"Mandy, I will be back soon. You have my word, but I have to go. Now."

"Of course you do. This is your career. It's important to you. And I have no desire to go to Hollywood. You're right about that." She paused, as if waiting for him to say something more.

"I can't let them ruin my book." He didn't give a damn about the book anymore. But if he tried to explain, he'd have to tell her about the divorce decree. And that he'd lied to her to keep her from marrying another man. He'd have to tell her he'd burned the decree. Things had been going so well between them that he'd almost forgotten the lies he'd told that first day. But, somehow, he'd almost rather she continued to believe he was a liar than that he was a sentimental fool.

"Naturally we can't let that happen." Her face was set. Amanda looked a lot like her father when she was angry and hurt, Evan thought. She pulled her mouth into a severe, stubborn line. "Your suitcase is already in the trunk. When does your plane leave?" Evan couldn't be sure if she was very angry or trying very hard not to cry. He suspected the former.

"The plane won't leave until I get there," he replied with unconscious arrogance. "They've chartered a Lear jet."

"Impressive."

Traffic was heavy on Midnight Pass Road. They didn't speak during the short drive to the public beach. Amanda appeared to be totally involved with her driving. She'd hidden her expressive gray eyes behind dark-tinted sunglasses. She stared straight ahead. He pointed out his rental sedan in the parking lot, and she pulled her small car up behind it. He couldn't let it end this way. He'd worked too hard to win back her trust over the past ten days. Why had he told her that cockamamie story about Murry being in Europe in the first place? *Damn it all to hell!* he cursed silently.

Evan unlocked the rental car, letting the door open to dissipate some of the heat, while his mind turned over one improbable scenario after another. He couldn't very well kidnap her and drag her off to Hollywood with him. She'd never stand for it, and in the end he wouldn't be any better off. She'd be back to mistrusting his writing, as well as his character.

Evan leaned his forearms on the open window of Amanda's car. She continued to stare straight ahead of her. They could have just as easily been separated by a hundred miles of desert sand as the few feet of beige upholstered seat that was actually between them.

"Why did you lie to me, Evan?" she asked tonelessly, and his heart sank. He could feel sweat break out along his spine, and it had nothing to do with the heat of the sun on his back. It had everything to do with the lies he'd started telling her back in the *Examiner* office that first day.

"Mandy, I want..."

"No more stories, Evan. Just the truth, for heaven's sake. You owe me that much."

"All right, the truth." His words were clipped. Amanda pretended to watch a game of two-man volleyball from the car window. Farther out on the beach, people sat under gaily striped umbrellas or paddled about at the water's edge. No one was swimming. The water really was too cold this early in the season.

"That's all I ask." She scooted around in the seat to face him. She hoped the tinted lenses of her sunglasses helped to hide the sheen of tears that she couldn't seem to blink away.

"I lied because I didn't want you trying to get in touch with Murry about the location of my copy of the divorce decree. It wasn't in his safety-deposit box. It never has been."

"Because you've had it with you all along." Amanda's voice was as cold as a March blizzard back in Maine.

"Yes."

"Give it to me, Evan."

"No! If I do, you'll run off and marry Tacett before the day is out."

"No, I won't. I only did something that impetuous once in my life, and I ended up regretting it," she shouted back, every bit as angry as he was. She pounded her fist on the steering wheel. "It was the only favor I ever asked of you."

"It's the only one I didn't want to grant." He looked down at his arms folded on the window ledge. His knuckles stood out white under the tan skin of his hands. He tried to unclench his fist, but couldn't seem to manage to do so. His whole body felt so tense he wondered if he could stand straight again without a painful effort.

"I want your copy of that decree," Amanda insisted.

"What happened to yours?" Evan demanded, striving to gain the upper hand by bringing up what was, after all, the cause of this whole fiasco. He'd run out of brilliant improvisations. Why had Murry picked this afternoon to call? Even five minutes later would have made all the difference in the world. They would have been on their way to paradise, alone, together. Now the scene he was playing out with Amanda qualified as a nightmare beyond any his imagination could conceive.

"I lost it when I moved down here. I told you that. It was an accident." She paused, then added emphatically, "Anyway, that's completely beside the point. Please quit playing games with me. Give me your copy of the decree. I know you have it. You can't run my life anymore, Evan. I love Robert. I want to marry him."

"Twenty minutes ago you weren't sure you loved him at all."

She made a strangled sound of protest. "I never said that."

"Okay, maybe you didn't." Evan conceded the point wearily. "But it doesn't matter. I don't have the paper anymore, either. You can look through my suitcase if you don't believe me." A carload of teenagers pulled up behind them on the narrow drive. Their radio was blaring, making a terrible din. Amanda looked in the rearview mirror, distracted, her hand going automatically to the ignition to move her car forward and out of their path. Evan stood up and made a threatening gesture that sent the youngsters backing up to the end of the row.

"Damn hoodlums."

"They're only kids." Amanda took off the dark glasses and pushed them into the auburn curls on top of her head. "What did you do with your copy of the divorce decree? Don't lie to me again. You never lied to me before, no matter how badly things went between us."

"I'm not lying to you now. I did have my copy when I came down here, but I don't have it anymore."

"I . . . I'm confused." She put her hand to her temple and shook her head. She was pale, and the bright blue of her blouse accentuated the pallor of her clear skin. Evan wanted nothing more than to open the car door and take her into his arms, but he didn't move a muscle.

"You may not love me anymore, but I think you're lying to yourself when you say that you love Tacett. I'm not giving him a clear field."

"Oh, Evan, stop talking in riddles. You're not making sense." This time she couldn't have stopped the tears no matter how hard she tried. She brushed at her welling eyes with an unsteady hand. "I don't understand you. Where is the decree?"

"I burned it, damn it." He pushed away from the car, putting another arm's length of immeasurable distance between them. "I burned my legal and official copy from the courts of the City of New York. Do you understand that? I didn't want to keep lying to you, even though I stupidly started out that way. And I didn't want you running off with Tacett. What it all boils down to is that you'll have to wait a few days

longer for your much-anticipated second marriage."
He turned and walked away before he blurted out the
rest of the truth. He wasn't going to lay his soul open
to any more pain. He wasn't going to break down and
tell her he loved her more than life itself so that she
could throw the declaration back in his face.

"Evan!" Amanda was standing outside her car,
blinking in the reflected glare of sun on crystal white
sand. "Evan, wait! That doesn't make sense."

"Then I'll make it as plain as I can." He slid behind
the wheel of the rental car, fished under the seat where
he'd hidden the key and turned it in the ignition with
so much force it nearly broke in two. He raised his
voice to carry over the sound of the engine.

"You have to wait now like the sleeping princess in
the enchanted castle. You have to wait until *I* come
back for you."

CHAPTER ELEVEN

THE SAND DOLLAR was crowded for a midweek afternoon, Amanda noted, as she let the heavy carved-oak door swing shut behind her. The clatter of silver and china was muted by the heavy linen tablecloths and the skill of the waiters as they moved quickly and efficiently through the press of late lunch patrons.

The maître d' bowed and motioned her forward as she moved down the short flight of tiled stairs into the main dining room. Here, the lighting was soft and muted, as though she'd stepped into a cool green grotto. The fixtures were polished wood, the plants lush and exotic, the splash and bubble of small fountains soothing and conducive to good conversation. The room was very much like the man who owned it: sophisticated, debonair and successful.

Robert was standing at the far side of the room, conferring with his wine steward. He saw her coming toward him and raised a hand in greeting. Amanda waved back, her heart lifting momentarily with a rush of affection. Robert looked so competent and level-headed in a lightweight gray suit and a sedate striped tie. Surely, now that she could be with him, unfettered by the invisible chains of Evan's charismatic presence, life would return to the safe, comfortable pattern they'd established together. It was the pattern she'd envisioned for their future. Amanda had decided that it was best that Evan had gone to Hollywood so suddenly. His absence had allowed her to think clearly for the first time in days.

At least she could banish Evan from her thoughts for hours at a time, although he hadn't allowed her to forget him entirely. He called every evening. The first time had been to apologize for his behavior at the beach. And after that he'd called just to talk. He told her about his meetings with the colorful, talented duo who were to produce and direct the movie based on *Demon's Spawn*. He confided some of his reservations about turning over control of his creation to them for translation into a cinematic presentation. She laughed at his jokes, sympathized with his problems and just simply enjoyed the sound of his voice and the pleasure of his companionship. That was, until he told her how much he missed her, how much he looked forward to returning to her—and sent her flying into Robert's arms. Or, at least, to the Sand Dollar.

Amanda stared for a moment out the windows that looked onto St. Armand's Circle, the focal point of the exclusive shops and gourmet restaurants that lined the street. She had to get Evan out of her mind. When he'd left, she had realized once more how unsuited they were for each other. She wanted a life here, in Sarasota, and a career of her own. Evan might understand those needs, but it didn't alter the fact that his life was a thousand miles away, in a city, in a life-style, that was as alien to her as the moon.

Robert had started moving in her direction, having dismissed his wine steward, so she banished her musings and tried to do the same with her worrisome feelings for Evan. Her hands were damp, and she brushed them down the front of her turquoise colored shirtwaist dress. Amanda didn't know exactly what she was going to say to Robert. She wasn't sure how she could find the right words to explain her erratic behavior during the last two weeks. One thing she was certain of. She wouldn't lie to him, or be evasive. She'd told Evan only the truth in that respect. She and Robert were honest with each other; they didn't play games. She wasn't about to start doing so now.

If she only held fast to her original hopes and plans for the future, everything would turn out right in the end. Evan was gone. He was a fever in her blood, she couldn't deny that, but they couldn't be happy together. She was still too wary to allow herself to love like that again, to be hurt like that again. She would be happy and content as Robert's wife. She wanted that future. It was the best and most logical choice. It had nothing to do with warlock's spells and magic rainbows and loving beyond all rational boundaries. It was reality, solid and true.

"Amanda. I thought I was hallucinating, seeing you standing there." Robert smiled and came up to take her hand, then bent to kiss her cheek. "I'm beginning to feel as if I've been trapped in this restaurant for a hundred years while the rest of the world goes on around me. It's almost as if some evil genie has woven a spell and imprisoned me inside. It's like being cast as one of those poor devils who end up in the *Twilight Zone*." Amanda gasped, and dropped her purse. "Here, let me help you gather those things up."

Robert knelt beside her as she groped blindly on the tile floor for her compact and lipstick where they had rolled after she'd dropped her purse. "It's nothing," she insisted. "The chain must have snapped." She held up the slim straw bag and inspected the gold link chain.

It was intact. Robert glanced at her quizzically as he held out his hand to help her rise to her feet. "I'm not going to get out of this by blaming it on shoddy workmanship, am I?" Amanda felt a hot stain of embarrassed color mount to her cheeks. "I'm just all thumbs today."

"Let's go back to the patio." Robert nodded a greeting to one or two of the diners as they crossed the room, but he didn't stop to exchange small talk. His hand was strong and firm under her elbow, familiar and comforting.

Swinging doors opened, and they entered the kitchen of the restaurant. Inside the big, high-ceilinged room, orderly chaos prevailed as chefs in tall white hats and aprons conferred about the dishes for the evening menus while their staff dealt with the remaining lunch orders.

Thick steam rose in savory, tantalizing clouds above huge stainless-steel pots of chowder on the stoves that took up one whole wall. In a cool, air-conditioned corner near a bank of walk-in coolers, the pastry chef labored over his creations. Amanda eyed the delicate confections longingly as she walked by.

"Do you mind using the staff patio?" Robert asked. "There shouldn't be anyone on break right now. We'll have it all to ourselves, and I can't guarantee that kind of privacy on the terrace." Amanda nodded her agreement with the suggestion, and walked with him toward the screened doors leading outside. They did find the small brick patio deserted. It was separated from the restaurant's outdoor dining area by a high stucco wall. Amanda halted before a wrought-iron chair in the far corner and found herself eye to eye with a small green chameleon clinging to a branch of the jasmine vine trailing over the wall.

The patio was colorfully furnished with castoffs from the main terrace, and the small groupings of tables and chairs were only slightly more faded and worn than the ones on the public side. The door to the kitchen through which they'd entered, and a small gate leading to the service area, were the only other signs that they were in the staff area. Amanda dropped her purse on the glass-topped table. The chameleon took offense at the noise and disappeared in the blink of an eye.

"I've missed you," Robert said simply, drawing her into his arms. He rested his chin on the top of her head. "Do you know we'd just be getting back from our honeymoon if everything had gone according to plan?"

"Don't remind me," Amanda replied.

"It's been too long." He smoothed his hand over her hair.

"For me, too." She lifted her face for his kiss. The touch of his lips was as welcome and pleasant as ever, but there was no spark of instant fusion, no burst of radiant heat and light within her as there always had been with Evan. As there still was with Evan. *It doesn't matter.* Amanda stepped back abruptly, afraid for a moment that she'd spoken the words aloud and nearly stumbled over a chair. Robert steadied her with both hands above her elbows.

"Is Cameron still bothering you, Amanda?" He looked concerned but not inclined to tiptoe around the subject, so neither would she.

"He's in Hollywood. He left here Saturday afternoon to try and sort out some problems with a movie deal he's involved in.'' Amanda shrugged to indicate she didn't want to elaborate on the subject. If she did, she might have to mention that she had considered— no, decided—to go away with him. She wasn't being evasive, she told herself firmly, it was only that she didn't know how to broach the subject. "He says he's coming back.''

"And..." Robert pushed her gently back into the chair. "You might as well start at the beginning. The last time we talked, you told me he didn't have his copy of the divorce decree either. Did you make any headway on that point?'' He wondered if she felt as strange about the way they'd conducted themselves over the last week or so as he did? He was in love with this marvelously complex and multitalented woman, wasn't he? He should have been with her as much as possible, the restaurant and his obligations be damned. At the very least, he should have threatened to punch Cameron in the nose if he didn't get the hell out of her life. Instead, he'd conducted himself like the perfect Southern gentleman, calling her now and then, giving her what advice and counsel he could, allowing her to come to terms with her past in her own way. Had he been too civilized, too much the gentleman? Was he going to lose Amanda to her old love because of his civility?

"Evan burned his copy of the divorce decree. Just as I did." Amanda wasn't aware of the tiny, private smile that played across her face. She was aware, however, of the hot bloom of color that once again tinted her fair skin. "He told me that . . . just before he left for Hollywood." *Just before he promised to come back for me.*

"That does complicate matters," Robert said evenly, hoping he was hiding the cold shaft of doubt in his vitals better than she was hiding her secret thoughts of Evan Cameron. "You two must be more kindred spirits than you want to believe." It was a leading observation, yet he had to know where he stood.

If Amanda wasn't still interested in her ex-husband, then she must never know that he was beginning to have reservations about their future. He was aware how badly she'd been hurt by the failure of her marriage. He knew how it felt to love and to lose, and to suffer that loss forever after. He wouldn't be responsible for hurting Amanda a second time; he cared too deeply for her. He'd do everything in his power to make her feel happy and secure.

But even though he hadn't wanted it to happen, in fact still couldn't believe it was happening to him, there was another woman in his life. He didn't know where it might go; he wasn't sure yet that his feelings for Teresa Harrington were any more than gallantry, protectiveness at finding a lovely and appealing woman whose loyalty to Amanda's father had involved her in a situation that was both dangerous and frightening for her. Or if he was experiencing something that could become a lasting and fulfilling attachment. It was an attachment destined to go nowhere as long as he was committed to Amanda.

"Evan has always been impulsive," Amanda said with a little shake of her head that sent flickers of sunlight dancing in her hair. Her words brought Robert out of his thoughts. He focused on her strained features with difficulty. "We did a lot of talking while he was here, Robert." She stood up and paced the length of the small patio. The breeze ruffled the palm trees whose fronds eavesdropped over the top of the walk but did little to alleviate the heat rising from the brick paving.

"What did you talk about?" Robert watched his own thoughtful expression stare back at him in the darkly reflective smoked-glass tabletop.

"Of shoes...and ships...and sealing wax...of cabbages and kings," Amanda recited whimsically. Then she spoke more briskly. "Mostly of what was right in our marriage. And about what was wrong." She shook her head in silent recollection of those memories. Robert sat quietly, staring at his hands. For the first time in his life, he wished he was a violent man; he'd like to have Cameron's throat in his grasp. Amanda had never looked at him that way and never would as long as Evan was alive.

"It made me realize that you and I...that we're making some of the same mistakes that Evan and I made. I don't want that to happen." Amanda turned on him beseechingly, spreading her hands in a gesture of appeal, asking for his understanding.

"In what way are we making the same mistakes, Amanda?" His tone was even, neutral—the way he tried to keep it when Evan Cameron was the subject of their discussions. He didn't think he'd succeeded this time when Amanda sighed and lowered her hands to her sides. Her great gray eyes were shadowed and apprehensive.

"About children, about a family. One thing I did promise him was that we would discuss the matter again."

"I thought we'd settled it, Amanda." Robert took a deep breath and let it out slowly, trying to hold onto his temper. He pulled at the knot of his tie, then made himself relax enough to lay his hands along the arms of the chair. It wasn't her fault. She couldn't know how much talking about children hurt—because he'd never told her the truth.

"I think it would be more accurate to say that you have settled it with yourself. And I . . . I agreed out of cowardice, I guess, as much as anything." She touched her fingers to her temple as though trying to order her thoughts. She moved to sit in the chair close beside him. She took his hand between her own. His skin felt warm and dry to the touch. Her own hand was cold and clammy. "I . . . I think I want to try again to have another child."

"Mine or Cameron's?" Robert couldn't help the coldness and anger in his voice, but he regretted it instantly.

Tears sprang into her eyes, and she blinked them rapidly away. "Yours, Robert," she replied with simple dignity.

"Forgive me, Amanda. That remark was uncalled-for. I apologize. But it's still impossible. I haven't changed my mind."

"Why, Robert?" She could sense he was infinitely more hurt than angry, and she pushed aside the pain of his earlier accusation. She'd been planning to say that she understood, but suddenly she found that she didn't understand. All at once it was the most important thing in the world that she know what this composed yet enigmatic man felt and thought, for his own sake as well as her own. "I'd be very proud and happy to be the mother of your child." At least she had that to thank Evan for. She'd faced one demon and defeated it; she wasn't afraid to contemplate becoming pregnant again.

"No, you wouldn't." Robert's harsh words cut through her heart like a blade. He stood up so quickly his chair nearly toppled over backward. He laughed at her expression of disbelief, and the sound was hollow and terrible to hear.

"How can you say that?" Amanda felt tears of grief and rejection stinging behind her eyelids. She was frightened and her breath came in quick, short gasps.

"The subject isn't open for discussion, Amanda."

She wanted to run and hide from the dull, aching pain inside her, but she couldn't. That way lay failure and agonizing self-defeat. "We can't just drop the subject. I care too deeply for you to just walk away from it." Her chin came up; her tone was thin, but steady and determined. "I won't run away, either. I did that with Evan. It was wrong. I won't make the same mistake again, and I won't allow you to either." She stood her ground, her jaw set but her eyes pleaded for his answer.

The stiff tightness left his back and shoulders as the silence lengthened and stretched out between them. When Amanda laid her arm on his coat sleeve he didn't resist her gentle insistence. He faced her, his eyes no longer blank and empty but filled with old pain and memories, at least as hurting as her own.

"I had a child, Amanda. His mother and I never married. He was...handicapped...severely, both mentally and physically. She wouldn't...couldn't accept him. He lived every day of his life in an institution. He died about five years ago. So you see, there are valid reasons for my decision." He looked up at the sky and saw nothing. Amanda took his hand, and he closed his fingers around hers gratefully. He looked at her, and the darkness receded.

"It might not happen again." She found herself taking Evan's arguments and using them to convince Robert that there was always hope. His skin was as cold as hers. She shouldn't have pressured him to resurrect his past.

"The chances are very good that it might happen again. You see, Amanda, there are things even more painful than losing a baby. One of them is having a child who will never have the opportunity to realize his potential in life at all."

"I'm so sorry, Robert." The words sounded inadequate. She squeezed his hand. "We won't talk about it ever again, not unless you want to."

"But it's going to make a difference between us." He looked deeply into her eyes. They were gray and clear and without guile.

"No, it won't." Amanda was emphatic; sorrow and compassion filled her heart. Perhaps now wasn't the time to voice her reservations. She was finding it truly didn't make a difference to her if she didn't have a child with Robert. She could live with that reality. *If I love him beyond life itself.* Honesty made her admit that, as yet, her feelings weren't that strong. They might never be. Where would that leave them in the future?

Evan had planted his seeds of doubt in her mind too well. They'd taken root and found fertile soil in which to sprout. Yet babies weren't the central issues: their lack of communication, their lack of total commitment were.

"I haven't talked about my son for a long time. I thought...I thought I would never speak of him again. Forgive me, Mandy. I didn't mean to deceive you."

"I know that. We'll work this out, too. We have all the time in the world, after all." He looked drained and exhausted, and it was all her fault. He needed her, as she'd needed him all these months. She couldn't fail him now. Amanda swallowed hard to clear the lump from her throat.

"Do we have all the time in the world, Mandy?" He seldom used her nickname, and somehow it made the moment far more poignant.

"I'll be here as long as you want me." Her resolve was strong once again.

Voices raised in altercation behind the fence broke the fragile illusion of privacy the deserted patio had provided. Robert offered Amanda a snowy handkerchief from his breast pocket to wipe her tears, but part of his attention was centered on the voices. Amanda was listening, too. She paused, the square of linen clutched in her hand. "That's my father's voice," she said in no uncertain terms.

Robert delayed a fraction of a second too long in denying the statement. "It's just some old wino trying to panhandle a dollar or two from one of the busboys. I'll get rid of him."

"It is not." She wasn't going to be put off. Robert wondered just exactly what he should do. Peter was supposed to meet him and Teresa here at three. Amanda's father must be early. He didn't dare look at his watch to check the time or he'd tip her off for sure. "That's my father."

Amanda stepped past Robert and looked around the gate of tall wooden slats just as a gray-haired, shuffling figure began to walk away from an indignant busboy.

"This old rummy won't get out of the alley, Mr. Tacett."

"It's all right, Mario. You go on into work. I'll take care of this." Robert waved his youthful employee inside. "Thanks, Mario."

"Sure thing, Mr. Tacett."

The derelict in a rusty black sports coat and faded denim jeans hung his head and backed away, but there was no doubt in Amanda's mind that he was indeed Peter Winston.

"Dad!" The old man didn't answer. He turned, darted down the alley, and was lost to sight in a matter of moments. "Robert?" Amanda turned to him in astonishment. "He ran away from me."

"Don't try to follow him, Amanda," Robert warned, catching her around the waist as she made to follow. Her feet dangled in the air as he lifted her off the ground. The authority in his voice clearly surprised her.

"I can't just let him go like that. I want an explanation." Amanda twisted in his arms. He released her but continued to hold her wrist in light restraint. "What's going on, Robert?"

"I gave him my word not to tell you. Your father knows what he's doing. He's capable and he's nobody's fool. You'll only get in his way if you go after him."

"I want an explanation." Amanda looked like a stranger. Her face was set, her expression stubborn and confused. From the way she looked, he wondered if she found him equally unfamiliar at the moment. He realized that their confrontation was producing something of a standoff and didn't know the best way to proceed.

The service door opened again, and Teresa stepped out onto the patio. She was dressed neatly, but plainly, in a dark skirt and white blouse. Her hair was drawn into a severe knot at the back of her neck. Amanda didn't notice her friend's apparel, but Robert recognized the clothes Teresa had been wearing on her visits to the shelter and frowned.

"Teresa? What are you doing here?" Amanda's eyes narrowed. "Were you coming to meet my father also?" Teresa looked quickly at Robert's grim face, then at Amanda's. She nodded. Released from Robert's hold, Amanda spun toward the door. "We have to catch up with him. I want the truth."

"You can't speak to him now." Teresa forestalled her by moving to block the exit. She looked almost nunlike in the sober skirt and blouse, but still enchantingly lovely with her head held high and her eyes bright with emotion. Robert decided to let her handle the volatile situation in her own way.

"I have the right to know."

"Yes, Amanda, you do. I'll try and explain everything." Teresa didn't look at Robert again, but he felt her wordlessly reaching out to him for reassurance.

"What's my father doing, running all over the city like a homeless wino?"

"I imagine he's on his way back to the shelter. He made Robert and me..." She paused, then laid a hand lightly on his jacket sleeve and withdrew it when he made a slight move to cover her hand with his own. "He made us promise to keep his secret. Now you mustn't do anything so rash as to put him in even greater danger."

"The shelter? I don't understand." The sun was making her head ache. She pushed at damp, straying tendrils of hair. It was hot on the patio, and barely a breath of air was stirring.

"He's undercover," Teresa said simply, devastatingly.

"Oh, God, what for?" Amanda raised her hand to her eyes and Robert saw her fingers tremble. He put his arm around her shoulders.

"Somebody in the Costa Verde government is smuggling assassins into this country," he said quietly. "Carmella recognized death-squad members among the shelter's residents."

"General Alexandro's power is waning. He's been forced to call special elections. If he loses, he's going to have to leave the country. He wants to come here." Teresa finished the explanation in her soft, low voice.

"And he doesn't want to be turned away like Duvalier or Marcos," Amanda said thoughtfully. "I'm all right, Robert, really." She moved away from the comforting circle of his arm with a brief caress of her fingers along his cheek.

"There are people already in this country who are opposed to Alexandro coming here. They are few but vocal." Amanda didn't hear the strained inflection in Teresa's voice but Robert did.

"And they have to be done away with so the man will have a better chance of gaining political asylum."

"Yes." Robert answered for Teresa. "And Peter is very close to finding the leader of the gang."

"But he won't tell Robert or me whom he suspects." This time Teresa's anxiety for Peter's safety was obvious even to a preoccupied Amanda.

"Teresa has been going to the shelter to pass on information." Robert indicated the plain, shabby skirt and blouse Teresa was wearing.

"I'm only an errand girl. Today we were supposed to meet him here."

"But he won't come back because I'm here," Amanda said tightly. "I'm going out to the shelter."

"You can't." Teresa's tone was sharper than any Robert had ever heard her use before.

"I'll...I'll pretend to be doing an interview," Amanda improvised. "That will work. No one will suspect who I'm looking for."

"You've never done an interview in your life. You're not a reporter." Robert thought it was time to bring the whole scene to a close. "Don't be so foolish, Amanda."

"I'm a newspaper publisher and a good one. I can manage to fake one interview."

"I don't think it's wise. Robert is right, Amanda, you have no experience." Teresa colored slightly, the blush darkening her pale olive skin as she heard the underlying appeal in her own voice.

"You'll only call attention to yourself and jeopardize your father's cover. You're out of your league, Amanda. We all are. Let him work it out for himself."

"I can't believe you've conspired to keep this from me." She looked from one to the other accusingly.

"Your father thought it best." Robert walked over to Amanda, but his legs felt as if they were made of stone. He bent to kiss her forehead and looked down at her, a rueful smile touching the corners of his lips. "I know I don't cut a very dashing figure in this business, but I did give my word. And your father knows what he's doing. Forgive me for keeping it from you, Mandy." The use of her nickname melted her anger.

"You have nothing to apologize for, but that doesn't alter the fact that I'm going after my father."

The stiffness in Robert's arms and legs seemed to be spreading directly to his brain. She wasn't listening to a word he said. How did he deal with her in this mood? "That's not wise." His words came out sounding stiff and formal.

"It's my decision." Amanda pulled her shoulders back and looked him directly in the eye. "My decision alone."

"Of course." Were they making a mistake, trying to go on as if nothing had changed between them, Robert wondered. Or had anything really changed? Had the heartache of talking about his son, the charged atmosphere of this confrontation over Amanda's father, simply brought to the forefront all the symptoms of a relationship going astray?

"Don't worry, Teresa," Amanda directed her next words to her friend. "I won't make a fool of myself, or the *Examiner*.

"Amanda." Robert tried once more to form an argument that would make her see reason. She didn't even look back at him, but disappeared into the restaurant. "Teresa?" He turned to the lovely, calm creature beside him. She was as cool and refreshing to look at as a stream in the desert. To taste her lips in a long, soul-satisfying kiss would be to drink its crystal-clear waters. He hoped the misery and indecision in his brain and heart hadn't seeped into his eyes, where Amanda might have detected it; he was certain Teresa sensed his anguish and his growing desire for her. She smiled at him, but her lips trembled and she refused to meet his gaze directly. When she did acknowledge him, her long-lashed brown eyes were shadowed and revealed little of her thoughts.

"I'm afraid she'll do something to put herself in danger also. What can we do?"

He wanted to take her in his arms but contented himself with taking her hand in his instead. Before he could answer, however, another voice made itself heard.

"She'll go barging in out there and blow my cover for sure." Peter was standing in the shadow of the partially open gate. "I didn't go far. I heard it all," he said succinctly. "There's nothing more you can do to stop her. I'll just have to be on my guard." He stepped onto the patio and looked from one of his reluctant cohorts to the other. Robert allowed Teresa to remove her hand from his.

"It's getting too complicated, Peter. Call in the authorities." Robert tried reason one more time.

"It's too late. I'm close; I can't back out now or the whole deal will go down the tubes."

"Robert is right, Peter. Please don't go back." Teresa looked from one man to the other. "Please."

"I must, Teresa. I have to be there when this thing goes down. I can handle it, don't worry." Peter didn't think, from the concerned looks of their faces, that he sounded as convincing as he wanted to be; and for a very good reason. He wasn't all that certain of the outcome himself.

PETER KNEW HE couldn't loiter at this dead-end corner of the corridor much longer. Someone was bound to come by and notice he'd been pushing his broom over the same three square feet of dingy brown tile for the last ten minutes. Damn, why couldn't Amanda have stayed away one more day? He'd roamed the streets until curfew last evening on purpose to avoid just such a confrontation. Now it was late afternoon and it was almost over. A manila envelope containing a computer-generated photograph of the man he was after was inside one of his ever-present plastic bags, passed on by Teresa earlier in the afternoon. He was almost ready to make his move.

But now his headstrong daughter was here, at the shelter, posing as one of her own reporters. And not doing a very convincing job of it, in his opinion. That meant his own chances of being discovered were greatly increased. The manila envelope included the identity of Alexandro's top man: Colonel Juan Silva. His image Peter had already committed to memory, but as yet he hadn't been able to spot his quarry. Thanks to his old contacts in Washington, he now knew who he was up against and could proceed accordingly. His adversary was a young man, barely half his age: intelligent, arrogant and totally ruthless. He had to keep up this masquerade for at least another twenty-four hours, until he could put the last phase of his plan into motion.

He'd already forbidden Teresa to come back to the shelter. And he'd made arrangements for Carmella and the girls to go to his sister in Biloxi. He had to stay at the shelter and in character until Silva showed himself. Only then could he be certain his quarry would be caught in the trap that was almost ready to swing shut behind him. And then he'd get the hell out of this mess and let the authorities do the dirty work.

The sound of Amanda's voice was coming closer. He had no place to go. He listened to her questioning the director of the shelter and hoped the man was too busy, too distracted with his own worries to notice the less-than-professional way Amanda was conducting her interview. If he got out of this thing alive, he'd have to give her a real talking-to, as well as a few pointers on getting a good interview.

"Dad." Amanda kept her voice to a whisper. It had taken her only a moment to catch up with the wheeled cart he was pushing at a slow half trot, half shuffle. She'd been almost rude to the director in her haste to break away and talk to her father. She'd make sure the poor man got some real coverage from the *Examiner* when this whole affair was over and done with. "Dad." This time he stopped and looked straight through her.

"What do you want, lady?"

The reality of the situation hit Amanda with a twist of fear deep inside that made her dizzy and light-headed. Teresa and Robert hadn't exaggerated their warning to assure her cooperation. The danger was real and present. She could almost feel it in the air around her. And this stranger wasn't the father she'd always known and loved. He was a professional investigative journalist, something she was not and would never be. The Peter she faced was a consummate actor, and he had to be good at playing his part—his life depended on it.

"Do you like living at the shelter?" she asked, striving to stay in character now that it was too late to turn back. She had put her father, Teresa, perhaps even Carmella and her daughters at risk by coming here. Why couldn't she have listened to the others, abided by her father's wishes and stayed away? Yet, now that she'd blundered into the middle of things, she couldn't just walk away and call even more attention to the two of them.

She glanced surreptitiously up and down the hall. Children's voices ricocheted out of the gymnasium where a lively game of soccer helped them pass the rainy afternoon. The sounds of food preparation and tables being readied for the evening meal echoed from the cafeteria to her left, but nothing more unusual than that. She relaxed slightly. There was no one to witness their talk but a monk of some kind dressed in a rough, brown robe and cowl. His hands were folded beneath his robe, and he seemed not to notice them.

"Lady, I said it ain't so bad here. You want to know anythin' else?"

"The food," Amanda stumbled over the simple phrase and cleared her throat, her hand tightening involuntarily on the microphone of the small tape recorder slung over her shoulder.

"The food's okay and I've got a bed to myself. It ain't bad, like I already said. Is that all, lady? I got work to do."

There was still not the faintest glimmer of recognition in his brown eyes.

"Yes. Thanks for your cooperation." She watched as he ducked his head and started to wheel the cart away, fidgeting with the big plastic bags hooked to its side. All her fear for him was in her eyes as she turned away to catch up with the director and finish this travesty of an interview.

From the doorway the cowled figure continued to stand quietly and watch. Amanda looked up and caught his eye for a brief moment. A polite smile began to form on her lips, then died as quickly as it began.

The hawk-nosed man wasn't watching her anymore. He was staring after her father with a calculating expression on his darkly handsome face. And he had the coldest, deadliest eyes Amanda had ever seen.

CHAPTER TWELVE

STORM CLOUDS WERE beginning to move inland, leaving the sky a dusky blue as the sun wheeled toward the horizon, a faded orange flower, blowsy, full-blown, dropping petals of sunbeams that drifted back toward the shore in broken stems of light. The heavy, oppressive heat of the past two days was gone, replaced by a cooling breeze. Amanda stared out at the scudding, tattered-edged clouds; the last relics of a day of soaking rain and heavy thunderstorms. More storms were predicted for the nighttime hours, but as yet they'd failed to materialize as anything but vague symptoms of what was to come: a restless, oily sheen on the Gulf, and a low, hazy smudge at the edge of the world.

It was also possible that the weatherman had miscalculated. Heaven knew, she'd made enough mistakes of her own lately that she couldn't sit in judgment on anyone else. Her mind drifted along with the marching clouds, touching on one sensitive point after another, as if her tongue was seeking out a sore tooth to test the pain, hoping to find it had gone away. But of course it had not. Each and every thought she brought to the forefront of her mind was too painful to contemplate for any length of time: her interrupted and unresolved relationship with Evan, her feelings for Robert and the hope she couldn't give up of their sharing some kind of future together, even the ambi-

guity of her emotions when her lawyer had called from
New York that morning to tell her the decree had been
located, duly copied and notarized, and turned over to
an express courier.

Nothing concerned her at the moment as much as
her father's whereabouts. Was he safe? Unharmed? At
the mercy of a madman?

That anxiety refused to diminish in the least, even
though at times she could banish her other problems to
the back of her mind—for a little while, at least. She
hadn't heard from Peter or seen him for almost thirty
hours. Not since she'd gone to the shelter yesterday.

She hadn't felt so alone, so lonely, in a long time. It
was a separateness almost as paralyzing as the first few
weeks after she'd left Evan. She hadn't ever wanted to
feel that alone again, but now she was.

She couldn't go to Robert. He'd made his position
clear that afternoon at the Sand Dollar. He believed her
father was capable of taking care of himself in a situation that was almost beyond Amanda's ability to
imagine. He saw no reason to interfere without Peter
asking him to do so. But Robert didn't know what she
knew, or at least what her intuition prompted her to
believe was the truth: the man at the shelter meant to
harm her father. She shivered and wrapped her arms
around her waist, unable to clear her mind's eye of his
hawklike features and his cold, cold eyes as he'd
watched her father shuffle away, unaware and so very
much alone.

Yet she also recognized that she wasn't being entirely fair to Robert. He would help her, despite his
promise to her father, if she told him everything, described the man in the monk's robe and his sinister
bearing. He would say they must go to the police, and

she'd agree. But the police needed proof, concrete evidence on which to act and she had none, only her own fear and the memory of a man's cruel eyes. So she'd done nothing but wait, and now she was running out of reserves of courage and patience.

It was as if her life were somehow held in thrall. She seemed to be existing in a curious kind of limbo; a microsecond out of sync with the rest of the universe, waiting, watching, reaching out to touch those around her and finding her hand pass through solid objects as if they were mist. Her control was slipping away, and her greatest fear was that her indecision might cost her father his life.

She needed someone to confide in, an objective observer whose opinion she trusted. A sad, enchanting ghost of a smile curved her mouth. *If only Evan would return*. She'd learned to trust him again over the past few weeks, and she'd always respected his intelligence. He would help her choose the right course of action—but he was two thousand miles away.

Amanda pulled a soft, ivory wool shawl closer around her shoulders as the damp wind feathered the curls at her temples and the nape of her neck. She shivered as another sharp dart of fear seared her nerve endings, raising gooseflesh on her bare arms. What should she do?

Max stirred restlessly in her lap as her disquiet communicated itself to him. Amanda bent her head to nuzzle the angora-soft fur between his ears as the cat stood and arched his back toward her. She pulled him close, wrapping her arms around her pet to savor his warmth and the low, nearly inaudible rumble of a purr deep in his chest. Max almost never purred, disdaining the obvious feline reaction as beneath his dignity.

He hopped off her lap in one fluid movement, landing almost soundlessly on the decking. Amanda stood too, but stiffly, the back of her apricot-colored sundress, even through the fabric of the shawl, feeling clammy from the slightly damp lounge cushions.

"You know, cat, I truly do wish Evan were here. How's that for a one-hundred-and-eighty-degree turnaround? Three weeks ago I planned never to see him again in my life. Now I have that damned divorce decree practically in my hands and I haven't told a living soul. What's the matter with me?" *You'd almost think I was in love with the man.* Before the echo of her thoughts had died away inside her, the silence of her living room was broken by a sharp knocking on the door.

Max moved forward a few feet and sat down, winding his tail around his legs. He watched the door with a great deal of interest, his hackles rising.

"Dad!" Amanda flew across the room, her feet scarcely touching the floor, no doubt in her mind who was on the other side of her front door. She swung open the heavy panel of wood and prepared to fling herself headlong into Peter's arms. But the man outside the door wasn't her father.

"Evan." She stopped so quickly that the skirts of her dress swirled around her knees with a swish of fabric. He was standing with one arm braced on the doorframe, one hand raised to knock again. He was wearing a dark, pine-green sweater of some soft, heathery material that looked as if it would be nice to touch. His face was shaded by a day's growth of beard, his eyes shadowed by both fatigue and the branches of the bougainvillea outside the door, so that she couldn't read his expression any more easily than she ever had.

"I told you'd I'd be back, Mandy." His voice was low and dark, matching the secretive twilight shades lingering beyond the brave square of yellow light outside the door.

"I'm not so sure I believed you."

He glanced past her as Max launched himself across the room to rub against Evan's ankles, purring loudly, then disappeared like a streak of lightning into the night. When Evan raised his eyes to hers again they were dark with secrets, the gold irises so dilated that they were almost brown.

Evan and Amanda stood silently a moment longer, each searching for something in the other's expression, bearing, gestures. She looked away first, suddenly light-headed, her breath coming in quick little gasps. She'd been so certain it would be Peter standing there, safe and well, that for a minute the disappointment was almost overwhelming. Yet below the disappointment there was a strong current of relief—and special joy. Evan had returned, and she was certain he would help her.

"You can always believe me." He made no move to enter her home. Amanda tried to pull her scattering wits back into focus and looked down. He didn't have any luggage with him. There was no other car parked in her driveway.

"Have you been to my father's house?" she asked, dizzy with new hope. "Your luggage . . ."

"I'm not staying that long, Mandy. I left my stuff in the Lear jet. I'll probably be using it to fly back to New York. . . ." He fell silent in his turn. Panic bloomed inside her, making her dizzier than ever. He didn't intend to stay. She ought to be relieved, but she wasn't. She was sad, so very sad, and still so alone.

Tears seeped into the corners of her eyes, although she willed them not to. *I musn't cry.* Amanda swayed a little with the effort it took to bring her emotions back under control, grabbing blindly at the door to steady herself.

She needed someone. No man was an island, and no woman, either. Her whole support structure was being torn out from under her. She didn't want to carry this great roiling fear for her father's safety inside herself any longer. But Evan wasn't going to stay and she had no right to ask him to share her fears, not anymore, not ever again.

"Amanda." He was over the threshold in an instant, his arms around her shoulders. "What's wrong?" It was certainly more than just the shock of his appearing unannounced on her doorstep. She wound her arms around his neck and held on so tightly he could do nothing but shift his stance to take some of her weight against him and pull her into his arms.

"I didn't mean to frighten you, just showing up like this," he teased gently. "I tried to call last night and again this morning before I left L.A., but no one answered." It wasn't like her to be so emotional. Something was definitely wrong. The decree. Was it here, in her possession? Had she already gone ahead with her plans to marry Tacett while he was gone? Was that why she hadn't answered her phone?

He didn't press her to tell him where she'd been. "We were so close to working things out the day I left...has anything changed?" Under his fingers her heartbeat began to accelerate. "I had to come back to you."

The words were simply spoken but devastating in their impact. Amanda's heart speeded up a little more but stayed in its proper place, no longer trying to float up into her throat and choke off her breath and her speech. "It's not anything you said or did, Evan. It's not even anything between us that's bothering me. It's my father. He's missing. At least I think he's missing." She laced her fingers through his and led the way to the couch. She sat down and he did the same, but almost immediately she jumped up again and started pacing back and forth in front of him.

"I don't know what to do next. I can't find Carmella. Teresa called in sick this morning and won't take any messages. Robert..." She tensed and turned back to face him. "I know I sound like a crazy alarmist. I don't have any concrete evidence, but I'm sure that my father is in danger."

"We could take your car—I came by cab—and drive by his house," Evan suggested quietly. There was a puzzled line between his dark winged brows. "Maybe his phone is out of order or off the hook."

"I don't think so. I know I haven't any proof that this time he's in trouble and not simply working on another lead."

She looked uncertain, and so damned appealing. He wanted nothing more than to scoop her up in his arms and carry her off into the humid moonlit night and make her forget all her cares and fears. He'd done what was necessary in California; he'd even gotten more than he'd intended to bargain for from the movie people with Murry's help, but his mind had never been wholly on the negotiations. He'd truly been alive only when he'd picked up the phone and made his daily call to her.

Was it possible he'd misinterpreted their conversations? Had they been far more one-sided than he cared to remember? In the end, he'd boarded the Lear jet and decided simply to show up on the doorstep. He hoped it was the right choice. Yet Amanda wasn't in any condition to deal with a personal confrontation between them. Right now, she needed his cooperation and his support. He intended to give it to her, with no more questions asked.

"Give me your car keys and start at the beginning," he said firmly to quell his own ambivalent musings. "I take it this has something to do with Costa Verde. Am I correct?"

Amanda nodded, silver flashes sparkling through the dark worry in her gray eyes. "Dad's on the trail of some of General Alexandro's hired assassins. Carmella recognized two members of one of his death squads. That's what set Dad off originally." Amanda grabbed her purse off the credenza by the front door and began rifling through the contents in search of her keys. She told him everything she knew then, as cleanly and concisely as she could manage, while he maneuvered her car out onto Midnight Pass Road and headed back into the city toward her father's home.

"And you're convinced this monk was acting suspiciously?"

Amanda sighed and shook her head in the affirmative. "He didn't make a single movement that was out of place. It was only his eyes. The way he looked at Dad. He had the coldest, deadliest eyes I've ever encountered—and don't ask me for any more objective description because I can't give it to you. The man was evil, and there wasn't any way at all I could go back and talk to my father. I shouldn't have gone. I'm no reporter, and that man knew it." She shuddered and hugged her arms around her body. "I wanted to warn my father about the man in the cowled robe but I never saw him again."

They were on Peter's street now. Amanda twisted her hands in her lap, glad that she'd let Evan drive her car because her eyes were dry and scratchy from lack of sleep. She closed them briefly and opened them again when the car slowed to a crawl. Her father's house was dark and obviously deserted.

"Wherever he is, it isn't here," Evan said unnecessarily. Then he lifted his fingers from the steering wheel to indicate he knew what a lame statement it was. "Now what?"

"Teresa's," Amanda said tightly. "I don't care if she's ill. I have to talk to her. She's been coming and going at the shelter, too. She might have seen this monk. Maybe she knows who he is, and then I can admit I'm being stupid and silly about the whole affair. If not, I want her to be warned. I've waited too long as it is to do something."

Amanda rang the doorbell outside Teresa's Lido Key condominium for the third time, punching at the round, lighted button as if that would make her friend answer the door more quickly. There was light coming through the window, but the drapes were drawn and Amanda could see nothing. The ground-floor, two-bedroom apartment had once been part of a lavish motel complex. A high wall enclosed the lawn, with access to the beach through an arched gate. There was a lush landscaped garden area, and a pool with a hot tub. One or two residents were taking advantage of the break in the rain clouds to sit outside in the dark quiet and soak away the day's tension. None of them had seen Teresa. Her car was gone, for the garage door was open and the stall empty.

"Another dead end. Now what, Evan?" she asked wearily, slamming the car door as she slipped into the passenger seat. She laid her head back and stared at the ceiling. "Teresa's gone. Should we go to the police?"

"What can we say?" Evan asked in his turn. "She might be out getting a bottle of aspirin or something to eat. We've got to have our story in good shape if we decide to go to the police. Let's get a bite to eat ourselves and talk this over." Maybe he shouldn't be putting forward such a mundane suggestion as food, but Amanda looked so fragile. Her skin had taken on a transparent luster across her cheekbones, and her lips were pale and bloodless. "When was the last time you had something to eat, Amanda?"

"I take it coffee and crackers don't count," she answered with an attempt at a smile.

"You're right, they don't."

"Then it was lunch. Yesterday," she admitted in an amazed sort of tone. "No wonder things keep sliding away from me now and then. There's a little place just down the road. Delmar's. Nothing fancy. Only the locals use it. Maybe Teresa's there," she added hopefully. "They have great chowder." Evan was trying to distract her from her escalating anxiety for a few minutes and she was grateful. She couldn't comprehend completely in her present, unsettled state just how good it did feel to have Evan back where she could look at him, listen to him, touch him and know that he would be there when she needed his help.

"Chowder sounds great. We can finalize our strategy there."

Thirty minutes later, settled comfortably in a high-backed wicker chair with a glass of wine at her elbow, Amanda spooned up the last of her thick, spicy chowder. Her face had regained some of its delicate peachy tint, and her eyes looked less bruised and waiflike. Evan pushed his bowl aside and leaned back in his chair.

"Feel better?"

"Yes, but I still haven't come up with any answers or any more ideas. Have you?"

He shook his head.

"It would have been too easy to walk in and find Teresa sitting at the next table, wouldn't it?"

"Yes." Evan began to trace patterns on the red-checked vinyl tablecloth with his spoon handle.

"So now what?" Amanda folded her hands under her chin and studied his guarded expression.

"We can go to the police and maybe blow your father's cover. Or we can sit on our hands and wait for him to tie things up in his own way. In either case the waiting is going to be brutal."

"We could go to the shelter." Amanda sat up straight and met his golden gaze head-on. "I'll bet my last dollar that's where both of them are right now. Teresa said Dad told her to stay away. But she's as stubborn as he is." Evan stared into his almost empty wineglass. It was a lighter shade of gold than his eyes, Amanda noted.

"It's too risky to go out there." He didn't try to soften the harshness of the pronouncement. "Your mad monk has seen you, remember? Showing up at the shelter would certainly tip him off. I'm not quite sure exactly what all is going on here, but going out there is probably the worst mistake you can make."

"I accept that." Amanda had picked up her wineglass as he spoke; now she set it down with a thump. "I'm going to go crazy just waiting. Evan..." Her voice was very small and quiet. "What if they've been kidnapped?"

"It's a possibility we might have to consider," he answered finally. Evan covered her hand with his own. It was cold, and he automatically began to massage warmth into her chilled fingers. "If we haven't heard from one or the other of them by midnight, we'll go to the police regardless, agreed?"

"Agreed. But what about your flight back?" She could have bitten off her tongue for even asking the question, but it had just popped out.

"I won't leave you to face this alone, Mandy. Unless you want me to go."

"I'd like you to stay." Her voice held a lost-little-girl note that went straight to his heart.

"We'll stop by Teresa's condo again when we leave here. She's probably back in her living room drinking herbal tea and watching an old Bogart flick on cable." He smiled, and Amanda rewarded him with a smile in return. "How about a walk on the beach?" Evan indicated the inky blackness beyond the floodlight at the foot of the small deck where they'd been eating. Thunder rumbled off in the distance, and lightning streaked down to dance on the surface of the water, but it was far away in time and distance. "It will help pass the time."

Amanda started an automatic protest, but he held up one square, long-fingered hand. "You've already left this number with the *Examiner* switchboard and at the Sand Dollar." His brows drew together in a slight frown, but he gave no other indication that he thought the gesture significant. "It's barely nine o'clock. I'll tell the waiter where we're going. He'll take a message if one comes in."

"Okay." Amanda gave in gracefully, not daring to contemplate the long hours stretching ahead of them. Even if the police believed their story, it would take time to authorize a search. Waiting was so hard; she'd never been good at it.

Evan pushed back his chair to go in search of the waiter who also doubled as the bartender. It was a small restaurant, with no pretensions of any kind to atmosphere or decor beyond a few draped fishing nets in the windows and the mandatory red glass hurricane globes over the candles on the tables. But the food was good, and it was quiet. Amanda rested her chin on her palm and looked out into the night, trying to empty her mind of all the thoughts scurrying around inside, trying not to let the growing tension in the damp air stretch her nerves even tighter.

Two elderly ladies, the only other diners, were conferring at a table along the wall. Amanda let their voices wash over her until Evan reappeared at her side. He held out his hand and she took it. She stood up just as the older of the two women came toward her.

"Please pardon my interruption, but aren't you Evan Cameron, the novelist?" the plump grandmotherly figure asked.

"Yes," Evan replied with a polite smile as he tucked Amanda's hand under his elbow.

"I'm a great fan of yours," the senior admitted coyly. Her hands set off a fluttering of voile scarves that gave her something of the appearance of a very plump butterfly. "I wish I had my copy of *Night Wanderers* with me," she lamented. *Night Wanderers* was Evan's current bestseller. "It was excellent. That's how I recognized you, from the photo on the dust jacket. It's a very good likeness."

"I'll take that as a compliment." Evan smiled down at his elderly admirer, no suggestion of restlessness or impatience in his stance or in his expression. "I could autograph something else for you, perhaps a menu?"

"Would you do that? I didn't like to ask. It seems such an imposition." Evan's fan turned to Amanda while he pulled a paper carryout menu from a stack on the bar and scrawled his name across the cover. "I do hope he's working on a new book."

"I believe he is," Amanda said softly and managed a smile. The elderly lady was walking on air, and Evan had handled the encounter very graciously. He really was more at ease with his fame than he had been during their marriage. He was at ease with his talent, his success, and in control of his writing, just as he'd told her.

"His stories are so wonderfully bloodthirsty...but never gruesome." The old lady laughed merrily as she accepted the menu from Evan. "I really don't know a better way to describe your books. It's his characters, I think." She directed her last comment to Amanda. "And his monsters. Diabolical is the only word. But they always have some redeeming qualities, too. I'm almost rooting for them by the end of the story!" She laughed, and it sounded a lot like Amanda's grandmother's laugh. She smiled at the pleasant recollection. "I am running on, aren't I? I can see you two young people want to be alone, and I must get back to my cousin, Blanche." She cocked her head to the left to indicate her companion, who was lingering over a drink of some violent shade of chartreuse with a Japanese umbrella and a fruit garnish that was large enough to feed two or three people.

"She's here from Buffalo," Evan's fan confided. "She's never seen a palm tree in her life. All she wants to do is eat seafood. I brought her here for the chowder. They have a fifteen-percent senior-citizen discount, you know?"

"That's very nice," Evan murmured, trying to hide a smile. Amanda shifted her weight from one foot to the other and tried not to laugh out loud.

"Well, thank you again. I'm going to call my daughter in Fort Wayne tonight and tell her I met you in Delmar's, of all places. She'll never believe me, but I have proof, don't I?" She walked off, brandishing the menu like a sword, her scarves trailing out behind her as though caught in the wake of a small hurricane.

"You handled that very well," Amanda said with the first real animation she'd shown all evening. Evan didn't want to break the lighter turn of her thoughts, so he smiled back at her and shrugged off the implied praise.

"I've been practicing. Besides, she looks like everyone's grandmother. I couldn't be rude." Amanda felt a twinge of sympathy. She'd only met Evan's maternal grandmother once before her death. She was as cool and disinclined to show affection as Evan's mother had always been. He had none of the rich, warm memories of his grandparents that she would carry in her heart all her life. She let him fold her hand back into the warm confines of his strong, lean fingers. The sexual tension was growing between them again, as it always did when they were alone together, no matter what the circumstances.

It made no difference that her conscious mind was consumed with the need to know that her father and Teresa were safe and well; her body needed the reassurance of Evan's touch, and nothing else would satisfy her. The reality of her commitment to Robert wasn't enough to still her desire to be caressed by this man, to feel his lips on her mouth and in her hair, to savor his body, heavy and fulfilling, on her and within her....

Amanda pulled her bottom lip between her teeth and bit down hard as they negotiated the stone steps to the beach. She had to stop this uncontrolled free-fall back inside the boundaries of Evan's sensual spell. He wasn't even staying with her this time, not really; he'd told her so himself.

She stumbled in the soft sand and stopped to tug off her sandals, setting them neatly side by side. "That's better." She managed a chiming little laugh. "I'm glad I'm not wearing panty hose. They make it extremely difficult to wiggle your toes in the sand." She suited action to words. For the next few moments she would let Evan's charismatic pull on her senses lull her fears. She would court renewed heartache and feel gloriously alive by doing so.

"You should always go barefoot in the sand if it makes you laugh like that," he said quietly, reaching out to secure the ends of her shawl in a loose knot. "It sounds like starlight on the water looks to me—diamonds dancing in moonbeams."

"You should have been a poet." Amanda hoped he didn't detect the strain in her voice as his fingers brushed very lightly over her nipples. The apricot fabric of her dress was only a flimsy barrier at best, and the warmth of his touch penetrated the material almost at once.

"The reviewers say I have 'an imagination equal in darkness to Poe's.' He wrote poetry also. Maybe some day I'll give it a try." Evan laughed and shook his head, holding out his hand to help her clamber onto the first of a projecting finger of large, flat boulders. A rumble of thunder, so low and far away it was more feeling than sound, punctuated his last words.

"The weatherman was right. It is going to storm again," Amanda observed before answering his last remark. "Your reviewers don't know you as well as I do." Amanda was watching where she stepped, and didn't see the quizzical look Evan directed at her.

"How well do we know each other, Mandy?" he asked, putting both hands around her slim waist to lift her onto a higher rock. A fitful breeze had sprung up while they'd eaten. Now it flirted with the full gauzy skirt of her dress, exposing a creamy length of thigh. She smoothed the material down absently.

"Far better than we did three years ago." She couldn't be more specific; she wasn't sure she wanted to be. But no matter how hard she tried to dismiss the fact, she couldn't: Amanda had never been so happy to see anyone in her life as she'd been when she'd opened the door and found him standing there.

Evan smiled as though reading her thoughts. It was the same heart-stopping private smile that had always been the power to melt her reason. She smiled back and draped her arms around his neck. She shivered a little, and he drew her closer. He could manipulate her emotions with the ease of a master puppeteer. She shivered again at the fleeting ghostly image of herself, wound round with never-ending cords of responsiveness.

"Come on," he urged, and there was a ragged edge to his voice that hadn't been there earlier. "Let's go out to the end. I can't remember seeing rocks like this anywhere along this coast. They're unusual, almost like a little chunk of moonscape plunked down at the edge of the Gulf.''

"Evan. We can't go any farther," Amanda pointed out practically as he lifted her over another foaming, water-filled space between two monoliths of stone.

Evan halted obediently but kept her tucked close to his side. In the diminished glow of the restaurant spotlights, he looked sleek and golden and elementally male. The planes and angles of his face were thrown into carved relief. His eyes glowed like topaz.

"Do you feel the life around us, Amanda?" he asked in a low, almost musical, singsong. "These rocks could almost be alive; silent repositories, vast untapped sources of knowledge or power we haven't the key to decipher."

"Libraries for your demon people." She laughed again, then saw the absorbed look on his face. "Evan, don't. You can't start plotting a book right here and now. In a minute you'll make me sorry I'm sitting here with you. I'll be believing these rocks—" She paused and thumped the stone underneath her "—are going to come to life and do some dastardly deed like all the other kooky monsters in your books. And regardless of what that dear old lady said, I dare you to make these piles of rock likable." She ended her speech on a whimsical note.

"It would be a challenge to give these suckers charisma." He scooted closer on the rocky ledge. The breeze strengthened and began to stir the curls beside her ears and lift wisps of hair along her neck.

"I never understood how you could take harmless, everyday things like buildings...or rocks...or babies..." Amanda hesitated, unprepared to explain or defend her words. "How you could turn them into

monsters, things that go bump in the night...
supernatural friends...." She let her voice trail away
as she searched his starkly etched features for his reaction to her teasing. Teasing? Was she actually teasing him about something that had caused her so much
anguish for so long?

He smiled again, resting his arm on his upraised knee
so that his wrist hung free. "Mandy, when you see a
rock, I see a rock."

"No, you don't." She was serious all of a sudden.
"And if you do, there's always something else there...a
demon child next door, an evil spirit inhabiting a wil-
low tree at the end of Lovers' Lane." She propped her
chin on her knees and looked down at her sandy toes
peeping out beneath the hem of her skirt. She heard the
sound of more thunder, but it was still so far away that
she could ignore its threat.

"Everyone sees something different. Everyone has
his own fears, his own hauntings, that only he can
identify, that he alone must deal with and defeat."
Evan's words were serious also, his tone a whisper of
sound above the wash of water against the rocks. A
thrill rippled over her nerve ends that was as real as the
sting of icy spray on bare skin.

"Have you ever been afraid of anything, Evan?" He
was silent so long she thought he might not answer. She
waited, and the world held its breath while some emotion, long suppressed, flickered to life behind his
shaded amber eyes.

"I've been scared to death I'd never see you again
every day for the last three years." He stared at the
churning, foam-filled chasm at their feet. It was there
again, the chance to bridge a chasm far wider than, but
just as real as, the one at his feet.

"I used to wonder sometimes, when I was lonely and alone, what situation you might have created to write me out of your life." Crystal tears shimmered in her eyes, silvering them in the fitful light. "I wondered what I would do if I found myself lost in one of your stories."

"You'd never be lost in my stories, Mandy. I'd never leave you alone to face the darkness by yourself, if you wanted me to stay."

"I thought . . . you wanted me to go." She was probing beneath the reflecting surfaces of his golden eyes, probing into his soul because this was something she desperately needed to know.

"When you left, I was the lost one. You plunged me into the midst of a living hell," he stated simply, without heat, without rancor. "All my life I was alone, until I found you. My mother never wanted me to know my father. She's proud of my accomplishments, she loves me, but she has her own life and career, and they're more important to her than anything or anyone. All those years I pretended not to care. Then I found you and by extension your father, a family of my own, and I could admit—but only to myself—how lonely I'd always been. I loved you. You loved me. I thought I'd never be alone again."

Amanda clasped her hands tightly before her to quell the impulse to reach out and gather him into her arms. The dark night and the restless, sighing ocean at their backs combined to isolate them once again in boundless, intimate space. Robert's diamond flashed its cold warning before she'd moved her hand six inches from her body.

"With you beside me, I could take out my fears, dust them off and look at them long and hard. Everyone's afraid of something, after all, so I tried writing about it. It worked." He chuckled ruefully, and the hollow ring of his laughter sent a shiver racing down her spine on tiny clawed feet. "Boy, did it work. Somebody at a cocktail party somewhere, or maybe a talk-show interviewer—I really can't remember—said I'd tapped some primal memory, some genetic chord that we all share." He shrugged and dragged his hand through his hair, and the light caught sparkles of moisture from the spray beginning to mount toward them. "But it got harder because I kept demanding more from myself with each book. And then you left, taking my protection, my talisman against my own personal bogeyman, and I was alone again. Trapped by my own hand into telling the world all the things that scared me and disguising them a hundred different ways so no one would guess there was really only one: living without you. And by the time I worked my way through the writing block I was getting pretty good at it. So most people don't know that in every book I write, it's me out there, alone in the dark."

"You've been doing very well without me," Amanda said, and there was sadness in her voice. "You might find you couldn't write again if I came back into your life."

"Don't ever say that, Amanda." Evan's voice was harsh. "I can do it alone, I've proved that. But with you, life will be so much better, my writing will be better."

The restless, dangerous longing to hold and comfort him stayed strong in her, for a moment blocking out even the anxiety for her father and Teresa. He was the same tender, loving man she'd married, the husband she had learned to know again these past few weeks. *The man I love more than life itself.* But no matter what he said, Amanda knew she'd destroyed what they had shared with her own blind, selfish inability to see and understand any suffering but her own. She wasn't sure she could undo the harm she'd caused.

"I should never have run away, and I'm glad, in the end, it didn't affect your writing permanently, but most of all I'm sorry it's too late for us to start again." She couldn't forget he'd told her he wasn't staying. The chartered plane was still at the airport, waiting to take him back to New York. Back to his life, a life she didn't share.

"Is it too late, Mandy?" He pulled her to her feet, his whisper-light kisses covering her face and lips, sending her thoughts to falter and be lost on the damp salty breeze. Was he getting through to her? Tonight she might be an enchanted princess in a castle, waiting for someone to free her from the darkness.

"They located the divorce decree, Evan. It's coming by express courier tomorrow." He tightened his arms around her.

"If I were writing that scene," he said, trapping her hands against his chest. "I think I'd have the monster swoop out of the bushes and eliminate the courier."

Amanda giggled and her laughter still sounded to him like stars and diamonds and moonlight. "Do monsters actually swoop out of bushes?" she asked.

"It all depends, but it would certainly hold up the wedding, which is the plot twist I'm looking for." Amanda sighed and pulled away from him a little. Her fingers traced the open collar of his shirt.

"Can you make me sure that I shouldn't go ahead with my plans to marry Robert?"

"In my book I could do it in a paragraph. Tonight . . . it may take longer, much longer." He lowered his head to kiss her again. The swirling mists around them were charged with desire, enshrouding, isolating them in a world of their own making. "Let's go home, Mandy."

She smiled at him; tears sparkled on her lashes. "I need to be alone with you, Evan. I've tried to make things come out differently while you were gone, but I didn't succeed."

"I'll make you a happy ending, Mandy. I promise." He kissed the tip of her nose and smiled. A shaft of joy and longing for her, so intense it took his breath away, raced through his body. "We'll check on Teresa and then go back to your place."

"There might be a message from my father." Amanda could feel Robert's ring like a millstone on her finger. She wasn't going to marry him. She couldn't, for both their sakes, but how to explain her decision? He'd only believe she wanted a baby too badly to take the chance of his never being able to give her one. How was she going to convince him that wasn't the reason? That it was something far more complicated, yet at the same time devastatingly simple; she couldn't marry him because she still loved Evan. And she always would.

They were almost back to the terrace. They halted at the bottom of the steps long enough for Amanda to pick up her sandals and brush off her sandy feet with the edge of her shawl. The air was growing heavy, weighing down on the senses as the storm approached from far out on the Gulf. He tried to shake the uneasy feeling. "Most likely Teresa is home with her feet up and a bottle of aspirin and a glass of orange juice by her side. She'll tell us where to get in touch with your dad, and we'll convince him to see reason and go to the police.''

Amanda snorted inelegantly and made a face, standing on one foot. Evan swallowed a smile at the sight. "That'll be the day," she said bluntly.

Evan didn't try to hide his smile any longer. "It might not be quite that easy, I agree, but at least then we'll have the time we need for ourselves. We have to decide what to do about the future." His fingers drifted into the curls at the nape of her neck as he cradled her head with his hands. He steadied her as the strap of one sandal dangled from her hand. He kissed her lightly, evocatively, while lightning danced over the ocean. He could almost believe in witches and warlocks and talking cats on a night like this. There was magic all around them. They might be standing on the edge of another world, their world, where they could count everything well lost as long as they remained forever in each other's arms.

As quickly as the illusion had been created, it was shattered by a voice cutting through the lovely, heated glow of their embrace.

"Amanda? Is that you?" Tacett. Evan didn't need to look up at the tall, distinguished man standing on the steps to know who he was.

"Robert?" One shoe still dangled from her hand. "How did you know we were here?" Evan could feel her tension as she realized that she was standing in his arms, her hair damp from sea spray and her lips swollen from his kisses. Thunder rumbled behind them, heightening the tension in the air.

"Where's Teresa, goddamn it?" From the look of shock on Amanda's face, Evan decided that Tacett wasn't in the habit of swearing in front of her. And he certainly looked distraught. He was white and shaken, his dark hair mussed and standing up in spikes.

"We don't know." His gaze swept past Amanda to rest on Evan. Their eyes locked, and Evan felt a surge of animosity toward the other man so strong it balled his hands into fists.

"She was supposed to meet me at eight-thirty. She never came."

Amanda held onto Robert's arm with one hand and put her shoe back on with the other. "She called in sick today. We've been trying to locate her and my father. Oh God, Robert. What's happened to them?"

"I told your father this whole damned affair was too dangerous to involve her in. Her car's in the *Examiner* lot. That's where I found out that you were here. Only I came all the way out to check at Teresa's apartment first.... It just isn't like her to break a ... an appointment. Her landlady said she'd left about five o'clock." He shook his head in self-disgust. "I should have made her stay in touch today."

"I left a message for you at the Sand Dollar," Amanda said. Her voice sounded small and scared. Evan moved a step closer, but didn't touch her again.

"I never got around to checking my messages. Christ, we've wasted a lot of time. It's after nine."

"I don't think we have any other options now, Amanda. It's time to call in the authorities." Robert looked directly at the other man for the first time. Their eyes met and held. "I'm Evan Cameron." He mounted the bottom two steps and held out his hand, conscious of the unspoken, almost primitive challenge that passed silently between them. "I don't think we've met before."

"I'm Robert Tacett." He didn't add, 'Amanda's fiancé,' but his meaning was clear. "You agree with me that something's gone wrong with Peter's plans to bring this group of hired assassins to justice?"

Evan nodded once. "I'm afraid so."

Robert smiled, but his expression held no mirth. "Damn, I was almost hoping you'd tell me I was a fool."

"We were going to call the police if Teresa or my father didn't contact me by midnight, Robert." He held out his hand, and Amanda accepted it in order to mount the steps. Evan stepped aside.

"Do you have any idea where they might be?"

"No, God help me, I don't."

"Robert, I went to the shelter."

"I assumed you would."

"There was this man, this monk." Amanda grabbed his arm and halted his rapid progress toward the door. "Do *you* think they might have been kidnapped, too?"

"I hope not," Robert said tightly. "But nothing feels right anymore. I don't know how to explain it. I think it's all going wrong."

Evan stopped by the bar. "If your feelings about something are that strong, there's usually a reason why." He took care of the tab for dinner by the simple expedient of dropping a large bill on the bar as they walked out the door.

The parking lot was poorly lighted. There were only two other cars alongside hers and Robert's. A van of uncertain make and model pulled slowly past the driveway. Robert stopped with the key already in the car door, and turned to Evan. "That van was following me when I turned into the lot. They must have been circling the block while we were inside."

"Are you certain?" Evan had started to unlock the passenger door of Amanda's car.

Robert shrugged. "No. The light's too bad out here. Maybe my instincts aren't as highly developed as yours, Cameron."

"You'd better lead the way, Tacett. You know the streets better than I do."

"Amanda can get you downtown to police headquarters if we get separated. I'll meet you there." Robert opened his door just as the van skidded into the lot from the opposite direction to that in which it had been traveling and blocked their path in a shower of sand and gravel.

"You will come with me, please." Amanda whirled around. A man in khaki fatigues emerged from the side of the nondescript van. He was of medium height, dark-skinned and round as a teddy bear. His voice was high and light. He looked like a nursery toy dressed up in army clothes.

"I don't understand. Who are you?"

"Keep quiet, Amanda." There was no lightness in Evan's tone. "He has a gun."

"What's going on?" Amanda didn't feel like laughing now. She was getting scared. Lightning flashed closer overhead and glinted on the pistol in the man's hand.

He motioned toward the vehicle and stepped inside. Behind him, two more men were kneeling in the opening. They also had weapons. "*Señores, señorita,* please don't make a sound. Get into the van. We are going to take a ride in the country."

Amanda stood rooted to the spot. This wasn't a nightmare. It wasn't a scene from one of Evan's books. This episode was for real, and she didn't know how it would end.

CHAPTER THIRTEEN

"GET IN THE VAN," the man repeated. The guns never wavered. Amanda stared at Evan uncomprehendingly. He shook his head almost imperceptibly, yet his meaning came through to her loud and clear. *Don't do anything foolish and brave, Mandy. These guys mean business.* He slammed the car door shut. Robert did the same.

The two men glanced at each other, their eyes locking for a brief second in mutual agreement to protect the woman they both cared for so deeply. Amanda was oblivious to the message that passed between them. She was just too dazed and too scared to take it in, but one thing she'd noticed on her own. The teddy-bear-man was nervous. And that made him more dangerous than ever.

"Move!" he ordered again, and then repeated the command in Spanish.

Evan's hand, firm and comforting on her back, propelled Amanda forward. She hesitated before taking the final step up into the van, looking back over her shoulder.

"We can't do anything here, Mandy," Evan said grimly. "Get inside." She didn't want to obey, didn't even want to acknowledge the ghastly truth in his words. She *couldn't* do anything about the situation. She hated being helpless, didn't want to believe such a thing was happening to her, to Evan, to Robert, here, in Sarasota, in the parking lot of Delmar's.

Again the wave of a gun barrel directed her movements. She knelt on the floor, near the back of the van, her mind whirling in endless, frightened circles.

They didn't even bother to tie her hands.

Somehow that brought home more vividly than anything else what had happened and the futility of trying to resist these men. Any act of rebellion, any attempt at escape by Robert or Evan, would be overpowered in a matter of seconds. She sat down with a thump as that awful realization penetrated her terror. Robert and Evan took their places on either side of her.

"Where are you taking us?" Amanda managed to ask at last, finding the silence hardest of all to endure.

"Keep your hands where I can see them and your mouth shut," their captor ordered as one of his henchmen climbed into the driver's seat and started the engine.

"I want to know what you've done with my father," Amanda continued stubbornly.

"You will be with him soon enough, *señorita*. Now shut up or I will make certain of your silence." The threat seemed all the more terrifying because it was so vague.

"That's enough, Mandy. Do as he says." Evan's tone was clipped but steady, and wonderfully dear to her. *Oh Lord, why didn't I tell him I love him back there on the rocks?* Now it might be too late; she might never get another chance. She searched his face for some clue to his thoughts. He smiled at her tenderly and privately, but his eyes, as always, were shuttered and deep lines bracketed his mouth from the strain. But for once Amanda thought she knew what was on his mind, and she wished she did not: Evan was thinking that they weren't going to make it out of this nightmare alive.

Amanda looked at Robert so that Evan couldn't detect the new horror that threatened to choke off her breath. She was certain her fear must be reflected in her eyes. Robert was staring straight ahead, his hands balled into fists, resting on his bent knees. He looked younger somehow in the white tennis sweater and lightweight flannel slacks he was wearing. Except for his face. He looked grim and determined and scared. As scared as she was.

The van pulled sedately out of the parking lot, but the high seats blocked Amanda's view of where they might be headed. Minutes passed, dragged out into small separate eternities by her anxiety and fear, and the continuous arguing voices of their captors. She didn't understand a word they said. Her Spanish was rudimentary, and now her frightened brain refused to deal with the few words she did recognize. What difference did it make if she understood the cause of these men's disagreement if it couldn't help her to get away from them in the end?

They crossed the bridge back into Sarasota and headed out of town, but what direction they were traveling, or what was to be their destination, Amanda still couldn't tell. Now she forced herself to listen for familiar words, phrases, anything that might give her a clue as to what their captors had planned for them. It wasn't any use, for her mind refused to cooperate.

The storm was drawing closer. Lightning flashes were brighter and closer together than they had been earlier on. Or was that only because they'd left the city behind and were traveling along a bumpy road, where high marsh grass brushed against the sides of the van, and the city's glow no longer diminished the wild dance of lights in the sky?

The van stopped. "Get out," the apparent leader said in English. Amanda wondered if he was one of the men Carmella had recognized. "Colonel Silva will be anxious to see you."

"That's not what your buddies seem to think," Evan said casually, not moving a muscle. "Sounds like they think it was a big mistake to grab us at all. Why don't you turn us loose?"

"Do you speak Spanish?" He seemed taken back by Evan's assessment of the conversation.

"Not much. But it isn't hard to figure out what you're arguing about."

"These men are peasants. They can do nothing on their own. They are like sheep. Get out!" He brandished the gun. "Move!"

Robert got out first and turned back to give Amanda his hand. "I'm sorry, Mandy. My instincts aren't so bad after all. They must have been following me." He smiled down at her sadly as she squeezed his hand. She knew her fingers were icy cold and gave away her fear. "That means they must have Teresa, too."

Amanda nodded, unable to speak because of the lump in her throat. "It isn't your fault, Robert," she said after taking a deep, steadying breath. "I'm the one to blame. I blew Dad's cover and probably Teresa's as well."

"We'll get out of this all right," Evan assured her. "We can't all just disappear."

Amanda was having trouble keeping her footing on the coarse sand as she tried to orient herself to their surroundings. The Gulf murmured restlessly, directly ahead; Sarasota lay to the north, a bright smudge on the low-hanging cloud cover. Venice was a smaller, hazy glow to the south. Dark shadows moved around them, like crouching men running for cover. If Evan had been writing this scene he would have made them police or soldiers come to rescue her, because he'd promised never to leave her alone in one of his stories. But this situation wasn't fictional, it was real. And there would be no rescue they didn't initiate on their own.

"Where the hell are we?" Evan asked, taking her arm to steady her at the top of the next dune. She looked back once more, and saw nothing but darkness. She stumbled again. She knew as well as Evan that she couldn't take off her shoes this time. The debris of countless storms, as well as sand burrs and broken shells, would make walking barefoot impossible, condemn any slim chance of escape to failure.

"I think this is San Marco Cove," she whispered back.

"Where's that?" Evan asked, never taking his eyes off the man walking about a dozen yards ahead of them, a huge flashlight in the hand that didn't hold a gun. The other two men were behind them, still arguing rapidly in Spanish.

"It's quite a way south of the city. Are those two still arguing over bringing us out here?" Evan pinched her arm, warning her not to speak loudly enough to be overheard.

"Uh-huh. Wish I knew a little more Spanish. My guess is that they were only supposed to keep an eye on Tacett. When he came after us, they recognized you. Then Fatso up there decided to haul us all in. Finish telling me about this San Marco Cove," he urged as she stopped to fish a sand burr out of her shoe.

"This place was going to be a big resort complex in the late seventies. It never got off the ground." She tried to put the greatest amount of information she could into each and every sentence. If Evan could see some hope of getting out of this situation alive, she'd do her level best to help. "One of the partners was embezzling. He even doctored the geologist's reports. There isn't any fresh water under this sand, and no way to get any out from the city." She took a deep breath because, even to her own ears, her voice sounded too thin and reedy. "All they ever built was the marina. It's in pretty bad shape, but kids come out here sometimes for beer and pot parties, and there's always someone saying that drug smugglers used it as a drop. Dad says that's a lot of bull. It's nearly silted in. It can hardly take a boat with a draft like his.... Evan! The boat. They've got Dad and Teresa here on his boat."

"You're probably right." Evan was silent for a long, charged moment. "From what you tell me, there's not much chance for the neighbors to call in the cops, right?"

"None." Robert replied before Amanda could form the word herself. "We're on our own out here."

"How well can you swim?" Evan was looking straight ahead, but Amanda could feel the taut determination in each and every muscle of his body.

"Forget it, Cameron. You might be dressed for cat-burgling, but Amanda and I aren't." Robert's voice was so low it barely carried the few feet between them. "There's no place we could go that they couldn't pick us out of the water like fish in a barrel." Amanda looked ruefully down at her pale skirt and had to agree with his assessment.

"Silence!" One of the men behind them moved forward and jabbed Evan in the small of the back with his weapon. He grunted in pain and stumbled from the force of the blow but didn't lose his footing.

"Stop it!" Amanda spun around and looked her captor fiercely in the eye. She didn't care if he hit her, too. She'd had about all she could take.

"Mandy." It was Robert's quiet, austere tone, his hand on her arm, that made her shut her mouth so hard her teeth clicked together but she held her peace. In her turn she touched Evan's forearm as he massaged the bruised muscles above his kidney. She could feel the rock-hardness of muscles tensed with pain beneath the softness of his sweater, but he shook off her hand.

"I'm fine," he insisted tightly. "He just knocked the wind out of me."

They struggled up the last hillock that separated them from the ill-fated beachside resort. Amanda could make out the silhouette of several sagging piers jutting out into the small cove. The scene looked like the last remnants of a failed dream. At the farthest pier, a light glimmered against the dark backdrop of the Gulf, dimly outlining her father's boat. A four-wheel-drive Jeep was parked alongside the ruins of the short pier.

The clean yellow light of a Coleman lantern illuminated several figures at the rear of the boat. Amanda's heart sank farther inside her chest. Even if her father and Teresa weren't bound and were able to help them, they were still outnumbered. And each of their captors carried a weapon.

The still-nameless teddy-bear-man signaled with the big flashlight. An answering signal blinked back through the night. "Now we shall see what Colonel Silva thinks of my prize."

Colonel Silva was the monk from the shelter.

"We've been expecting you, Ortega. I want to get underway before the storm hits." Even Amanda, who spoke no Spanish, could understand his meaning as lightning arced down to the water and thunder split the night. She had no need to guess his next words.

"Ortega! Who the blazes is this?" The monk's robe was open to reveal a green-and-white Michigan State T-shirt that explained why Colonel Silva's English was spoken with a flat midwestern twang. The prisoners were clearly visible now that Ortega had hopped on board the boat. "Amanda Winston?" He rounded on the other man. "You idiot. Why did you bring the woman and her lovers?"

He didn't bother to switch back to Spanish, and Amanda realized that despite his surprise at their appearance he saw no reason to keep anything from them. Had he decided that quickly that none of them would leave this desolate stretch of beach alive? Or was he simply so arrogant that he saw no need for the precaution of speaking in his own language?

"Hostages?" he snorted in response to Ortega's halting explanation. "You've jeopardized the whole mission, you fool. I should cut your heart out for this."

Flustered, Ortega sputtered out further excuses in Spanish, but Silva raised a hand imperiously and ordered him to be silent. One of the two men from the van prodded Amanda forward roughly. The other jumped onto the boat and began to make preparations to depart. "Bring out the old man and the woman,"

Silva commanded, dragging the monk's robe over his head and tossing it angrily aside. "I have nothing but fools and incompetents to work with; it is no wonder that the regime is floundering."

Peter emerged from the doorway of the small cabin, his head bent, his hands tied loosely in front of him. He was dressed as Amanda had last seen him at the shelter, in a threadbare gray shirt and jeans. He looked old and lost and on the verge of collapse. A light spattering of rain on his head caused him to look at the sky in confusion.

"Daddy." She stepped forward and shook off the restraining hand of her captor without a backward glance. Her father raised his head at the sound of her voice, his face shadowed by the rim of a disreputable White Sox baseball cap. Only his eyes were out of keeping with his abject appearance; they were familiar, bright and steady, and completely in command. "Dad?"

"Hi, Mandy." She had to strain to hear him, his voice was so weak, so confused-sounding. It didn't match the strength of purpose in his brown gaze, but then nothing made sense to her anymore. Evan sucked in his breath behind her, stiffened and stood a little straighter, his eyes riveted on the older man. "Hi, Evan." Peter shifted his stance and smiled pathetically. He stumbled a little and took a moment to right himself. "When did you get back from California?"

"A couple of hours ago."

"It's good to see you again, boy. You'll take care of Mandy for me, won't you?"

"Are you okay, sir?"

"So-so." Peter tried to laugh, and his words ended in a hacking cough. He lifted his bound hands to his mouth. It wasn't raining any harder, but the wind was stirring up waves as it gusted ahead of the storm. Peter stumbled and nearly fell as the boat rocked beneath him.

"Daddy." Amanda would have braved the devil himself to get to her father then. "Can't you see that he's ill?" she shouted helplessly at Silva. "He needs help." Peter waved her off with a fearful glance at Silva.

"I'm all right, Mandy. Did they hurt you?"

She shook her head, too angry to speak.

"Where's Teresa?" Robert stepped forward, almost to the edge of the pier and looked at Peter long and hard.

"I'm here, Robert."

Amanda couldn't restrain a gasp as Teresa came out of the cabin, standing for a moment to catch her balance on the rolling deck. Her friend's hands were tied also. Her white blouse, the same one she'd been wearing when Amanda last saw her at the Sand Dollar, was streaked with dirt and torn at the sleeve. There was a purpling bruise on her cheekbone.

"You bastards." Robert's voice was hoarse with suppressed fury.

Amanda was certain Robert would have gone for Silva then and there if a man with a machine gun hadn't barred his way.

"I'm not hurt, Robert," Teresa hastened to assure him. "Please, don't do anything foolish and get yourself shot." Her voice wasn't quite steady, but she managed to smile.

"She was not cooperative at first," Colonel Silva said with a shrug, his brilliant dark eyes fixed on Robert's set, drawn face. Amanda couldn't believe anyone could look so sinister, so evil, in a ratty old T-shirt and jeans, but this man did. "I didn't believe she was only planning a dinner date with you. I assumed that you must know something of importance, so I had Ortega follow you."

"She was telling the truth, damn it! But if I'd known anything at all about you, I'd have killed you myself before you could lay a hand on her."

"Very gallant, *señor*. But an empty threat, I think, in view of the circumstances."

"It looks to me as if it's your bad luck as much as ours." Evan said in a tone that was so carefully controlled it lacked any inflection at all. "Ortega's taking matters into his own hands has fouled up your plans, hasn't it? You might have gotten away with killing off an old man and a woman, but now there are five bodies to dispose of. That's a fair number, even for you guys. How did you plan to pull it off, anyway?" he asked, gesturing to Peter and Teresa, still looking only idly interested in the answer.

"Very simply," Silva replied, equally mildly. "An old man, as you said, a lovely younger woman, a secret love affair—" He turned and made a travesty of a courtier's bow in Teresa's direction. "A boating accident, naturally—when I've finished with the vessel."

"My boat." Peter sounded on the verge of tears. Amanda's nails cut half-moon grooves in her palms. She'd driven her father to attempt this dangerous undertaking, and now it was going to cost him his life.

"Shut up, you old fool. It would be a nine days' wonder, don't you agree?" He directed the statement to Evan, who nodded shortly. "Very titillating, but as soon forgotten, when some other scandal comes along. That would leave only the Molina woman, and she can't identify me, or Ortega. Only these two." He pointed to the two men who had been with Ortega. "So even if we don't find where she's hiding, it doesn't matter. Who would believe her?" He dismissed Carmella with a snap of his fingers.

"I'll go with you if you want but let the others go." Peter sounded humbled, defeated, and Amanda wanted to cry; she had to have imagined that flash of spirit in his eyes. He was nothing more than Silva had said: an old man, confused and defeated.

Silva's handsome features hardened into a mask of steel. "Whatever makes you think you could outwit me, old man? Now I may have to settle for just that condition. Damn you, Ortega, you've made a shambles of everything I've worked for." He issued a series of orders in Spanish, raising his voice to carry over the noise of wind and waves. Thunder rumbled but still the storm held off. Ortega jumped to do his bidding, a grimace of hate and fear twisting his roly-poly features. He laid his pistol and flashlight on the deck railing and disappeared below.

The engines sprang to life with a roar and choking cloud of diesel fumes. Amanda almost screamed in frustration. She'd been straining to hear above the slap of waves against the pier. What was it? The far-off beat of an engine, a boat out beyond the curve of the cove? Perhaps she hadn't imagined the crouching figures among the dunes? She just couldn't be sure. Now, of course, with the steady throb of powerful diesels only a few feet away, she couldn't hear anything at all.

"What makes you think you can go back to Costa Verde with your network of hired assassins coming down around your ears?" Evan asked, still in that bored, uninterested tone. His voice made Amanda's skin crawl, and it was more than apparent Colonel Silva found it abrasive.

"I have done the best I can. It is Ortega here who will be blamed for failing, if it becomes necessary to find a scapegoat." He shrugged eloquently, each movement fluid and beautiful to watch, but deadly, like a cobra before it strikes. "General Alexandro is on his way out. He has many friends in this country, it is true. But the opposition is growing stronger each day. Soon it will be impossible to hide the atrocities he has sanctioned, or the extraordinary extent of his misuse of government funds. Then I don't think it will matter how many people he planned to silence. It will be too late for him to find asylum here." He spread his hands in a gesture of dismissal.

Amanda felt sickened at the cruelty and utter lack of caring for so much innocent suffering barely hidden behind the genial expression. "At that time I may find it prudent to change my allegiance, possibly expose what remains of this network of assassins. There is always a place in a new government for a bright young man who has seen the error of his ways."

"And one who knows where the skeletons are buried. My congratulations, Silva. It seems you've covered all your bases." Evan bent his head in his own mocking bow. "It would be a pity to leave a lot of bodies lying around to complicate matters."

Behind Amanda, their single guard was growing restless; she could feel him looking back toward the low dunes more and more frequently, as though he expected an attack from the rear.

"You still have to get out of the States and back to Costa Verde."

Peter's head came up abruptly. "You can't expect to make the trip in my boat. She'll never make it in these rough seas."

"My transportation waits just outside the legal limit. You haven't been listening to a word I've said, have you, old man? You can stay with your boat and die at sea. *Amigos! Vámanos!*" He gestured to the man at the wheel to pull away. Someone started to throw off the last bowline just as the night exploded around them.

Later Amanda would find that, try as hard as she could to recall the next few minutes, it would be in a series of set pieces, almost as if individual frames of film had been spliced together to create a number of vignettes of terror and confusion.

A helicopter came streaking in low from the south. Armed men erupted out of the scrub and marsh grass with spotlights and bullhorns, demanding the surrender of the boat in the name of the government of the United States. Amanda couldn't be sure who they were: Sarasota police? Immigration? The Coast Guard? Later, she would learn that all three law-enforcement agencies had been involved.

For a few stunned moments no one moved. Then the man guarding Robert knocked him to his knees with his gun butt and made a desperate running leap for the boat. At almost the same instant, bullets flying around them, Evan dragged Amanda down beneath him. The downdraft from the helicopter's rotors sent stinging clouds of sand blindingly into the air. Broken shell fragments dug into her cheek and knees. The noise of the aircraft and the boat's engine combined was deafening. Amanda wanted nothing more than to cover her ears and stay safe and protected in Evan's arms.

But her anxiety for her father was too great. She wiggled free of Evan's shielding grasp long enough to see what was happening on the boat.

It looked like a scene from a madhouse. The helicopter's spotlight was relentlessly trained on the small craft. Waves churned around the vessel. The sound of thunder and lightning competed with the shriek of bullets on the ground. Ortega was attempting to go over the side, single-mindedly intent on escaping Silva's promised vengeance. He cannoned into Teresa, who was standing paralyzed by the shouts and blinding lights. The impact sent her over the rail, her face white with shock and terror. Her scream was lost in the melee going on around her. Robert, still on his knees trying to shake off the guard's blow, was gone off the pier almost in the same instant in a low shallow dive that brought him alongside Teresa in two swift strokes.

Silva spun around, making a dive for Ortega, catching him around the knees and throwing him to the deck. With a vicious backhand he left him broken and crumpled against the rail. The last thing Amanda saw before Evan covered her with his body and rolled them both off the side of the pier was a nightmare scene that would stay in her memory for the rest of her days.

Her father was wrestling with Silva. His hands had been freed somehow from the ropes that had been bound loosely around his wrists. Now they were locked on Silva's gun arm. The Colonel's face was stark with fury and rage, her father's, white and set. They grappled silently, endlessly it seemed, as men screamed and bullets thudded into the deck around them. Then Amanda heard nothing as Evan twisted beneath her to take the brunt of the short drop to the ground.

Amanda lay still, too stunned to move, the breath locked in her chest, not from the force of the fall but from what she had just seen. Her last glimpse of her father had been terrifying beyond all description. Silva, with a violent burst of strength, had shaken free of Peter's hold. With a snarl he'd turned on the older man, almost pitching him over the rail. Peter had managed to scramble onto the dock while his opponent was thrown momentarily off balance as the boat skidded sideways preparing to take off. But as Silva fell, he fired the gun.

"Daddy!" Amanda knew she'd screamed the word, but it never got past the constriction in her throat.

So, when she closed her eyes, it was to the repeating image of her father slumped on the pier, blood already staining the sleeve of his dirty gray cotton shirt.

"JEEZ, THAT HURTS." Peter twisted his head to watch the police paramedic work on the gash in his upper arm.

"You should be in the hospital," Amanda scolded, still so frightened that it took a physical effort to stop shaking. Tears continued to threaten every time she opened her mouth. "Gunshot wounds are dangerous. I should have insisted that you go in the ambulance to get checked out in Emergency like Robert and Teresa."

Peter snorted. "I don't think those two would have appreciated the extra company." He looked at Amanda intently, but the pointed sally seemed to have sailed right over her head. She was staring at his arm, and her face was several shades paler than normal.

"This isn't a gunshot wound, Ms Winston," the young man explained sympathetically.

"I cut myself on a loose piece of metal when I rolled onto the pier." Peter laughed then, and if the sound was still strained around the edges, it was so close to normal that it could be ignored.

"You should have a tetanus booster, sir," the paramedic cautioned. "You might want to have your family doctor take a look at it, but I don't think you need stitches." He wound a gauze bandage competently around the wound and taped it into place.

"You mean ... Silva's bullet ..." Amanda felt her knees getting weak just thinking about that awful moment.

"Missed me by a mile," Peter said, waving his uninjured arm expansively. "I tell you, Mandy, your showing up like that sure put a crimp in my game plan."

"You can say that again."

The last statement was issued from the front seat of the police van where they'd taken refuge from the rain. The thunderstorm had finally rolled inland, just as Silva made his escape into open water. "It certainly didn't make my job any easier, young woman." The bald, middle-aged police lieutenant who'd spoken scratched the short fringe of hair above his ears. "I'd have had one hell of a time explaining to Washington why the medicos were pulling bullets out of a best-selling New York writer and one of Sarasota's leading businessmen."

"Not to mention answering to me if my assistant editor or my one and only daughter had been seriously harmed." Peter's voice held no hint of jocularity; he was in deadly earnest.

"Dad, I brought this on myself by going out to the shelter and blowing your cover." Amanda leaned forward and kissed her father on his roughly bearded cheek. "I'm so sorry. If anything happens to Teresa I'll never forgive myself."

"She'll be fine, Miss," the paramedic answered again as he helped her father back into his shirt. "I checked her out before they left. She's suffering from shock and exposure. She's got a bruise or two here and there, but that's all."

"Robert will look after her." Again Peter waited, as if he expected Amanda to comment on the fact that Robert had accompanied Teresa to the hospital.

"I was never so glad to see anyone in my life," Amanda replied fervently. "When Robert carried her out of the water I..." She made a steeple of her hands and covered her mouth for a moment until she could get her emotions back under control. Evan slipped his arm around her waist, and Amanda leaned back against the strong, comforting warmth of his chest.

"Tacett did the smart thing, staying under the pier until the fireworks were over." The low rumble of Evan's voice communicated itself through bone and muscle and set up a tingling reaction all around her heart.

"He saved her life," Peter replied simply. "There were so many things that went wrong tonight ... I'm getting too old for this sort of thing."

"Come on, Peter. We were ready for just about any contingency."

"Except Ortega showing up out of the blue and snatching the three of us," Evan put in.

"Ortega was pretty much an unknown quantity in my equation," Peter acknowledged. "I didn't think Silva would have an outside contact we could trace, but I was wrong. Teresa recognized him right away when his picture came through this afternoon...or I guess it's yesterday afternoon now. She'd seen him talking to the monk...Silva...She came back to warn me, and that tipped them off to her."

"Silva was already suspicious of you because of my visit," Amanda repeated. "It's still all my fault."

"Only partially." Peter's incorrigible grin took the sting out of his words. "I've been coordinating with Lieutenant Daly back there, and some guys at the State Department, from the beginning. I only wish I could have spotted Silva earlier."

"Where are Carmella and her daughters?" Evan asked. The warmth of Amanda's body, so close to his in the confines of the van, kept his breath short and his blood hammering in his veins long after the rush of adrenaline from the danger they'd faced had run its course.

"Safe and sound with my sister in Biloxi. Teresa put them on the bus yesterday."

Lieutenant Daly cleared his throat.

"Now what?" Peter eyed his cohort darkly.

"Carmella Molina and her two little girls showed up at headquarters about an hour before we began to deploy out here."

"She what?" Peter came halfway up out of his seat before he remembered the low ceiling and sat down again.

"She wanted to tell us everything she knew, she said." He hesitated a moment, as if an unfamiliar emotion had caught at the words. "She said she wasn't going to live in fear anymore, or run for her life ever again. She'd risked everything she had to come to this country. She intended to live in peace and freedom. And she knew that wasn't possible for anyone, anywhere, as long as men like the ones she'd recognized at the shelter were not behind bars.''

"Well, I'll be damned. I shouldn't have kept her so much in the dark. And I should have confided in you, too, I suppose." He gave Amanda a rueful look. "Where are Carmella and the children?"

"Safe and sound. I have a policewoman staying with her and the little girls at a downtown motel. We'll bring them out to the shelter in a couple of days."

"Well, I'll be damned," Peter repeated softly. "You take them home bright and early in the morning, Jim. And remember, home is my place, don't forget."

"I won't." The policeman swiveled his seat to the front and motioned the driver to move them out.

"And I'll never underestimate your abilities again, I swear." Amanda hesitated, twisting a fold of her skirt between her fingers until her father reached out and covered her hand with his own. She could see the faint red lines of rope burns on his wrist, and another involuntary shudder rippled through her.

"You thought I'd gone round the bend, didn't you, Mandy?" Peter asked softly. "I am sorry I kept you in the dark, but I thought it was best. I wanted Silva off guard. I'd taken every precaution I could. All the phones were bugged. The boat's bugged, too. That's why I won't give up hope we'll get her back if she rides out the storm."

"You let Silva get away." Evan took Amanda's cold hands in his own warm grasp as Peter began to work at the buttons of his shirt, now minus the left sleeve, which the paramedic had cut away.

"In the long run, we think it's the best solution," Jim Daly confirmed.

"That decision came from Washington," Peter revealed flatly. "General Alexandro is a political embarrassment these days. Silva told the truth when he said he still has powerful friends, though. But I think he was also right when he said the truth will be known. I don't think we have to worry about the soon-to-be-ex-President of Costa Verde moving in next door anytime soon."

"What about the assassins?" Amanda was having trouble taking everything in. She sat back, grateful once more for the comforting strength of Evan's body to lean against.

"Silva set them up in cells, like the underground used during World War II." Peter also leaned back in his seat as the van began to pick up speed when they turned onto the main road.

"There were probably only three members in each cell, Mandy." Evan took up the explanation as the paramedic handed Peter two pain pills and a thermos cup of water. "Only one member of a cell knows who the contact is. That way, if anyone is caught, they can't betray anyone else."

"And Ortega was the main contact," Amanda said, beginning to understand something of the scheme. "Now there's no way to filter information down through the cells."

"Yes," Peter agreed with satisfaction. "And no time to get another system of cells set up and into place. Somehow I don't think Ortega's men will sit around for months waiting for word that never comes. If you ask me, in a matter of weeks they'll start heading back to Costa Verde, or just disappear into the ocean of illegals already living here."

"And Carmella?"

"She's a brave lady. She's no threat to them anymore. The only men she could identify are on the boat."

"And Silva will come out smelling like a rose, with Ortega to blame the whole fiasco on." Evan shook his head.

"I like to think he's overestimating his chances of coming out of a change of power on the high side," Peter said grimly. "But, for all our sakes, I just hope we gave him enough rope to hang himself back in Costa Verde." He laid his head back against the seat and closed his eyes.

"We'll drop you off at headquarters, and a patrol car will run you out to Lido Key to get your car if you'd like, Ms Winston," Daly offered.

Amanda's shoulder slumped a little as she calculated the extra time that would take. It was after midnight. The formalities had taken far longer than the actual raid. Evan must have sensed her fatigue because he proposed an alternative.

"Just drop us at Ms Winston's home. I'll pick up the car in the morning." Amanda turned her face up to find him smiling down at her with a low kindling flame shining deep in the burnished gold of his eyes.

"Okay by me," the police officer agreed. "We've got both your statements. If we need you for anything, Mr. Cameron, will I be able to reach you there?"

Amanda held her breath. All at once a vision of the Lear jet, engines roaring as it prepared for takeoff on the runway pad, filled her thoughts and brought an aching sense of loss to her heart.

"I'll be there," Evan said with quiet conviction. "For as long as you need me."

CHAPTER FOURTEEN

AMANDA'S HANDS refused to stop shaking as she tried for a third time to insert her spare key in the front-door lock. The feeling of detachment that had started to overtake her on the way back into the city wouldn't go away. Knowing the sensation was the result of fatigue and the aftereffects of facing a life-and-death situation didn't make it any easier to cope with. She felt more and more as if she'd stepped through the looking glass. There had been some small tear in the fabric of her reality, and now she couldn't find her way back. It was frightening and unnerving; it scared her almost as much as the whine of bullets and Silva's timeless menace had.

Evan reached around her and steadied the key in the lock. It slid home with a scrabbling sound of metal on metal and opened with a click. The door swung inward to reveal the muted colors of her home, glowing dimly in the light of a single table lamp. Max awoke, uncurling himself from a pile of floor cushions, stretching one leg at a time with typically feline enjoyment in the action before jumping lightly down from his sultan's perch.

"I put the key back on the window ledge," Evan said, coming up behind her so quietly that she jumped.

"Thanks. Are you sure you saw my purse on the car seat? I can't remember having it after we got to the restaurant." Amanda shook her head helplessly. Max sauntered across the floor to greet and inspect the two humans in the doorway. He looked up at Amanda, unfazed by her tatterdemalion appearance, but his unblinking emerald eyes narrowed as she turned up the lights. He switched his attention to Evan, then opened his mouth to reveal a raspy pink tongue in a large, unabashed grin. He glided closer to rub himself repeatedly against Evan's trouser leg, his roaring purrs reverberating throughout the quiet room.

"I'll put him out," Evan said, scooping up the big tomcat while Amanda sank onto the floor cushions by the empty fireplace, her knees suddenly too wobbly to support her weight. She winced in pain as she bent her leg, then noticed the tear in her skirt and the dark stain of blood on the hem for the first time.

"I scraped my knee," she said as though making a great discovery. "I never even noticed it until right now." She pushed the apricot linen of her skirt higher on her thigh to show Evan the nasty scrape. "It hurts like the dickens, all of a sudden."

"It needs to be washed off," he said tightly. *God, if anything had happened to her out there tonight I'd have killed Silva with my bare hands, gun or no gun,* Evan thought.

"It's nothing, don't bother." Amanda dismissed the injury with a wave of her hand; directing him to the first-aid supplies was more than she could cope with at the moment. But Evan was already on his way to the bathroom, and he ignored her directive. "Should I call the hospital and check on Teresa?" she asked when he returned with a bottle of antiseptic and a wet cloth.

"She's resting comfortably. They're going to let her go home first thing this morning. Daly called the hos-

pital just before the van dropped us off, remember?''
He smiled tenderly as she shook her head in an amazed
negative. "I thought you fell asleep there for a few
minutes.''

"I was only resting my eyes." Amanda's indignant
statement ended in a breathless yelp. "That stuff stings.
Besides, it's so old it's probably not worth painting on
me.''

"Indulge me," Evan said, and there was a low, exciting quality to his voice that raised gooseflesh on her
arms. She could feel his desire across the small space
that separated them. His power over her senses hadn't
diminished in the years they'd been apart; if anything,
it had increased in intensity and scope.

That intensity of feeling proved she couldn't marry
Robert. If she hadn't been so determined to drive
Evan's very memory out of her heart and her thoughts,
she would have admitted that to herself a long time
ago. She cared for Robert—as a friend, but nothing
more.

Had she spent so much time fighting the inevitable
that it truly was too late to go back to what she had
shared with Evan? At the restaurant a few hours ago—
a lifetime of fear and danger ago—he'd said he wasn't
staying. Why should he? She'd thrown up so many
barriers, both real and imagined, that he'd evidently
gotten tired of beating his head against a stone wall. He
would be going back to his life in New York as quickly
as possible. He couldn't know how desperately she
wanted him to stay. He'd never know unless she told
him. "Evan..."

He was gone from her side when she looked up. He
crossed her line of vision to put the bottle of disinfec-
tant on the kitchen counter and dispose of the soiled

cloth. She watched as he moved to pull the sheer drapes across the windows. He remained in the deeper shadows, a dark figure silhouetted against the pale oblong of light, while she studied his expression for a clue to his feelings.

It was no use. She couldn't see anything, wouldn't see anything of what he was feeling unless he wanted her to do so.

"Take off your shoes, Mandy."

"What...?" Whatever she had expected him to say, it wasn't that. She shook her head in confusion. "My shoes?"

"Take off your shoes," Evan repeated patiently, moving out of the shadows. "You're tracking sand all over the floor. It'll get on the cushions if you're not careful."

"Oh." Dumbfounded, she glanced down at her sandals and at the damp sand that was caked on them. Obediently she stepped out of the heeled slippers. Evan knelt beside her and began to dust the dried sand from her feet.

"I was so afraid we'd have to try and run away from Silva and I'd hold you and Robert back," she said in a breathless little voice that still held traces of her terror. "I knew I couldn't take them off; there were so many broken shells and bottles." She choked on the last words and took a deep breath to steady her voice. She reached out a trembling hand to touch his face. "I was afraid you'd both be killed because I knew you wouldn't leave me behind. I don't think I'll ever buy another pair of high heels in my life." Amanda tried to inject a light note into her voice, but the deeper emotions she felt were obvious. She shuddered, and Evan drew her into the haven of his arms.

"Never wear high heels to dinner if there's the possibility of being kidnapped before dessert." Strong arms held her against the rock wall of his chest before he pushed her back slightly and then smiled down into her eyes. Amanda tried to smile in return and knew she must have succeeded pretty well because she had the satisfaction of watching the grim lines at the corners of his mouth relax. His eyes smiled too, she noticed. They were clear and unshaded, the color of fine old sherry. "I was scared to death out there, Mandy. Scared I'd lose you forever."

"I'm so glad you came back, Evan. I needed you so tonight." It was as close as Amanda could come at the moment to confessing just how much she had always needed him, and would always need him. "But I'm all right now. You don't have to stay.... The Lear jet..."

"To hell with that damned plane. I think you're a closet snob, Amanda. You bring up the subject of that jet at the drop of a hat." His hands slid up over her shoulders, and his fingers slipped into the glowing tangles of her hair.

"You said you weren't staying." She searched his face for a clue to his thoughts. He returned her scrutiny steadily.

"Forget what I said earlier. I'm not going anywhere. I thought we settled that out on the rocks." His voice was thick with longing. The tremor in his hands, when he moved them to rest on her shoulders, sent delicious, echoing shudders through her. "If Tacett hadn't come looking for you..." He gave her a little shake to emphasize his next words. "You'd already be mine again. Just as you have always been. Just as you always will be." Max howled from beneath the window and Amanda closed her eyes, too bemused to deal with her warlock and his feline familiar, too.

Evan was casting his sensual spell over her yet again, and she couldn't escape the pleasing, enslaving words. She didn't want to. "Will you always belong to me as well, Evan? I've never asked you if there is someone waiting for you back in New York." She'd never asked because she couldn't bear to hear that there was.

"Would you believe me if I told you there hasn't been a woman in my life at all for the past three years?" There was no shielding of his thoughts now. She could look into his eyes and see deep into his soul. And what she saw there was love, deep and abiding, lasting beyond time.

"I believe you." She lifted her arms, taking his face between her hands to hold him close and still. "I believe you, Evan. But do you truly believe there's a future for us...together?" Her voice held a lilting thread of wonder that acted on his senses like a potent drug.

"I've known that we had a future almost since the first moment I walked inside the door at the *Examiner*. But I'm damned near as stubborn as you are." He laughed triumphantly, hooking one arm around his knee. Amanda folded her hands in her lap and hid a smile of her own. "It's been hell waiting for you to come to your senses," he went on, suddenly serious. His voice was raspy with strain. "God, I'm tired of waiting." Exploring, massaging fingers returned to the softness of her hair, sending pins flying in all directions. They landed with little explosions of sound on the tile floor, on the glass tabletop, the marble hearth of the fireplace. His hand roamed downward, grazing the skin of her throat, pushing back a curling tendril of hair to trace the delicate shell of her ear.

"I haven't talked to Robert about us, Evan," she said haltingly, unable to come up with the right words to explain her hesitation. Tears of remorse and regret filled her eyes. "He doesn't know yet..." *That I love you,* she thought, but couldn't say. "I..."

Evan touched his finger to her lips, trapping her words in her mouth. "You don't love him," he insisted fiercely. "Don't lie to yourself any longer. If you loved him you wouldn't respond to me like this." He brushed his palm over the tip of her breast, and her nipple tightened instantly beneath the light, clinging fabric of her dress. He covered the soft warmth of her breast with his hand and he was filled with a great longing. *Damn it, why does she have to keep bringing Tacett into it?* Couldn't she tell how it ate at him to know that she still felt herself bound to the man? She was his; she always had been his; she would always be his.

He cupped her chin with his hand, more roughly than he'd intended, as the force of his emotions threatened to take control of his actions. He imprisoned her head, and his mouth covered hers in a demanding, unrelenting kiss. "Don't you see our bodies know what is right for us, even if our minds say otherwise?" He felt Amanda stiffen in his arms as he molded her to the lean, corded hardness of him. His lips were insistent; his arms pushed her down into the nest of cushions on the floor. His kiss compelled her surrender, and her mouth opened under his with a small moan of defeat.

Immediately the harshness of his embrace ended, gentling to a caress so devastatingly tender it bound Amanda more securely than physical restraints could ever have done. Evan drew back from the kiss to watch her. She was aware that the echo of desire that gilded his face also shimmered in her gray eyes. "Come back to me, Mandy. Let me love you as you deserve to be loved."

Come back? Amanda closed her eyes and felt him settle his weight more firmly atop her lower body. She stared at the ceiling in momentary confusion. Was he asking her back into his heart? What exactly was he offering her? A life in New York, where she didn't want to be? She held up a trembling hand to smooth his tousled blond hair as he nuzzled her neck, nipping softly, tantalizingly at the slender gold chain that was the only ornament she wore—except for her engagement ring.

"We haven't settled anything." She tried to inject a note of sanity into what was happening, but the magic of his spell was too great.

"No more details, Mandy," Evan said hoarsely. "Trust me this time. I know what's best."

"But..."

"There'll be answers for all your questions... later."

Robert's ring winked in the pale glow of the lamp on the table. She wasn't free, not yet. Couldn't Evan understand that simple fact? Then he kissed her again, and the world tilted on its axis as it had the first time their lips had touched so long ago. Suddenly, none of the questions still unanswered between them was of any importance. Robert Tacett ceased to exist for Amanda. There was only Evan in her universe now—his hands, his lips, his body, so heavy and exciting above her.

"Let me love you, Mandy. Let me bring back all our yesterdays and make you see we belong together." He waited for her to speak, his eyes probing deep into hers.

If she told him she loved him now, would he respond by renewing his vows to her?

"I don't feel free to make love with you tonight, Evan," she said with painful honesty. She held out her hand to make him look at the outward sign of Robert's claim on her. She stared at the ring, and then back into his shaded topaz eyes. "Can we still go back? Can you take me back with you to what we used to share?" She spoke so quietly Evan had to bend his head to catch the whisper. Her lips were only inches from his. Her breath touched his skin with warmth; a sheen of tears sparkled like dew in her eyes.

"I can make you forget everything you don't want to remember..." He touched the corner of her mouth with the tip of his tongue. "And I *can* give you back all our yesterdays." Gently, slowly, he took her left hand in his. Amanda watched in dreamy silence as he kissed each pearl-tipped finger in turn. Then, with a fierce, exultant gesture he tugged the dully gleaming stone from her hand and dropped it onto the table beside the couch.

Amanda looked at her hand. There was only the palest of circles to show where the ring had been. She looked up into Evan's glittering amber eyes. He didn't smile. He looked tense and guarded. Suddenly she felt lighter than air. A great weight lifted from her heart. This was so right; this was what she wanted with all her being, this man, and this coming together. She placed her hand in his.

Evan carried it to his lips and kissed her palm. "I've waited so long for you, Mandy. I won't let anyone or anything spoil it for us again. When I'm through loving you there won't be room left in your heart for another man." He reached around her to lower the zipper of her dress in a single fluid movement. The garment fell to her waist with a little sigh of material. "Amanda," Evan whispered, repeating the syllables over and over again as if saying her name only once was not enough. With calm precision he divested her of the dress, her clinging, lacy half-slip and panties.

A small whimper of wanting escaped Amanda's lips as she gave herself up to his embrace. As his hands kneaded the rounded fullness of her hips, everything else receded. He pushed her back into the cushions. Her hair spread around her face in a fiery halo; he buried his fingers in its softness. Their bodies fused together. "Your hair smells so good," Evan said, inhaling its fragrance. "Like lemons and raindrops and the sea."

Amanda banished the faint, lingering stirrings of honor and conscience with heady abandon. She deliberately ignored the knowledge of right and wrong, time and place, that had stayed her before. She knew now that there had been no room for Robert in her life since Evan had walked through the door of the *Examiner* building and back into her heart. She would always care for Robert, value him as a friend, but nothing more.

Her thoughts began to scatter; her logic became nebulous. She was aware of only a single, elemental truth—she needed to be one again with Evan, to be joined once more with the laughing boy she'd married, with the man he'd become. She slid her hands under his sweater, straining toward him as she splayed her fingers over the sleek sinewy contours of his back, entreating their coming together with silent eloquence.

Answering the primitive, meaningful sounds of desire coming from deep within her, Evan released her clutching hands. He trailed a line of tiny kisses across her brow and eyelids as he straightened to pull off his sweater and kick his shoes away.

Amanda watched in silence as he turned off the lamp, unfastened his pants in the moonlight, then stepped out of his briefs and bent to take off his socks. Naked, he came back to her, and she drew him close. His hands weren't quite steady as he gathered her against his chest, and that pleased something timeless and feminine deep within her. He wanted her as much as she wanted him.

His eyes never left her, and every millimeter of her flesh reacted to his visual caress with fiery delight. Her breasts still tingled from their contact with the heathery material of his sweater, but now she wanted to press herself even closer without the barrier of his clothing to interfere with her pleasure. She reached up to pull his head down to her breasts. Her hands skimmed the broad sweep of his shoulders, trailed down the corded muscles of his arms as he held most of his weight from her.

He kissed her breasts, slowly, lingeringly, and she moved with sinuous grace beneath him, heightening his pleasurable torment as well as her own. With daring fingers she snaked over the flat muscles of his chest, outlining the almost hidden nipples, twining her fingers through the dense, curling hair that covered his brown skin.

"I love you, Mandy. I loved you before time began. I'll love you long after this world is no more."

"I know, Evan. Don't talk anymore. I only want to feel you with me." Her voice was soft and beguiling in the silvery moonlight that streamed in through the sheer curtains. He loved her! How wonderful it was to hear those words again.

Evan held himself above her, his knee parting her thighs, his hand cradling her bottom as he prepared her to accept him. "Do you belong to me, Mandy?" he asked, and his voice sounded bemused, strangely hollow in the near-darkness. He lifted his hand from her hip to caress her nipple, tugging gently at the dusky tip, stirring memories of desire as old as her knowledge of her womanhood.

Amanda closed her eyes against the rush of need his touch provoked. His fingers grazed over the taut, smooth skin of her stomach, moving lower, closer and closer to the very center of her. He was waiting for an answer, his fingers becoming more aggressive and determined with each passing second as he felt her immediate reaction to his exploring, invading caress.

"I belong to you, Evan," she managed to say as she drew breath on a tiny moan of delight, mesmerized by the translucent flames that flickered deep in his eyes. She wrapped her arms around his neck, wanting to tell him more, to tell him how much she loved him. But it had been so long since he had touched her in just this way. It was achingly familiar, his knowing caress, but strangely new and exciting at the same time, and she couldn't find the words. She couldn't even speak. Perhaps she'd already told him she loved him? The words were echoing so loudly within her mind that she thought possibly she had spoken them aloud a thousand times.

Evan shifted his weight to string a line of sharp, demanding kisses along her collarbone to the place where her neck and shoulder joined, where her pulse beat light and fast.

Amanda could no longer restrain or control the answering choreography of her body as his knowing fingers probed more daringly into the warm intimate places that no other man had ever possessed. Her legs tangled with his, and she moaned again as his lips and teeth fastened on her nipple. Her agony was exquisite, but achingly incomplete, as tiny shudders rippled through her body with increasing frequency.

This was lovely. It was enchanting, but it was not enough. Amanda opened her mouth to tell Evan so, but at that moment, as though sensing that she was nearly at the limit of her control, he settled his weight on her, completing their union in one fluid movement that sent Amanda careering toward the edges of oblivion.

It had been so long since she'd known such joy. She had been so lonely. The hours and days of their separation flowed away as he melded her to him. She drew his head down to hers as she began to move in the ancient coupling dance that, once learned, could never be forgotten.

Amanda claimed Evan's mouth with a passion equal to his own, branding him as hers, acknowledging him as the perfect complement to her femininity. Their kiss mimicked the joining of their bodies, deepening as Evan moved further within her and her body adjusted to the unfamiliar intrusion, softening and warming to welcome him.

For Evan, all rational thought stopped. He didn't care that she hadn't told him she loved him. She'd admitted that she belonged to him, would always belong to him. For the moment, buried deep within the heated core of her body, it was enough. She did love him; he was certain of it. Later, when the fire that was burning too hotly between them had died away, there would be time for them to talk. Now, only the sensations of passion, and the need, the overpowering need for her and the pleasing, dizzying rhythm they were establishing between them, was reality.

He gloried in the additions, the subtle variations Amanda contributed to his theme. She clutched him tighter as he felt her carried nearer to the edge of completion. He felt so heavy, as if his weight would press them both deeper and deeper into the swirling opalescent currents of fulfillment. Amanda moved demandingly beneath him, urging him on, synchronizing their movements as they traveled into the rush of a gigantic wave that tumbled and curled beneath them, straining their bodies toward a distant shore. She arched against him, absorbing the power of his thrusts, matching each with her own arcing response as they gained momentum, caught up together in an endless tide of longing, united beyond the need for words.

"Mandy!" Her name was torn from his throat by the convulsive release of his body.

"Evan . . ." Her response was equally breathless as he felt her satisfaction come in a series of building tremors. "Evan..." He thought he heard her say *'I love you'*, but the rush of blood still pounding through his veins obscured her words.

It didn't matter, not now, not anymore, not as long as he held her in his arms. Evan settled himself to sleep, his body still locked with hers as they were swept away, coming to rest on warm, peaceful sands.

AMANDA AWOKE WITH her customary slowness, consciousness returning in bits and pieces, but also with an unaccustomed sense of peace and rightness. Her dreams had been happy ones. A small contented smile curved her lips as she recalled the shared passion of the night before. Evan had been with her, gloriously, undeniably real; he was no longer the phantom lover of her most private fantasies. From the first intimate fusing of their bodies, she'd been unable to hide her need for him; and once unleashed, Evan had demanded—and given back in return—all the love she could ever wish to experience.

She stretched with lazy grace, sore muscles mildly protesting the action. She was only a little surprised to find she was lying on the couch. Sometime during the night they had moved there, she supposed, and Evan had gone into the bedroom to find a blanket to cover them. She snuggled under the light cover and looked around the room. He was standing by the window, one arm on the frame, one hand stuck in the back pocket of his pants. He wore nothing else, and the dawn light outlined his wide shoulders and narrow waist vividly.

Amanda pushed herself up against the couch pillows. He turned at her movement, smiling down at her sleep-smooth face, and she glimpsed again the lowering of the barriers that normally shaded the depths of his eyes. "Good morning, Mandy. Did you sleep well?"

"Very well," she murmured, a flush of color stealing over her face and throat. Actually they'd slept very little, as he was well aware. She liked being teased at dawn, she decided. "Good morning, Evan," she added as an afterthought. She held out her hand. He moved away from the window, crossing the room toward her with lithe grace, the dark material of his slacks complimenting the teak shading of his skin.

"I couldn't sleep," Evan said, as she pulled the blanket up over her breasts and bunched it around her knees so that he could sit beside her on the couch. "We've got a lot of things to plan this morning."

The words struck an odd note in Amanda's brain, sending a flickering jolt of unease across her skin. She rubbed her bare arms absently and curled her legs up under her. *Plans.* She'd used that word so often when discussing the future with Robert. Guilt gnawed at her. "What plans, Evan?" she managed to ask.

He smiled, but there was a quizzical twist to his lips. One arm rested along the back of the couch. Amanda could feel the slight tensing of his muscles and knew he'd picked up on the strain in her voice. "Not very important things. Just where we're going to live. Your job. My writing." He ran his hand through his hair in the characteristic gesture that had always betrayed his agitation. A rough shadow of beard darkened his cheeks and accentuated the strength of his jaw, the planes and angles of his profile. He hooked his hands between his knees and studied his bare feet.

"I don't want to leave my home, leave the life I have here in Sarasota," Amanda said before she could stop herself.

"I know that." Evan felt like kicking himself. Her eyes were as big as silver dollars. The regret she felt for sleeping with him was plain to see. "We should have talked this all through last night...." He tried to go on with what he wanted to say, but sudden fear that she would reject him closed his throat.

"Last night all I wanted was to make love with you," Amanda said candidly. She smiled, and was rewarded by seeing his special private smile reach all the way to his eyes.

"I was afraid I'd rushed you again." He traced the tip of his finger along the line of her collarbone and dipped down to skim across the swelling curve of her breast. "You do strange things to me, lady. I don't think all that straight when I'm holding you in my arms."

"Everything that happened to us last night... I hope it was a once-in-a-lifetime experience." Amanda took a deep breath and reached out to touch his cheek. "Everything except what happened in this room. Our being together. I want that to last forever."

It was Evan's turn to hold his breath. Was she going to say she loved him now? He'd waited so long; he needed to hear the words so badly. He knew that need was irrational, but it was achingly real nonetheless. He'd made so many mistakes with her in the past he couldn't be sure of how she felt now. He couldn't read her thoughts, or her wishes, only her desire. Amanda remained silent, and Evan felt his insecurity grow stronger, like a cold hard stone in the middle of his heart.

"We can make last night last forever," he said with more conviction than he felt.

"That would be nice, but not very practical." Amanda couldn't keep the little tremor of emotion from spoiling the light effect of her words and her smile. She dropped her head to hide the intensity of her reawakening desire to be held and caressed. From the corner of her eye she caught sight of her ring. Her engagement ring. The outward symbol of her commitment to Robert Tacett. The diamond sparkled in the new light, recalling her to a sense of duty and guilt so strong it covered her in a suffocating weight. She had no business discussing a life together with Evan until she had freed herself of her promise to Robert. She owed Robert that much.

Without conscious thought she picked up the ring from the end table and slipped it onto its accustomed finger. *After all,* she thought stupidly, *what did one do with a ring when one was wearing nothing else?* Robert's forgiveness and understanding meant a great deal to her peace of mind.

"Don't put it on again, Mandy." Evan's voice was cold. He lifted her numb fingers as if to remove it. She curled her fingers into her palm protectively.

"I owe him an explanation, Evan. Besides, I don't have any pockets in this outfit." Again, her small attempt to lighten the situation in order to deal with her emotions fell flat. She tried to smile up into his hard, set face, but her own lips felt as brittle as glass, and she couldn't manage to bring it off. "What's wrong?"

"I don't want you running off to Tacett as soon as you get out of my bed." *God,* Evan thought, *now I really do sound like a sexist, pompous ass.* No wonder she was looking at him as though he'd suddenly sprouted horns. He raked his hand through his hair again, standing it on end. If she'd only told him she loved him. She'd admitted she belonged to him, but not that she still loved him as much as he loved her. She couldn't still care for Tacett, could she? he asked himself. Robert was a good man; Evan wasn't going to fool himself in that respect. He'd make Amanda as happy as he could, give her everything in the world she desired, never cause her a day's grief, a moment's unhappiness. Could Robert persuade her to reconsider not marrying him if they were alone together? Could he let her go to Tacett and risk that happening?

"Your bed." Amanda was angry, and he didn't blame her.

"Sorry. I didn't mean that the way it sounded. It's just that you..." Evan clamped his teeth shut on the end of his sentence. It was such a simple question. Why couldn't he ask her straight out if she loved him?

"I owe Robert an apology. I have to explain to him what's happened between us. I'm confused, Evan...." Amanda twisted the diamond on her finger, then deliberately put her hand down at her side where Evan couldn't see it as she caught the angry scowl he directed at the jewel. "Robert and I would have been married now if things had worked out differently." She almost said, "If I hadn't burned my divorce papers." The decree; it would be here today. *Perfect timing,* she thought miserably. "I promised..." Tears filled her eyes like puddles reflecting a rainy gray sky. Why couldn't Evan understand that this was going to be one of the most difficult things she'd ever had to do in her life? Why couldn't he understand she cared for Robert enough to hate having to cause him pain? Were men the only ones allowed to feel bound by their honor?

"Stay with me a while longer, Amanda." Evan's tone was suddenly cajoling as he lifted her chin with his finger, forcing her to meet his eyes. Even in her growing misery, his sexuality called to something wild and unquenchable within her. His hand moved up to caress her breast through the thin material of the blanket. Her breathing grew shallow and uneven; she leaned into his touch and hated her lusting body for compelling her to do so. "Stay with me, Mandy, and leave the rest of the world out there where it belongs."

"I gave Robert my promise, Evan. Please don't ask me to love you again until I've freed myself from that obligation."

Evan had been denied the solace of her arms for so long that he found it hard to think when she was so close, her body so pliant, so responsive to his touch. Why was she so insistent on getting to Tacett? Why wouldn't she admit that he didn't mean a thing to her? If he could make love to her once more, she'd forget all about the other man. They would belong to each other again. "Stay with me, Mandy." He kissed her slowly, evocatively. Her lips parted and opened to him. Her head fell back among the pillows, and she moaned softly under the caress of his lips. He let his hand follow the curve of her body to rest heavily between her legs. He could feel the heat building within her; he increased the pressure of his fingers, and she moaned again. "Stay with me, forget Tacett. Forget he ever existed."

"No." Amanda jerked her head away from Evan's seeking lips. She stared at him, anger and hurt warring for supremacy in her gray eyes. It wasn't like Evan to be so possessive, so uncaring. What was the matter with him? Hadn't she proved she loved him last night by making love with him even though she felt herself in honor bound to another man? Last night had been lovely, and fulfilling beyond her wildest dreams; but it hadn't worked a miracle. She still couldn't seem to understand the way Evan felt, the way his mind worked.

"I gave Robert my word." She repeated the phrase because her need interfered with her mind's ability to function intelligently. She didn't want to enter into a renewed relationship with Evan encumbered by guilt. "I have to go to him . . . now."

Evan stood up so abruptly it made Amanda dizzy. She fixed her eyes at the level of his belt buckle and refused to meet his stormy golden eyes. "I won't be here when you get back."

"Evan, that's so unfair." Amanda tried again to be reasonable, to understand what was causing his jealousy. They'd overcome so many of the old misunderstandings, but this behavior on his part was totally unexpected. What was wrong? He loved her; he'd told her so. And she loved him. He wouldn't really go, leave her, would he? Not now, not when they'd come so far along the path to reconciliation? "I don't want you to go, Evan," she said, and there was only a quiver of unsteadiness in her voice. "But I have to talk to Robert."

Evan was pulling on his sweater, and his voice was muffled by the fabric. "You do what you have to do, Mandy." He didn't look in her direction again until he heard the bathroom door open and shut. He'd done it again, shut her out of his life. He'd told her again and again how much he'd changed, but he hadn't, not enough. He needed some time to think, to regroup, to work himself out of this mess he'd made of their reunion. He'd take a walk, cool down and then tell Amanda everything that was in his heart. He wasn't the same man who'd broken her heart three years ago. He just needed a little time to come to grips with his jealousy. The doorbell cut short his disjointed inner dialogue.

Inside the blue-tiled bathroom, Amanda leaned her head against the door. She was repeating the same self-defeating pattern that had driven them apart three years ago. Evan wasn't an unreasonable man. Surely, if she found the right words, he'd understand her need to clear things up with Robert before she could feel completely free to give herself to him again? If she pledged her love to him, explained that she had to return the ring before she could be released from the burden of the guilt that plagued her peace, he'd understand. They were both new at revealing their feelings so candidly to each other. Emotional intimacy, as well as physical intimacy, was adding a new dimension to their relationship. She couldn't give up this easily.

Grabbing her robe off the hook, she pulled it on with trembling fingers. It was up to her to shatter yet another transparent obstacle to their understanding. She'd make Evan stand there and tell her what was bothering him. This honesty-of-emotion business worked both ways. They had come so far; but they still had some distance to travel. Last night, the magic they had shared had been real and true. Their love was real and true—and it would last beyond time if they gave it a chance.

Amanda hurried back toward the living room before her newfound courage dissolved in a wave of cautious, defeatist second thoughts. The cushions where they'd made love still held the impressions of their bodies. Her clothes were in a small colorful heap on the floor. Evan was nowhere to be seen. Instead of the man she loved sitting on her couch, she found a large blue-and-white envelope with the name of a well-known courier service emblazoned across the front. Evan's initials had been scribbled on the receipt.

The divorce decree. Drat the courier's efficiency. It was the last thing she wanted him to see, the means to allow her to marry Robert if she so chose. Amanda walked to the window with slow, heavy steps. She looked out at the dawn-pink crescent of beach with seeking eyes, but the sands were as empty as the room behind her. Where had he disappeared to in such a hurry? Was he gone for good, as he'd threatened?

She didn't think so, but she simply couldn't be sure.

Only Max was present to see the hot stinging tears splash down her cheeks as he sat patiently cleaning his luxuriant whiskers before the sliding glass doors, waiting sphinxlike for her to let him in.

She was alone again.

CHAPTER FIFTEEN

WHERE IN SARASOTA had he ended up this time, Evan wondered idly. Somewhere close to downtown would be his best guess. It was his turn to exit the small airconditioned bus. The driver eyed him suspiciously, and he ran a hand over the dark stubble of beard on his chin. He probably did look like a mass murderer—or at least an embezzler on the lam in his wrinkled slacks and too-heavy green sweater.

He got out of the bus. It didn't really matter where he was; he might as well get off here as the next stop. Stepping onto the sidewalk he nearly collided with an elderly gentleman in Bermuda shorts and a ball cap perched jauntily on his bald head. He was in a hurry to cross the street and sidestepped Evan with surprising agility for someone of his age.

The sharp distinctive crack of leather on wood gave Evan the answer to the senior's haste, and indirectly answered the question of where he was. Baseball. It was the last week in March, the end of spring training, and White Sox Park, the winter home of the Chicago White Sox, was across the busy street from where he stood. The small stadium was close to downtown, near the courthouse and the *Examiner* building. Evan wondered if Peter was in his office this morning. He could use the older man's advice on how best to handle Amanda.

He wanted to go back to her, back to the house on the beach that he was already starting to think of as home. But he didn't have the nerve. He should have kept his hands off her one more night. No, he smiled wryly to himself, that was asking too much of any mere mortal. But this morning he shouldn't have pressured her to respond to him. She did owe Tacett an explanation; he accepted that. But unfortunately he'd let his emotions and insecurities overpower his intellect. And then that blasted courier had to show up with Amanda's divorce decree just at the worst possible moment. He cursed himself for being a fool. But he wasn't going to be a bigger one by running back to Amanda until he'd settled things in his own mind, and given her a chance to break things off with Tacett—if she intended to break the engagement. He couldn't erase the image of Amanda wearing Tacett's ring from his thoughts.

"Evan, boy! What are you doing here?" Peter Winston's voice carried over the cheer that rose from the crowd inside the stadium as the White Sox starting lineup was announced. He was wearing clean, neatly pressed slacks and a loud green plaid shirt. A White Sox ball cap covered his iron-gray hair. Peter eyed the younger man's tired face and beard-roughened chin. "I know last night was no picnic, but you look like hell. Where's my daughter?"

"With Tacett, I think." Evan answered the query with reluctance, aware that Peter's deep-set brown eyes were watching him with calculating interest from beneath the bill of his cap.

"Ummm." Peter changed the subject abruptly. "The Coast Guard found my boat this morning. Evidently Silva was able to ride out the storm and meet up with his ride back to Costa Verde. Or maybe the bastard drowned, who knows?'' Peter shook his head mournfully. "My poor boat.''

"Is she in pretty bad shape?'' Evan asked, grateful for the new direction of the conversation. He turned automatically and followed Peter when he started across the street toward the ball diamond.

"Beat-up but still afloat, thank God. They've got her under tow. She'll be back in port by evening.''

"You don't think Silva drowned, do you?''

"He most likely got away scot-free. If you ask me, those bigwigs in Washington decided he was more valuable in Costa Verde stirring up trouble than he would be here in the States in jail.''

"A political embarrassment to the administration.'' Evan shook his head in agreement with Peter's assessment of the situation.

"Maybe they think he can prop up Alexandro for a few more months until they can come up with a plan for new elections that will oust the old man but save face on Capitol Hill? Maybe they think he'll take over from Alexandro and we can bargain more constructively with him?'' Peter snorted in disgust. "Hell, who knows how those yahoos at State and Defense think? All I know is that Silva's gone from here and we put a stop to his dirty little scheme.'' Peter appeared to decide that he'd let his feelings show more than he meant to. He looked around, searching both sides of the street outside the stadium. "Come on, let's go in and watch the game. I'm supposed to be meeting Carmella and the girls, but they're late. The girls have never seen a major-league team play, and this is the last game before the season starts up north.'' They took their seats and watched the game in silence for a few minutes.

Without consulting his companion, Peter signaled a passing vendor and provided them both with mustard-lathered hot dogs. Evan was more than hungry enough to oblige his ex-father-in-law. "Thanks." He raised an inquiring, appreciative eyebrow when Peter also produced a stainless-steel flask from his hip pocket.

"Scotch. Chivas Regal, to be exact. By way of celebrating my official return to the *Examiner*."

"No more paying lip service to Amanda's plans for your retirement?"

"I intend to die in harness," Peter decreed. He took a long swig from the flask. "Damned near accomplished that. I appreciate your help out there last night, son."

Evan swallowed a bite of his hot dog. "My help? All we managed to do was get ourselves snatched by Ortega and his goons. By the way, what do you think will happen to him?"

"If he isn't already shark bait, Silva used the best word for it. Scapegoat. I could never get close enough to the two hit men, the ones Carmella recognized and the ones who helped kidnap you three and Teresa and me, by the way, to zero in on Ortega until it was too late."

"They were probably the first cell, right?"

"Yep. Like most maniacs, Silva liked to talk. Why shouldn't he tell me everything he had planned when we both knew he intended to kill me in the end? He's brilliant, I'll admit that, but he must have seen too many old movies as a kid. They set up those cells to be airtight. My guess is, with Ortega and those other two guys out of the picture, there's no way they can accomplish anything."

"Thank God."

"Amen." Peter took a sip from the flask. "And that little diversionary tactic isn't going to stop me from thanking you for keeping my daughter safe. I couldn't have handled that scene alone. I'm too old for that cloak-and-dagger stuff, I'll agree with Mandy on that account." He shuddered and passed the flask to Evan. "I was in over my head and I know it. Jesus, I was scared when they dragged Teresa onto the boat. And when Ortega showed up with you three, well . . ."

Evan accepted the flask with a grateful nod. The fiery liquid burned its way down his throat and landed in his stomach with a smooth, warming glow. "I thought you had everything worked out with Daly and the Feds."

"I did, as far as we could plan. But then suddenly, you were there, and bullets were flying all over the place. I was only supposed to have my own hide to look out for. It was a miracle nobody was hurt." Peter was solemn. He flexed his arm as if it bothered him. Evan was reminded of his injury when he glimpsed the sheen of a white bandage below the sleeve of his sport shirt. Peter reached for the flask, and Evan passed it over. "Robert was right. I probably should have let the authorities know what was going on as soon as Carmella came to me. But no. I still wanted to prove I had it in me for one last big story. If Mandy hadn't been pushing so hard . . ."

"Amanda is a stubborn woman." It was Evan's turn for the flask. The excellent liquor was already starting to loosen his tongue.

"We're going to have to have a long father-daughter talk in the very near future," Peter said, shaking the empty flask. He put the cap back on reluctantly. "We'll come to an equitable agreement in the end. She's never any harder on others than she is on herself. Are you planning to carry my daughter back up north with you anytime in the near future?''

Evan didn't have an answer to the blunt query right away. "I'd like to be alone with her somewhere, somehow," he finally responded with a trace of self-pity, engendered by good Scotch and a nearly empty stomach. "But I think I'd like to live down here, if she'll have me. She won't give up the *Examiner* and I won't ask her to. I could be happy living here," he repeated as the players on the field wobbled up and down in his field of vision. Evan closed his eyes against the glare of the sun.

"You sure don't act like it." Peter rested his chin on his fist, eyeing Evan with perplexity.

"The divorce decree came this morning," Evan said with a tipsy logic that made the statement perfectly clear to him.

"Then what's stopping you from carrying her off somewhere and marrying her again?"

"Tacett. She's with him now."

"Returning his engagement ring." Peter's words were rewarded with a scowl that might have daunted a less determined man.

"I'm not so sure of that."

"I seem to have missed an episode or two of this little soap opera," Peter said bluntly but not unkindly. "I assume you spent the night with my daughter. I think you'd better tell me what's going on."

Evan rested his forearms on his knees and tossed the paper that held his hot dog under his seat. "Mandy and I've come a long way to getting back together since I came down here, but I'm still making mistakes." His tone was rueful, his smile a tight, hard caricature that still qualified as more of a scowl.

"Let me guess. You took off in a snit this morning because Amanda hasn't had time to settle things with Robert, is that it?"

"Close enough."

Peter snorted, then asked abruptly, "Do you love my daughter?"

"Yes."

"Then get yourself back to her. I've always hoped you two could work out your problems someday. That's why I stayed out of it when you showed up down here. Seems to me it's as simple as one, two, three. You either love her enough to go tell her so, or you don't."

"I love her, damn it." Evan was getting angry. "She's never said she still loves me." There, it was out in the open.

"You're moping around here, paying no attention whatsoever to the game, ruining my afternoon, drinking my Scotch, because of that? Go ask her, if you aren't sure. But you should be. I saw what you two had was special from the beginning. Do you think I'd have let any other man run off with my little girl the way you did?" He balled his hand into a fist and banged it on his knee. "Do you think I'd stand by and let any other man walk back into her life and turn it topsy-turvy the way you have these last couple of weeks, if I didn't think you belonged together?" There was no levity in Peter's words. He was deadly serious.

"She couldn't get to Tacett with those papers fast enough this morning." Evan couldn't stop himself. He'd had too little sleep and too much Scotch.

"To end it, man." Peter thumped Evan on the back with enough force to emphasize his point. "Amanda's harder on herself than she is on anyone else, you know that, or you ought to. She'll blame herself for not loving Tacett enough. You probably got caught in the overflow this morning." He chuckled and shook his head at Amanda's intensity. "Just like her mother, that girl." He took a deep breath and went on. "Look, Robert Tacett is a good man. He'll understand. Don't make problems for yourselves where none exist. It'll be dark soon. Get yourself back out to her place. Do you need a car?"

Dazed, Evan answered with automatic politeness. "No. I'll take a cab. I need a little time to clear my head." He didn't say anything more. He stood and held out his hand. "Thanks for the advice."

"You'll do fine, boy. Just remember one thing. Don't make Amanda guess how you feel. Show her, tell her, and for both our sakes, never let her out of your sight again as long as you live!"

"I'll do my best." Evan stood up and started to make his way out of the row of seats.

"Evan."

"Yes?"

"Be sure and ask my daughter what she did with *her* copy of the divorce decree."

AMANDA LOOKED AROUND the crowded restaurant in dismay. It hadn't occurred to her that the Sand Dollar would be this busy in the middle of the afternoon. It was possible Robert couldn't spare the time to be private with her at all. Then she'd have to come back later. The thought caused a quiver of apprehension to race up and down her spine. It had taken her most of the morning to plan what she wanted to say to Robert; it had taken nearly that long to get up the nerve to come to the Sand Dollar at all.

To be truthful, she'd kept hoping Evan would return before she left the house to pick up her car. He had not.

And now she could put this reckoning with Robert off no longer. The headwaiter smiled as he noticed her standing indecisively at the foot of the steps. "Mr. Tacett is in his office," he said, then bowed with practiced grace. "Would you like me to tell him you're here, Miss Winston?"

"No, thanks. I'll go on back." Amanda pushed the strap of her purse higher on her slim shoulder and held on tight. With her head high, she marched the length of the restaurant, the gauzy skirt of her olive-green cotton shirtwaist swinging about her knees with every step.

There were two entrances to Robert's office. The first opened off an alcove at the back of the main dining room, the second exited into a short hallway leading into the kitchen. Amanda chose the dining-room entrance and knocked, rather more timidly than she'd planned, on the walnut panel.

"Come in." Robert was sitting behind his desk working at some sort of ledger. Amanda was too nervous to notice many details. A half-finished sandwich and glass of wine sat at his elbow. The room seemed quiet after the commotion in the dining room. It smelled faintly of furniture polish and Robert's spicy after-shave.

The silence, which neither of them did anything to break, hung heavy in the tastefully decorated, masculine room. "Amanda," Robert said finally, then stood up and walked toward her. He was wearing a light-weight gray blazer and pale gray slacks, and looked very much at home in his surroundings. "I was hoping you'd spend the day resting, but as usual I underestimated you. I planned to call you later."

He refused to meet her eyes directly as he spoke, but Amanda, for her part, was staring at his chin and missed the slight hesitation in his speech and in his expression. When she finally did look at him, his features were composed and noncommittal. "I picked Teresa up at the hospital and drove her home this morning. It put me behind schedule," he explained in a slightly hurried tone. He kissed her quickly on the cheek, a fleeting caress that she barely felt. Robert motioned her to take a seat in the upholstered chair in front of his desk. Amanda sank into it gratefully. At the moment her knees didn't seem to want to hold her upright. Robert leaned back against the big mahogany desk and crossed his legs at the ankles, one hand curled over the carved edge on either side of his body.

"You took Teresa home? That was good of you, Robert. She's okay, isn't she?" Amanda blushed at what sounded to her own ears like a very offhand show of concern for her friend. "I meant to call . . . I still don't have all the details straight from last night. . . ." She shook her head in bewilderment. "You saved her life, Robert."

He waved aside her praise. "I had to get off that pier, didn't I? The bullets were flying too fast for me." He looked up at the ceiling for a moment. "Teresa is fine. She swallowed a little salt water, that's all. She didn't suffer any more ill effects than the rest of us, thank God."

"I'll run out to Lido Key later.... Robert." Amanda changed the subject before she could lose her nerve. "I came here today for a reason." She could feel tears stinging behind her eyelids and threatening to clog her throat so that the words wouldn't come. She swallowed and began again. "I came to say..."

"That our wedding is off?" Robert bent forward and took her hand between his own.

Amanda nodded. "I'm sorry, Robert." Her voice cracked on a sob. It was even more difficult than she'd envisioned to hurt this man so.

"Don't cry, Mandy. I'm not blind. I've seen it coming, even though I pretended not to." He looked down at their joined hands. If he noticed she was no longer wearing his ring, he didn't say so. "I care for you a great deal, Amanda. I want you to be happy."

"But you don't love me." The statement just missed being a question. Amanda slid forward in the chair, bringing them so close their knees almost touched.

"No, Amanda. I thought I did...." He smiled, and it was bittersweet.

"We confused friendship with being in love. You deserve so much more than I can give you." Amanda didn't care how hackneyed the sentiment might sound. She meant it with all her heart.

"And you deserve more than I felt able to give you." Robert stood up, pulling her with him. His eyes carried the faint ghost of haunting memories.

"You could give me everything I want...if we loved each other enough. I began to understand that the day we talked on the patio; when you told me about your son." Amanda did nothing to hide the sparkle of tears on her lashes, the crystal drops falling on her cheeks. "If I loved you with all my heart and soul, being with you would be enough. The two of us would be enough." She began to cry softly.

Robert groaned, taking her in his arms. "Shh, Mandy." His voice was low and comforting.

"I'm so sorry about your son. About..." Her words were muffled against his shirt. His heart beat strong and steady beneath her fingers.

"It's all right, Amanda. And you are right, you know." There was a faint tone of wonderment in his next words. "I've never thought of it in just that way. If I had loved you with all my heart and soul, I would have found the courage to tell you about him sooner. And I would have found the courage to give you a child, if that's what you wanted."

"I do want children. I finally quit lying to myself about that. But you see..." Amanda struggled to find the best words. "*I* couldn't have asked you to take the risk along with me."

Robert put a finger against her lips, stopping her words. "Because friendship isn't always enough."

"Yes."

"But for some things it's the very best of beginnings." A memory flitted past his mind's eye, recent, but no less precious because it was new. Dark expressive eyes filled with terror watched him, and as he touched her cheek to reassure her the terror faded away to be replaced by relief and love. Her lips turned up in a smile, sweet and pure and meant for him alone. Beautiful eyes, beautiful lips. Teresa.

"I'll always be your friend, Robert." Amanda held out her hand. Robert took the ring lying in her palm. He stared at it for a long moment, then put it into his pocket. "I hope you find your special someone very soon."

"I think I will, Mandy." He smiled, and a bright spark of happiness kindled in his clear blue eyes. "Very soon."

CHAPTER SIXTEEN

ANOTHER DAY WAS dying in a palette of warm orange-and-gold hues far out on the Gulf. Amanda walked onto the deck of her home, her arms wrapped tight around her cat. She was tired of waiting, and beginning to doubt again.

The hope that had buoyed her when she returned to find Evan's suitcase in her foyer hadn't been able to outlast the strain of his continued absence. Max yawned and stirred in her arms, impatient with her introspective mood. He struggled in her grasp, and Amanda let him jump out of her arms. In the flick of an eye he was off the deck and melting into the shadows of palm and palmetto at the edge of the beach.

She was lonely, so alone. There were so many things she had to say to Evan, but she was afraid all her carefully nurtured courage would fail if he didn't return to her soon.

He came walking out of the evening twilight so quietly it was almost as if she'd conjured him up once more. Max reformed out of the same shadows, brushing himself against Evan's leg, waiting to be scratched behind one pink-lined ear. Evan dropped to one knee, and the two remained silhouetted against the darkening sky for several moments, looking, as they always did, as if they were exchanging secrets of great importance.

"I've been waiting for you." Her voice was husky with suppressed emotion and anxiety. Evan looked tired, she noticed when he got close enough for the light from the windows to allow her to see his features clearly. He'd found time to shave as well as to change his clothes sometime during the day. His hair was clean and soft, shining, lifting off his forehead in the light sunset breeze.

"I've been doing a lot of walking. And a lot of thinking," he answered slowly, with the rough, intimate note she loved threading in and out of his words. He stared up at her with narrowed, disturbing topaz eyes. "I wanted to give you time to think, too."

"You left without a word this morning." She gripped the railing so tightly she could feel each and every groove in the wood.

"I'm sorry." He wondered if he could ever tell her just how scared he'd been that she might not be waiting here for him to return? Someday, perhaps, he would. "I spent some time with your father today. He told me to ask you this question before we discussed anything else."

"Yes?" Amanda was almost as intrigued as she was puzzled. He looked very masculine and desirable standing there so casually. His shirt was a deep, rich coral that set off the bronze of his skin and the dark gold of his hair and eyes. But the nonchalance was a shield. She knew him too well now; she could see past the pose and into his heart. He was as anxious as she was, and just as vulnerable.

"What exactly did you do with your copy of the damned divorce decree in the first place, Amanda?"

She laughed. She couldn't help it; the sound rose around them in the dusk like a gathering of fireflies. "My copy?"

"Yes, damn it. Your copy." He didn't think this was a bit funny. *What the hell was Peter up to?* "I want to know."

Amanda walked to the top of the steps and looked down at him. He looked half defiant, half rueful, and she smiled in heady relief. He was here beside her, with her, and she never intended to let him out of her sight again.

"Ashes," Amanda said softly, all levity gone from her voice when she spoke. "Ashes, three years ago. I burned mine years before you ever thought of doing it."

Evan laughed, too, and there was a world of relief in the sound. He scooped her up in his arms and whirled her in the air. "God, I love you, Amanda."

"And I love you, Evan Cameron. I always have. I always will." Just that easily she said it, said the words that had tortured him for a night and a day.

"You don't know how badly I've wanted to hear you say those words."

"I said them last night," she insisted, looking up to see the darkness of remembered sorrow in his eyes.

"No, you didn't. Not once." Evan held her close. "Do you see why I came apart when you put Tacett's ring back on your finger? Why I acted like I did?" He lowered his head to kiss her but Amanda stepped back, though still remaining in the strong circle of his arms.

"I had to go to Robert first, this morning, before I could feel free to make love to you again. I expected you to know that. I wanted you to read my mind, but of course you can't, not really." She tilted her head, her words ending on a whimsical note that was almost questioning. She reached out to twitch his shirt collar into place and, once bidden, her shaking fingers refused to detach themselves from the material.

"It didn't make it any easier to wait. When you put that ring on your finger... Then that damned courier showed up.... I couldn't have planned the timing for the monster to put in an appearance any better if I'd written the scene myself." He shook his head in consternation. "I just took off, started walking. I wanted to come after you, but I didn't."

"Why not?" Amanda asked, intrigued.

"Because I trust you," he said simply. "You were entitled to the time to say goodbye to Tacett on your own terms. In your own way."

"Thank you, Evan," she said with a catch in her voice. "Robert is a good man. He just isn't the man for me."

"I am." His hands rested lightly, on the curve of her waist.

"Yes, you are." She lifted her hand to twist a button on his shirt, unfastening it with tantalizing slowness. Her hands grew bolder, working at her task with fierce concentration, pushing aside the material to slide her palms across his chest with sweet boldness. "I want to make love with you now, Evan. You promised to take me back to what we used to share. Last night we came so close."

"I want the woman you are today, Amanda. The fulfillment of the promise that girl I married possessed. My love, my wife, the mother of my children." It was his turn to ask the question on which their future happiness might depend. Amanda had been tracing the shape of the buttons on his shirt as she spoke.

Now she stopped, becoming very still. Evan didn't move a muscle. She was holding her breath. He could feel the tension in her. He knew there was something else that had to be brought up and examined, settled between them before they could go on.

"Evan, some days I'm so afraid of the future." Her next words were barely a whisper. "What if I miscarry again?"

"We won't try until you're ready. Everything will go right this time, you'll see."

"I believe you." She buried her head in the hollow of his throat, inhaling the faint, spicy aroma of his skin. She did believe him. And if they weren't as lucky as he predicted, she was strong enough now to bear the pain—especially since she wouldn't have to bear it alone this time. "I know our babies will be happy and healthy."

"Florida is a good place to raise children." His soft, rumbling words caught at her heart, piercing her soul with joy. His hand on her shoulders compelled her to return his steady regard. She did so with tear-bright gray eyes.

"I do love you, Evan Cameron." One thing they'd both learned was that loving meant sharing and compromise. "With Dad coming back to the paper full-time, we'll have extra time to be together." She rested her head on his shoulder in dreamy contentment. "Time for my husband. Time for planning a baby." Evan's grip tightened. He turned his head to meet her lips. They kissed, tenderly, slowly, deeply.

Amanda turned and led the way to her bedroom. The lamp on the small table beside her bed dispelled the night. "We've wasted so many precious days, Mandy," Evan said with sadness as he traced a hand over her breast and up to touch her cheek. "Forgive me for all the pain."

"We're lucky. We found our magic again."

He dealt with the buttons of her dress in the space of two heartbeats. It took only a moment longer for her to rid him of his shirt. The rest of their clothes followed just as quickly. It had become imperative that they renew their commitment with more than words. Amanda smiled as Evan lowered her onto the bed and followed her down to lie on the cool white sheets. She lifted her arms to encircle his neck, capturing his mouth as she moved against him with seductive intent, inviting their joining, the intimate merging of their bodies.

AS HAD HAPPENED so often before when she lay in Evan's arms, time had slowed and stopped for Amanda. She wakened with a smile on her lips and the pleasant weight of a man's body beside her. She looked out the window at the moon-bright sky. Max was howling plaintively outside the sliding glass doors. Amanda slid out of bed, careful not to waken Evan.

There were certainly going to be a lot of changes in her life, and she intended to meet them head-on. She tugged on her brown-and-gold Chinese silk robe. There would be no more hiding, no more running away. She wanted her career. She wanted to give Evan children. She could do both and be successful at it. And most of all she wanted to spend every minute of the rest of her life with one loving, exasperating, extremely successful writer of novels of horror and the occult. Maybe, with Evan by her side, she'd even get up her nerve to read one of them.

And, of course, there was Max. She giggled, coming down from the clouds in a hurry as she spied her pet: dirty, tattered and battle-weary outside the glass doors.

"Good grief! What happened to you?" she asked, bending to inspect the damage to one velvety ear. A fluid, moving shadow of sinuous brown caught her eye, and she straightened in time to see Ming Le's haughty, erect tail slipping back toward the Ellery bungalow.

"Max . . . you promised."

"Promised what?" Evan was standing in the shadows. He'd pulled on his briefs, but wore nothing else. Amanda sucked in her breath at the sight of him.

"I didn't want to wake you. Max has been out carousing." She pointed to the battle-scarred cat.

"If he's the successful suitor, I'd hate to see the other guy."

"He does look like he's been dragged through a hedge backward." Amanda bet Ming Le had given as good as she'd gotten.

"He's a mess," Evan said with a distinct lack of sympathy.

"I'll have to clean him up." Amanda sighed. "It's four o'clock in the morning, you beast."

"He's fine." Evan interrupted. "Come back to bed with me, Mandy." His voice was a low, seductive whisper. "It's very late. The moon is waiting to watch us make love." He gathered her close and pointed to the silver disk low on the horizon. "We have hours of the night left to spend together."

"Ummm, and all the nights to come." Max seemed to have disappeared as they spoke, but it didn't take long to locate him.

"Out, Max," Evan ordered as he took one look at the bedraggled feline in the middle of Amanda's bed. The cat eyed his mistress with a sad-eyed glance as she seconded Evan's order to vacate in a softer tone. Accepting defeat gracefully, he jumped down and curled himself on the rug. "He looks worse than ever in this light."

"Poor Max, he'll need a bath tomorrow. You can give it to him."

"Maybe." He pulled her back down into the tangled nest of sheets and pillows they'd vacated only minutes before. His briefs were gone. Nothing lay between them but the silky cloud of her robe. He let his hand slide upward to tug loose the tie, brushing aside the silk to cover her with the heated vibrancy of his lips and tongue. "Let Max get his rest, love. Ming Le is quite a lady. And so are you," he added in a choked voice as she boldly folded her hand around him.

"We are," she agreed with a satisfied smile that would have done justice to Max's lovely companion. "Evan." Amanda's voice was soft, nearly lost in the rush of blood through her veins. "How *did* you learn about Mrs. Ellery and Ming Le?"

Amanda's once and future husband chuckled low in his throat, an exciting, beguiling sound that raised a delicious shiver along her spine. "Warlocks have their trade secrets, just like writers, my love."

"I'm sure I never mentioned either of their names, yet you knew them." He was kissing the curve of her ear, her throat, the hollow between her breasts, and she was having trouble forming intelligent sounds as her breath came in quick, hard pants.

"Would you believe I talk to cats?" Evan moved to blanket her slender body with his own hard warmth. The warlock glint was bright and strong in his golden eyes. Amanda shivered as she felt a heady primal thrill. For a fleeting second she thought she glimpsed a strange shifting of color in his pupils that spoke of other worlds. She half-believed he might have the ability he claimed.

"No, I don't believe you talk to cats." She got the words out with difficulty as his lips began tracing a heated path from her lips to her breasts.

"Good. I'm glad that's settled, Amanda. I'm only a man, nothing more." He smiled down at her, reveling in their coupling. The strange dancing tint was gone from his eyes, replaced by the clear liquid amber of his all-encompassing love for her. "I met Mrs. Ellery and Ming Le walking on the beach. She cataloged Max's faults in great detail. Are you disappointed there's such a commonplace explanation?"

"No," Amanda managed to say, even though her growing passion threatened to take the power of coherent thought away. Evan was moving strongly within her and with her. Nothing about him was at all commonplace. His sensual power, at least for her, was every bit as potent as a warlock's spell. "No, Evan, my love," she admitted with a sigh. Another powerful wave of ageless, timeless delight washed over her. "I have nothing to feel sorry about at all."